Merry Christmas
and a Wonderful Year
in 1981 to the Whole
Hockensmith Family —

from "Aunt" Margot Griffith —

THE SATURDAY EVENING POST

Christmas Stories

THE SATURDAY EVENING POST

Christmas Stories

THE CURTIS PUBLISHING COMPANY

INDIANAPOLIS, INDIANA

President, The Curtis Book Division: Jack Merritt
Managing Editor: Jacquelyn S. Sibert
Editor: Amy L. Clark
Editorial Assistant: Melinda A. Dunlevy
Proofreader: Helen L. Weyerbacher
Design Consultant: Caroline M. Capehart
Designer/Art Director: Pamela G. Starkey
Art Assistant: Jinny Sauer Hoffman
Compositors: Patricia Stricker, Penny Allison,
                Kathy Simpson
Production Manager: David M. Price
Staff Artist: Lucian Lupinski
Technical Director: Greg Vanzo

A Carol of Gifts

By Richard Burton

The gift of the Christmastide!
  A time of right good cheer,
When the door swings open wide
  And the fire leaps blithe and clear.
    Where once walked folly and fear,
      Ring the shouts of the young at play:
    And indoor mirth makes joy on earth
      And a spirit of holiday.

The gift of the loving heart,
  When the kindred ties of home
Draw close the far apart,
  Make mates of those who roam:
    Be they tossed on the ocean foam
      Or dwelling in strange, sad lands,
    In soul they meet and fondly greet
      Through the gift of the clasped hands. (1903)

One touch of Christmas
makes the whole world kin.

Contents

CHRISTMAS BEHIND THE SCENES

CHRISTMAS SCENES IN FACT AND FICTION

CHRISTMAS SCENES OF THE PAST

CHRISTMAS BEHIND THE SCENES

René Bache

Letters to Santa Claus

The faith of childhood in Santa Claus and his gifts makes a good deal of business for the Post-Office Department during the Christmas season.

Little boys and girls know only two ways of communicating with the jolly Christmas god—by the chimney and by mail. A letter, dropped into the fireplace just before bedtime, may be expected to reach him. The smoke, when the fire is lighted, will carry it up the flue; or, if it is not safely conveyed in that fashion, Kriss Kringle will come for it. In fact, a mere list of toys and other articles desired, when similarly deposited, will accomplish the purpose in view.

But these are days when postal facilities are employed much more generally and widely than was the case fifteen or twenty years ago, and the channel of communication with Santa Claus by chimney has been to a great extent abandoned, the everyday mails being preferred on account of their greater promptness and sureness of delivery. Hence it comes about that, at Christmastide each year, thousands of missives addressed by children to their patron saint are dropped into post-boxes all over the country.

They are directed in a great variety of ways— sometimes simply to the "Arctic Regions," but oftener to a more definite locality, such as "Ice Land," "Snow Land" or "The North Pole." Occasionally a European capital, such as London or Paris, is mentioned as the address of the saint, and in such a case the missive is duly forwarded— to be returned to the United States, a month or two later, with the words "Not Found" officially stamped upon it. If mailed without a postage-stamp it goes just the same, because the charge for carrying a letter to a foreign country is collectable at the other end, if not paid in advance.

Such letters, strange as it may seem, sometimes travel about all over the continent of Europe in pursuit of "Mr. Kriss Kringle," being forwarded from place to place by postal officials who seem to entertain no suspicion of their true character.

Eventually, of course, they are returned to this country, where they find their final haven in the foreign division of the Dead Letter Office in Washington. It is an interesting fact, worth mentioning in this connection, that French, German and even English children are frequently imbued with the notion that Santa Claus resides in America, and address their Christmas petitions accordingly.

The Hartz Mountains, in Germany, where such quantities of toys are made, are understood by many children to be the good saint's headquarters. Last Christmas a small Quaker girl in Philadelphia addressed in obedience to this notion her letter, which, in winding up a series of requests, said: "I will not ask thee, dear Santa, for a live baby, for I am sure that either my grandmother or my aunt means to give me one. And I know thee is so busy."

Another little girl wrote from Baltimore to Kriss Kringle at the "North Pole," asking for a pony and cart, and explained that though her Papa had no stable, there would be room for the pony in the playroom closet. Somehow the missive got as far as New York, but was sent thence to Washington with the inscription "No such post office in this State" stamped on the envelope. Technically, "Santa Claus letters," as they are called, come under the head of "fictitious" mail matter, and those which are directed to such impossible places as "Snow Land" or "Arctic Regions" are so marked at the local post offices and forwarded to the Dead Letter Office.

It is held by the Post-Office Department that such children's letters are entitled to the same privacy and respectful treatment as ordinary first-class mail enjoys. When they reach the Dead Letter Office they go through the regular course of procedure, being opened, examined for valuable contents—once in a while small sums of money are found in them—and returned to the senders in case (as often happens) their addresses are appended. If they lack stamps, for missives of the kind are liable to be dropped into the post-box "on faith" and without prepayment, the writers, if practible, are notified. The letters whose senders cannot be reached are burned.

"I would like a woolly dog," wrote one boy last Christmas. "I would like an alive one. I have a woolly dog on wheels, and he barks. I do not care for the alive one unless he can bark, too."

This is an example of the kind of letter that is dictated by the child to a sympathizing parent, who takes it down verbatim, addresses it to the North Pole, or to Peking, China, and shows the youngster how to drop it into the mailbox on the nearest corner. When, on Christmas Day, the woolly dog makes his appearance, it is obvious that the communication must have been received by Santa, and no further questions are asked.

Most Santa Claus letters are dictated in this way, but many children prefer, and are encouraged, as soon as they have acquired the art of printing words, to forward their petitions in autograph. Done in large angular letters, last Christmas, was the confidential missive of a small Washington girl, who wrote:

Please bring me a doll, and some candy. I like candy. Dear Santa Claus, bring me some green candy. 2410 G Street. That is all.

Now, why should this little girl have preferred green candy? Was it because she had found green sweetmeats more toothsome, or (as seems more likely) because she admired the color?

Here is another, from a small boy:

My dear Santa Claus: I hope you will come to my house, and don't forget. I want a drum, a bote, an engin, and a story book. And a trumpet. Yours truly, Stephen Fink, 709 24th st., N.W.

There is no art more difficult for a child to grasp than that of epistolary composition. Hence it comes about that nearly all Santa Claus letters are written with more or less help from the grown-ups. But there are occasional exceptions, of which the following is seemingly an example:

Deer Santy Claws: Maggy nex dor had two dollys last Crismus, and i had nun. I cride all day. She don't nede enny dollys this crismus. So don't giv her enny, and giv me two.

Now, is that not just like a child? Really, when one comes to think of it, children are very interesting, anthropologically considered. They are many thousands of years older than we are. We adults are of to-day, but they, in their nuances of thought and expression, represent the infancy of the human race, ages before the first civilization dawned on the earth!

It is a curious fact, noticed in the Dead Letter Office, that the children of the rich write comparatively few letters to Santa Claus. And the reason why is not far to seek. It is not that they have less faith in the myth but because they have no anxieties as to the gratification of their wants. They know that, when Christmas comes, they are sure to get whatever they desire, and it is not worth their while to bother with petitions.

When the writer was himself a little boy he was told that the chimneys of the houses of the poor were so narrow that Santa Claus could not make his way down them, and so he carried his toys and other gifts elsewhere. It was a pathetic, picturesque way of expressing the idea of the *res angusta domi* which forbids many of the best blessings of life to those who cannot afford to buy them.

Just before Christmas of last year there came to the War Department in Washington, from the Dead Letter Office, a letter from a soldier's little boy, addressed to "Santa Claus, Alaska." It was "returned for better direction," and read:

I would like you to send me, if you please, good Santa Claus, one steam car, one little red wagon, one stocking full of candy. Much Oblige. Your little friend, Daniel Le May, Jr.

The hearts of the bureau officials, toughened by official hard knocks and the influence of unsympathetic red tape, were melted by this childish appeal, and a collection was promptly taken up, the sum obtained being sufficient to purchase a locomotive and train, a miniature automobile and several pounds of fairly digestible confectionery. These were at once shipped to Master Daniel Le May, with a letter bearing a huge seal and ribbons, and stamped "Palace of Santa Claus, Alaska." It read:

My little Friend: My last train of reindeer, skimming over the cold snows and ice of my faraway home, brought me a big bushel-bag of letters from my little friends, and among them I found yours. After lighting my pipe and telling my man to close all the doors of my palace so as to keep out the cold winds, I made him get out of my factory some things for you; and, after having them packed, I told him to harness my two fleetest reindeer, Blitzen and Vixen, to my sled, and take them to the post office for you. I hope you will get them in time for Christmas. With my best wishes for a merry Christmas, I sign myself, your friend,

Santa Claus.

Done at the Palace of Santa Claus, this Christmas, A.D. 1902, under seal.

On more than one occasion the clerks at the Dead Letter Office in Washington have put their pennies together to buy gifts for children whose chimneys (as suggested by pathetic letters at Christmastide) were too narrow to let in good old Kriss Kringle.

"Please bring me a dolly," writes one scrap of femininity. "And please, Mr. Santa, brig it up the steem-heeter, and not down the chimny, so she won't get her hair burned."

A small boy writes: "Dear Saint Nicholas: I love you next to God. So, please, if God don't mind, bring me a billygote."

Goats are evidently in great demand at Christmastime. Another boy writes: "I want my billy goat to have horns, so he can but, and a tale, so I can pull it."

Equally characteristic is a Christmas petition from a youngster who has an aquarium. He writes: "Please, Mr. Santa Claus, giv me a bull-frogg. I want one that can sing."

A little girl says: "I would like some munny for myself to spend. The munny you gave me last Christmas Mamma put in the bank. I want the munny to buy candy."

Another writes: "I am a little colored girl. I want a white doll-baby, with gold hair, and eyes that shut. And a red dress, please."

Santa Claus' Christmas correspondence is full of humor and pathos. From whatever sources it emanates, the mansions of the rich or the most untidy slum, it is the literature of an innocence as yet unspoiled by the world. (1903)

Edgar S. Nash

The Origin of Christmas Customs

There are a few things in existence to-day which have not been changed or moulded in the hands of Progress. One by one legends and customs have been disproved and overthrown, yet none has dared attack the legends and the customs sacred to Christmas-tide. Here and there a savant has tried to prove that December 25th does not mark the birthday of Christ. Men and women read, smile, pass on.

The time of year corresponding to our Christmas-tide has always been a period of rejoicing. It marks the winter solstice. The days begin to lengthen, and the sun no longer journeys away from earth, but enters upon his return. It is a promise of renewed light and warmth, of the approach of the summer days, and men hailed these signs with every expression of gladness.

In Rome the Saturnalia, or feast of Saturn, fell at about the same time as our Christmas, and it marked the greatest festival of the Roman year. The city abandoned itself to gayety. Unbounded license held sway; universal mirth was the order of the day; friends feasted friends, and foes were reconciled. There were no slaves, no masters; all social distinctions were laid aside. Work was stopped throughout the city, and no war was ever entered upon at this time.

The tree as the emblem of life also figured conspicuously in the earlier religions. In Egypt the palm tree put forth a new shoot each month, and at the time of the winter solstice it was the custom among the Egyptians to decorate the houses with a branch of palm bearing twelve shoots. In Rome the fir tree was regarded with veneration; during the Saturnalian festivities, halls and houses were hung with evergreen boughs.

In England, in the days of the Druids, the houses were decked with evergreens in order that the sylvan spirits might repair to their grateful shelter and remain protected from the nipping frost and the icy winter winds.

Farther to the north the wild Teuton tribes worshiped their god in wooded places, and they looked upon the fir tree as his sacred emblem. The period corresponding to the Roman Saturnalia was the festival of Thor. This festival, like the Roman feast, was given over to the most barbaric pleasures and the wildest forms of enjoyment. Among these peoples the festivity was known as Yule-tide.

When Christianity spread abroad, men knew that in the story of Christ's nativity was realized what they in their blindness had striven to typify. So they adapted the old customs of their ancestors to the new order of things.

Among Northern European tribes a great fir tree was set up in each household at Christmas-tide. At its base were placed representations of Adam and Eve; in the branches coiled the Serpent, and on the top-most bough gleamed a candle, symbolizing that Light of the World through whom alone was victory over the Serpent possible. Later in history the tree was more profusely decorated with gaudy knick-knacks, all of which were at first symbolical. But the children were not allowed to see the tree till Christmas morning.

To account for its appearance there, the parents used to tell the children a Chaldean legend. Years ago it was the custom for every Saxon household to burn the Yule log on Christmas Eve. This was a great, knarled root or tree-trunk, cut the day before Christmas and brought into the hall on Christmas Eve with great ceremony, and accompanied with music. Each member of the household would sing a Yule song, standing on the centre of the log.

Then an attempt was made to drive the Yule log into the great hall as if it were a stubborn horse. The cry was given that the "dun" refused to move, and the whole company was summoned. All took a hand, and, loudly shouting, dragged it to the great fireplace. It was lighted with the charred remnant of the former year's log, which had been carefully preserved for this occasion, and which was supposed to insure the house against ill luck.

The children were told that during the night the Yule log gave birth to the Christmas tree which they found in the hall on Christmas morning loaded with gifts.

The Christmas tree was introduced into England by Prince Albert, consort of Queen Victoria. From the palace the custom spread, until now the Christmas tree is a necessary feature of an English Christmas.

In Germany and other European countries it was believed by the children that the tree glittering with candles and bright baubles, and the gifts found beneath the tree, were the work of jolly old Saint Nicholas, Sant Nicholaus, or Santa Claus, as we know him. This kindly saint was no legendary character. He lived about 300 A. D., and was a noted Bishop of Asia Minor. He was looked upon as the patron saint of generosity because of his liberality.

Three daughters of a poor nobleman could not marry as advantageously as they should because their father could give them no dowry. But one night one of the daughters found in her room a purse, shaped like a stocking, filled with gold, evidently thrown in the window by some one from without. The next night the second daughter found a purse

in her room, and on the third night the father caught Saint Nicholas in the act of throwing the third purse in the window.

From that story originated the custom of hanging up the stockings on Christmas Eve. Thereafter the young girls at the convent schools would hang their stockings on the door of the Mother Superior's room on Saint Nicholas night. On the following morning they would be found filled with gifts and dainties, and a little hint from Saint Nicholas as to the appearance and character of their future husbands.

Carolers making "a joyful noise unto the Lord"—a special part of the Christmas season.

Saint Nicholas is the patron saint of Russia, and his festival used to be celebrated earlier in December than the 25th, but now his name is synonymous with Christmas festivities. In parts of Europe he is known as "Pelsnichol," or Nicholas with the fur, because he is supposed to be clad in furs from head to foot.

The idea of Saint Nicholas traveling in a sleigh which was drawn by reindeer originated in the cold Northern countries. The reindeer were the swiftest animals known, and they must needs fly like the wind to carry Saint Nick the rounds of the world in one night.

In certain parts of Germany it was commonly held that on Christmas Eve the Christ-child—Criss Kindlein, or Kriss Kringle—visited earth, and, as He passed over the houses, dropped gifts through the roof for the deserving and the good.

But aside from the customs which relate to gifts and the spirit of giving at Christmas-tide, there are several observances which are indissolubly linked with this time.

Christmas is never really Christmas without the holly wreath and the mistletoe. Christians venerated the holly, or holy tree, because to them the little thorny leaves and red berries made in a wreath typified the crown of thorns and the bloody drops. Doubtless they introduced this solemn reminder at the joyous festival in order not to forget the sacredness of the occasion in the general festivities.

The mistle bush, mistletod—or mistletoe, as we know it—owes its use as a festal decoration to pagan times. According to the Scandinavian legend, Baldur, the most beloved of all the gods, had a premonition that death impended. Thereupon, his mother, Frigga, besought everything that was begotten of earth, air, fire or water to swear not to harm her son.

But in her request she overlooked the insignificant little mistletoe. Loki, the god of destruction, disguised as an old woman, visited Frigga, and, learning of her oversight, hurried back to where the gods were assembled. There they were amusing themselves by hurling all manner of missiles at Baldur, and all were turned aside. But Loki, with an arrow made of mistletoe, pierced Baldur's heart.

In reparation, the mistletoe was given to Frigga to do as she saw fit, provided it touched not earth. And she, to show that she bore no ill, hung it up, and every one who passed under it received a kiss as a token that, instead of hatred and jealousy, the mistletoe now stood for love and forgiveness.

Among the Celtic nations the mistletoe was an object of veneration, and at the festival of the winter solstice the Prince of the Druids himself cut a bough of it. The people were assembled, and then were led to the woods by the priests, who drove in advance of the company two snow-white bullocks. When the oak tree was found which bore the mistletoe, the plant was cut with a golden sickle, and the bullocks sacrificed.

At present it is the custom for the young men to carry out the doctrine taught by the Scandinavian myth and print a smacking kiss on the lips of any maiden thoughtless enough to stand beneath the suspended mistletoe bough. But for every such kiss one of the white berries of the mistletoe must be removed, and when all the berries have been kissed away the spell is broken.

Almost as important as the gift giving and gift receiving on Christmas Day is the feast of dainties spread on that festal occasion. But even the Christmas dinner has its origin in the dim, distant past. Feasts were always the accompaniment of any festival. In Egypt, at the winter solstice, every family killed and ate a goose as a religious observance.

In the hieroglyphic language of the Egyptian, the figure of a goose was the word "child." The people had noticed that the goose was remarkable for the way in which it protected its young, hence it was looked upon as the symbol of great love—that love which is willing to sacrifice itself for the object of its affection. This trait was also believed to belong to the god they worshiped, so the Egyptians celebrated this festival by killing and eating a goose.

We preserve the custom of eating fowl on this day, but the toothsome turkey has more generally supplanted the goose. The plum pudding as a dish in the Christmas feast has its meaning. The number and richness of its ingredients represented the rich gifts the Kings laid at the feet of the child Jesus.

In earlier days the mince pie, then a great pastry dish, filled with forced meat and fruits, was made box-shaped, to typify the manger in which the Child had lain.

The celebration of Christmas-tide is as old as the human race, and many of the customs have lost their origin in the hazy past. We preserve and hand down these customs because we respect their age. But pagan customs have survived in our Christian festival, not so much because of their age, as because it was necessary at the start to preserve them.

When Christianity was in its infancy, men who embraced it refused to give up the old festivals, so in view of the great end to be obtained, the leaders of the early church allowed these customs and festivities to stand, but sought to put into them some Christian significance and meaning.

But to such strict sectarians as the Puritans and the Quakers in England the Christmas festivities appeared to be little better than pagan orgies. These worthy people thoroughly discountenanced the festival, and when the Quakers and Puritans came to found a State in the New World, they made rigid rules against any such form of festivity.

The Dutch colonists, however, were enthusiastic in their observance of Christmas-tide, and, though far from home, they celebrated the happy time in the old way. From the Dutch colonists in America spread the Christmas cheer, and the frowns and resolutions of the staid Puritan and Quaker colonists availed nothing against the infectious spirit of Christmas cheer and good-will which the Dutch brought into the new country. (1898)

Paul Gallico

Silent Night

'Twas the night before Christmas, when all through the house
Not a creature was stirring, not even a mouse...
CLEMENT C. MOORE

But on the night of December 23 in the year 1818, in the little Austrian village of Oberndorf by Salzburg, on the banks of the frozen River Salzach, a mouse did stir.

He not only stirred; he invaded the organ loft of the church of St. Nicholas. There, because he was a cold, hungry mouse, he perpetrated a deed and initiated a chain of events that were to resound to the farthest corners of the earth.

It was the following morning, crisp, cold and clear, that an important gentleman in a black frock coat and stock let himself into the church of St. Nicholas and sat down at the organ.

His name was Franz Gruber, and he was a dark-haired, pleasant-faced man 31 years of age, with a longish nose, cleft chin and friendly eyes. The world never heard of him, but in the small ponds of the neighboring villages of Oberndorf and Arnsdorf he was a very large frog indeed. For in Arnsdorf he was the schoolmaster and in Oberndorf he was the organist of the church.

Now he flicked his long coattails out of the way, adjusted the organ bench, trod the pedals and pressed the keys. But no music issued from the pipes—only a soft, breathy sigh.

Before Herr Gruber had time to investigate this unhappy phenomenon he heard a sound by the door and turned to see his friend, Joseph Mohr, himself a musician and utility priest, who had been sent to Oberndorf on temporary basis until a permanent pastor could be found. Gruber cried, "*Grüss Gott,* Joseph. What has happened?"

The young priest—he was then 26, with merry eyes and a gay air—raised his arms in a helpless gesture and beckoned for his friend to follow.

He took Gruber to the loft behind the keyboard, where the leather bellows supplied the wind for the instrument, and pointed to the hole in the worn fabric of the leather. "I discovered it this morning. A mouse must have gnawed it, and at the first tread the whole thing gave way."

Gruber inspected the damage. A Christmas Eve Mass without music was unthinkable. He cried, "*Donnerwetter!* Here is a fine fix. What is to be done?"

"Well," Father Mohr said somewhat shyly, "I have written a little poem." He coughed and corrected himself. "Actually some words for a song."

The schoolteacher smiled at his friend and said, "I'll wager you have. You were always more of a poet than priest. I can't imagine why you ever chose the cloth."

Father Mohr replied with some asperity, "It isn't *that* kind of song."

Herr Gruber smiled again at the vehemence of his friend, for it was known that Father Mohr did enjoy *that* kind of song, the kind of song you sang with the peasants and rough rivermen when the new wine flowed and the zithers twanged. This was what caused grumbling among the more pious parishioners and brought frowns to the brows of the church fathers.

It was no wonder, Gruber thought, that his young friend was a bit wild. His mother had been a poor seamstress of Salzburg, abandoned by her husband, and she had no one to sponsor her infant boy Joseph or his baptism. Eventually it was the public hangman who agreed to stand up for the child. Later one of the monsignors had the boy educated and inducted into holy orders.

Gruber glanced down at the poem and read the first stanzas. A strange chill ran down his spine. It was indeed not *that* kind of song. It seemed to lay its hand upon his heart and speak to him gently, simply and movingly. Gruber was stirred by the words as he had never been before. Already he was beginning to listen to distant music waiting to be born.

Father Mohr said almost apologetically, "I only thought, since there is not a tone to be had from

Hallmark Cards, Inc.

the organ, that you might be able to arrange something for our guitars with perhaps a simple chorus for the children."

Gruber said, "Yes, yes, perhaps we could. Let me have it; I will take it and see what I can do."

All through the hour-long trudge homeward through to Arnsdorf, Gruber was composing. He passed three Christmas mummers in the guise of the Three Kings and didn't even see them. Words and music were already beginning to blend.

Silent night, holy night;
All is calm, all is bright.

Like deaf Beethoven he was hearing all of the notes inside himself.

Holy Infant so tender and mild,
Sleep in heavenly peace.

The chorus he would write for the children's voices rang through his brain.

He sat at his spinet in his simple room with its

scrubbed light pine floor, porcelain stove, few pieces of furniture of painted pine, and crucifix on the wall. The words unlocked melodies, and the music flowed forth.

That afternoon there were collected in the priest's study, beneath the wreaths and garlands of evergreen, 12 little boys and girls, scrubbed and shining in their warm woolen stockings, jackets and pinafores. The two men strummed their guitars and rehearsed their charges.

"So, now, Hannes, Eva, Peterli, you sing like this—'ta, ta, ta, ta, ta, ta, ta!' And you, Gretel, Liesel and Johann, you sing, 'da di, da di da, da.' "

The two men looked at one another with satisfaction. A little rough. A bit of trouble in the third section, but it could be easily remedied. It was going to work.

Christmas Eve! There was a crust on the snow. Beneath, it was so dry that it crunched and squeaked under the heavy boots of the churchgoers. Their cheery "*Grüss Gotts*" rang through the still night. The air was sharp and crystal-clear and hurt the nostrils when inhaled. The stars seemed to hang from the sky and glitter like Christmas-tree ornaments.

Bells pealed from the tall, whitewashed tower of St. Nicholas' church. Within, hundreds of tapers and candles reflected from the golden plates and chalices, softening the stiff, Gothic-carved Madonnas and endowing them, for all their woodenness, with gentle grace. The church was decorated with pine boughs, evergreen and holly berries. The congregation sat on the hard benches, the men in their lumpy woolen garments, the women in bright aprons and shawls.

There was a rustle of surprise as the 12 children, with Mohr and Gruber carrying their guitars, appeared before the altar. The sour-mouthed pious noticed with disfavor the gay streamers of red and green hanging from the necks of the instruments. Ribbons of the same colors were woven into the corn-colored plaits of the little girls and tied to the boys' stockings.

Gruber nodded. The strings vibrated, and the tenor of Father Mohr and the basso of schoolmaster Gruber filled the church.

Thus the Christmas hymn "Silent Night" was heard for the first time—and the next day it was forgotten. No single, solitary soul of that congregration, least of all the minor poet and the minor musician who had put it together, could guess what would happen—that it was to sweep the world. No one dreamed that genius had burned for a few hours in two simple men who never would be heard from again, and that through the magic of their collaboration on a Christmas Eve in an Austrian village something deathless had been born.

It was an accident that saved the masterpiece from oblivion. The master organ repairer, Karl Mauracher, who came up from the Zillertal that spring to repair the damaged bellows, asked what they had done without music at Christmas.

Gruber told him. "It was just a trifle," he said. "I wouldn't even know where to lay my hands on it. Mohr is not here any longer. Wait. . .if it were anywhere it would be——"

There was a small cupboard at the rear of the church, and there, crumpled and dusty amidst old papers and records, he found the song.

The organ repairer's lips moved as he read the score, and a deep humming of the melody came from his massive chest. "It has something," he said softly. "Do you mind," he asked, "if I take this with me?"

Gruber laughed, pleased that their little effort had this belated moment of approval. "By all means have it for no one will have any further use for it once you have mended our organ."

Herr Mauracher shouldered his bag of tools and leather patches and departed. Franz Gruber forgot the incident. And in this manner the words and music of "Silent Night" journeyed to the lovely Zillertal Valley, thus beginning its never-ending encirclement of the world.

The song spread from Austria to Germany as folk music. Only in later years were Mohr and Gruber acknowledged the creators, though not a penny did they ever earn. It crossed borders; it went to sea with German emigrants.

Mohr and Gruber died as poor as they were born. But Gruber's old guitar still sings for him, for it was preserved and handed down in the family. Now each Christmas Eve it is brought to Oberndorf and the children's chorus gathers around the Christmas trees in the snow before the memorial chapel which stands on the site of the old St. Nicholas church, erected to the memory of the two men. There once more it sounds forth the background melody of one of the most famous, best-loved songs in the world. (1962)

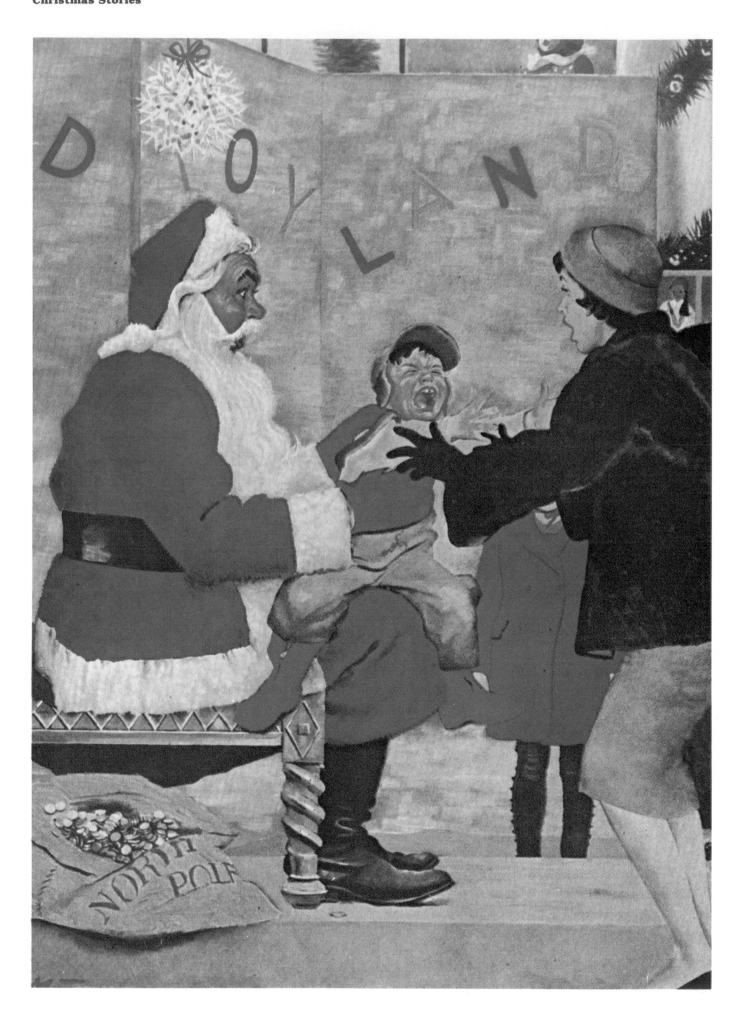

Nat B. Read, Jr.

How to be Santa Claus

"Ho! Ho! Ho!" So they've asked you to play Santa and you said you would! Well, listen, you jolly old elf, you, there's a lot more to being Santa than going "Ho! Ho! Ho!" As a matter of fact, you shouldn't even go "Ho! Ho! Ho!" at all. It scares the little kids!

Playing Santa is one of the greatest thrills this side of the North Pole. It'll make you laugh—and cry—and give you moments you'll treasure for all the Christmases to come. But if you're going to step like Clark Kent into a change of clothes that makes you all-knowing and all-powerful, you'd better do a bit of boning up on *how to Santa*.

Whatever you do, don't make a mistake that most rookie Santas blunder into while playing their first season suited up: Don't refer to "Mom and Dad" with a child you don't know. Maybe the kid doesn't have a Mom or doesn't have a Dad . . . or doesn't have either one. How do you get around that one? Simple: Always refer to "the folks" and you can't go wrong.

And even more basic than that, remember the surrogate Santa's cardinal role. It's the golden, unbreakable, iron-clad law of Santa-ing: *Don't promise anything*. Whatever else you might not remember, don't forget for the twinkling of an eye the consequences of Santa *himself* promising something that the child might not get. Tell the child you'll "see what you can do," or "see if the elves have made enough to go around," or simply "I'll surprise you!"

Don't ask a child what his or her name is. Santa's supposed to know that. (Say "young fellow" or "young lady.") But do act as if you recognize them and are glad to see them again. One of the safest openers is "My, how you've grown since last year!" It's a safe line since every child has grown in a year's time, but most children are genuinely awed that Santa recognizes them so quickly and remembers them from Christmas Past.

Another safe line of conversation is to encourage some development in the coming months. You ask them to be more helpful in keeping their rooms straight and in finishing their dinners during the coming year. Almost all children have room for improvement in those areas, and they always marvel at Santa's knowledge about their deficiencies.

If you see calluses on their thumbs, ask them not to suck their thumbs so much. Or you might ask them if they know their address or telephone number. If they don't know it, ask them to learn it for you. Children should know both as young as possible, so you're being a good teacher as well as a sly Santa.

After a few dozen kids, you'll begin to recognize the different attitudes the various age groups hold about Santa and the different challenges they present. The 1½- to 2½-year-olds are perhaps the most difficult. They face the prospect of meeting Santa with screaming terror or petrified silence. Don't touch a child unless it's obvious he or she appears comfortable with body contact. That's true of children of all ages, but especially the very youngest. If the young child balks, ask the parent to accompany him or her to the throne. You'll need to spend a little more time with children of this age generally to let them warm up a bit to such a foreign idea as red-suited, great-bearded Santa Claus.

Perhaps the most fun of all comes with the talkative 2½- to 3½-year-olds. They're old enough to have a trace of logic but not old enough to keep that logic untangled. They're the age group that teamed up with Art Linkletter to say the darndest things. You won't need much advice about handling this group; just allow them plenty of room for creative thinking.

The oldest of Santa's client groups (ages four to six) represents the biggest intellectual challenge. These postgraduate preschoolers are in the twilight years of their St. Nicholas fantasy. They're just on the verge of challenging the myth, or they're in the existential midst of Santa doubt, or they've recently crossed the bar into the huge fraternity which is in on the Big Secret. Whichever of these three stages they happen to be in, they're busily researching their budding intellect for the most penetrating and the most troublesome questions and tests of your Santahood.

This is the age that will examine your whiskers closely for telltale signs that your chin has a false front (a reminder to prepare yourself thoroughly), that will ask you to name your reindeer (you'd better know them!) or ask you about that other Santa in the store down the street ("One of us is just a helper; can you figure out which one?").

Or another common question is "Where are your reindeer?" Don't make the common novice Santa mistake of telling him they're in the parking lot, because sure as the hair on your chinney-chin-chin, he'll circle the building to check. So what's your answer? *I left them on the roof!* (It's logical and he'll just have to take your word for it. There's no way he can check out *that* line!)

Perhaps typical of this age's thinking is the San Francisco lad who wanted $500 in cold, hard cash. "Why so much?" Santa pressed. The lad replied that after this year he wouldn't be believing in Santa Claus anymore and he'd be needing the cash to buy his own Christmas gifts from now on.

Expect the best of children, but prepare for the worst! Beard-yankers are perhaps the worst. Watch closely to make sure they don't give your false hair a tug, but if they do, don't forget to yell "Ouch!" Santas have been jabbed with forks (to see if they are real) and kicked and hit (because they didn't bring the right things last year). Santas have frequently gotten their beards caught in children's hooks, zippers and buttonholes and one unwatchful Santa even had his beard ignited by a fiendish kid's lighter.

If you've never played Santa before, you're in for a surprise when you begin hearing the repetitious litany of Christmas gift requests from the child of today's society. You'll hear very few requests for ponies, bats and balls, model railroads, toy airplanes and other generic toys. Instead you'll hear a replay of the top toy companies' television advertising appeals. Children will ask for very specific brand-name toys. They'll want the Six Million Dollar Man, Baby Alive, Evel Knievel toys, Tenderlove dolls, Hush Little Baby Doll, Baby Baby Doll, Tuesday Taylor Doll, Wake Up Thumbelina, Don't Cry Baby, G.I. Joe and Stretch Armstrong. Today's child is recorded feedback of what has been programmed into its "want" bank by Saturday morning Madison Avenue mastery every week.

Occasionally, though, a bit of creative thought still breaks through the solid wall of television commercial replays. Like last year's California child who asked for a Kentucky Fried Chicken franchise. Or the lad who asked Santa last year for "a whole bunch of racehorses—real ones!" Perhaps the most optimistic child to petition Santa last year was one who asked simply for "all the money in the world."

Several years ago a child in Massachusetts asked Santa for a bird that couldn't fly. "Why a bird that can't fly?" Santa asked. "Because the bird you gave me last year flew away!" the tyke replied.

One of Santa's most puzzling questions last year came from an El Cajon, California, youngster who wanted all of last year's presents back. "What happened to them?" Santa wanted to know. "The duck took them!" was all the explanation Santa got, leaving him to ponder the mystery the rest of his life. One child wanted an Evel Knievel motorcycle, but made it clear he didn't want just the toy version. He wanted the real full-sized machine!

One of Santa's young patrons a few years ago asked him for a wedding gown, "so that I can marry my daddy," but a surprising number each year ask for new daddies or mommies in place of the ones they're mad at this year. One wanted a new daddy because the one she had was "wearing out on top."

Although his ancestry goes back quite a few centuries, Santa Claus is as American as Barbie Doll and the Six Million Dollar Man. It was only around the turn of the century that his image was clearly focused into the precise Santa that we know today. Before that, different people had different ideas. He was like the Easter Bunny today. Each artist pictures a slightly different rabbit: some fat, some thin, some with clothes of one sort or another, and some without. Santa Claus came in a variety of versions, too, until the emerging magazines of the late 1800s and early 1900s began to settle on a unanimous version of Santa Claus. The version they settled on was that of cartoonist Thomas Nast, widely circulated in *Harper's Weekly*.

Thomas Nast's Santa Claus drawings brought together a little bit of the Dutch *Sancte Klaas*, the Bavarian Pelz-Nicol, and the colonists' St. Nicholas and decided once and for all that Santa would be obese, would wear a red suit trimmed in white fur, would wear a stocking cap and black boots.

St. Nicholas was the patron saint of New York in the days of the early colony. (Some cynics say he still was up until the city went broke a couple of years ago!) St. Nicholas was not the same as our Santa Claus at all. St. Nick wore white instead of red. St. Nick was the patron saint of the sea while Santa Claus (if he is patron saint of anything other than profits) is patron saint of the air. St. Nick rode a white horse; Santa rides a red sleigh. St. Nick brought only sweets; Santa brings you anything within your credit range.

St. Nicholas was the figurehead on the Dutch ship, *Goede Vrouw*, and the Dutch quickly erected a church in his honor in their new colony. The children of the colony came to believe that St. Nicholas arrived on "the Christmas ship" from Holland on December 5 (which at that time was Christmas Eve).

The St. Nicholas figure descended from a real person, the Bishop of Myra, which is a town in Lycia, halfway between Rhodes and Cyprus. That was in the fourth century. St. Nicholas was a wealthy man whose "thing" was to help those who needed help—but to remain anonymous. Then someone found out who he was (maybe an investigative reporter) and thus, when good things were done for people, St. Nicholas got the credit for doing them.

Then along came a professor named Dr. Clement Clark Moore, teacher of Biblical Languages at General Theological Seminary in New York City. Dr. Moore undoubtedly taught his seminary students much about the sacred meaning of the religious Christmas observance, but history will remember him for his hallmark of the secular Yuletide.

It was Dr. Moore who composed a bit of verse to amuse his children and ended up amusing children for a century to come. Dr. Moore's little poem began, " 'Twas the night before Christmas, when all through the house. . . ." When his poem became widely known in Dr. Moore's later years, it got coupled with Thomas Nast's drawings and together they pretty well locked Santa Claus into the form we know today.

How did the stockings get hung by tradition on the fireplace mantel? Well, it seems that one year St. Nicholas dropped his purse down the chimney, and instead of falling on the hearth as it was supposed to, it got stuck in a stocking that had been hung there to dry.

Now you are all ready . . . ready for the greatest thrill of all. Step out of the drab, humdrum life you've been living, into the magical red suit that will make you more important than the President of the United States, wiser than any university dean, more interesting than a World Series pitcher and more powerful than any inhabitant of the Pentagon . . . at least to the children who are dreaming at this very moment of having a chance to meet . . . YOU! (1977)

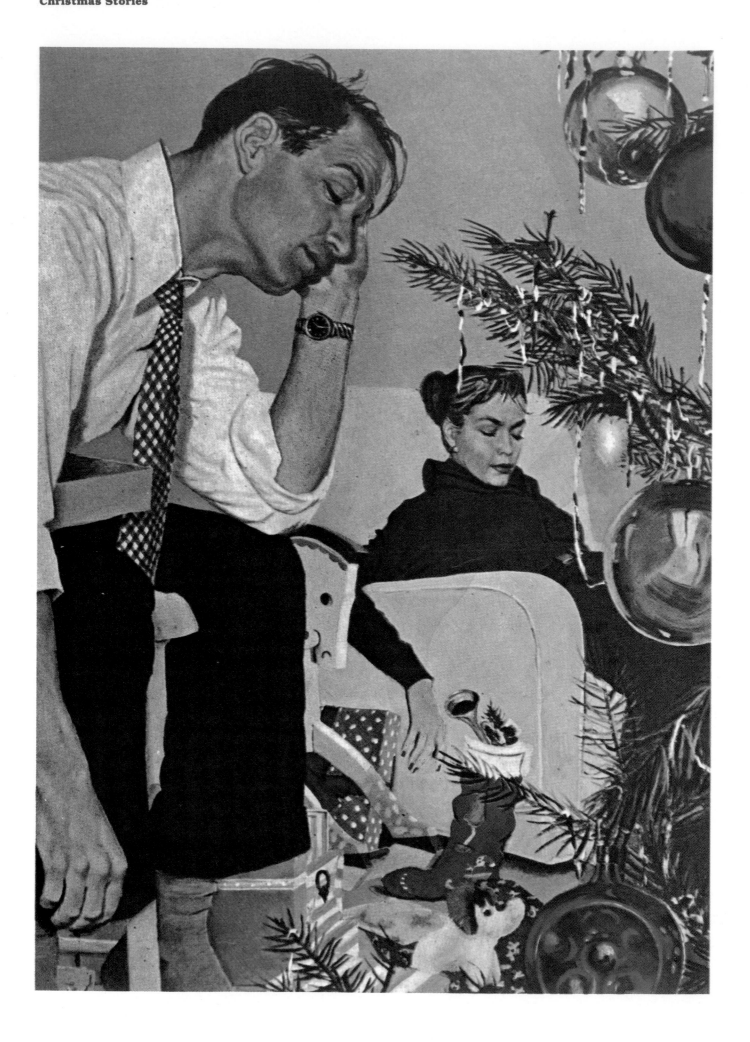

Robert M. Yoder

Merry Christmas in Ten Pieces

Yes, Virginia, there is a Santa Claus, and he has a home up near the North Pole, where it is colder than a bathroom floor. But don't believe that story about his having a lot of little dwarfs who put toys together for him, singing as they hammer. Nobody puts toys together, until Christmas Eve. Toys come in sixteen pieces, with one missing, and are put together by a large band of Involuntary Elves who call ourselves Santa's Press-Gang Helpers. We don't exactly sing, either, although a certain low, ominous murmur can be heard rising from a million homes on Christmas Eve. Put it this way, kid: That ain't no dwarf; that's your old man, beaten down. The luckless peon bought the toys; now he is learning that he has to finish manufacturing them, too, and by one A.M. his mood will make Scrooge seem like Sunny Ebenezer.

The first thing your frightened eye lights on, in the store, is a nice little red wagon, and you think, in your fatuous adult way, that this is just the thing to brighten the young heart. If you weren't partially paralyzed by the fear that you are shopping too late, you would realize that if the kid wants a wagon at all, it isn't this chaste little model. He would want one twice this size, with demountable tires, a ram-jet engine, electric lights, an overdrive and a windshield wiper, at $79.75. The kid next door has had one like that for two years and uses it only to haul his good toys in. Then you see the rocket-firing antiaircraft gun and realize that this is the answer. While it will not do bodily harm, and is therefore a partial bust to start with, it is a realistic-looking little number, and you buy it, at an exceedingly realistic price.

About the hour on Christmas Eve when you are in mild shock for fear the thing won't arrive, the delivery man stumbles in with a large package that can't be anything else. Will you put it under the tree that way? Or will you have it out in the open, so the child may see this splendid

sight first thing in the morning? Full of Christmas sentiment, you decide to expose the gun to full, gladsome view. So you tear off the wrapping. Here is a dial, here is a leg, here is a muzzle. You thought it would look like the store model, did you? Well, Santa has a little surprise for you. It's in pieces, and you are going to have to put it together. Merry Christmas, in at least ten pieces.

There is a sheet or folder of directions which could not get under your skin worse if they were in Spanish. They are written in the special language of directions, a mechanical gobbledegook achieved by writing the directions first in Ruthenian and then allowing the translation to curdle. A stop sign from the same mumbling pen would take 200 words. In the language of directions, "close the door" would read like this: "Grasp door-opening device with right knob-grasper and exert pressure outward until Panel A fills Aperture B. If scream is heard, other hand may be caught in opening." Along with being as turgid as possible, the directions are printed in a miniature type face known as Myopia Old Style, which is two sizes smaller than pearl and is otherwise used only to print the Declaration of Independence on souvenir pennies.

Well, lying there in pieces, the gun looks like nothing at all; it's got to be assembled. The first line you encounter in the directions says: "Using ring grasper from Assembly Kit, grasp collector ring near tube spar tightening guide rod" . . . but, thank heaven, that goes with some other toy. Your own directions start out more simply: "Connect round opening at end of Feeder Spring A with hooked end of trigger lock restraining bar by placing round opening over hook and pressing." What'd he think you'd do—spot-weld it? (The answer, unfortunately, is that he expects more than that, but not just yet.) Now the guy begins getting esoteric.

"If retaining mechanism fails to admit trigger, horizontal opening of drum impeding stopper should be widened horizontally." He means if the damned trigger won't go into the guard, you got to cut more room, and sure enough, it won't. This is going to be the only gun in the neighborhood with a demountable (falling out) trigger, unless you fix it. If retaining mechanism fails to admit what it's supposed to retain, then it should never have left the factory, but it's too late for that kind of recrimination now. Getting a hammer from the basement, a good paring knife and a screw driver, you manage to make the trigger go where it should, with one very bad moment when you think you've split the thing.

Well, the barrel, H, slides into place nicely; maybe things are beginning to go your way. The next step is to fit Firing Platform Z on Tripod, the Tripod being made by inserting Metal-tipped Ends of Legs into Sockets, which is child's play. Now all it takes is two bolts, L and M, which you slip into place with great efficiency. They must be firmly in place, the directions say, or gun will

not swivel on Platform Z; you might say, it won't swivel on any platform. A neat little bag contained the bolts, and in it you find the nut for Bolt L. But half an hour later you are still rummaging through wrapping paper in a grim search for the other nut, the crucial nut, the nut without which, as the Latins say, nothing. You may have 128 nuts of assorted sizes in a jar in the basement, but you will not have one that fits Bolt M. That is a freak size used nowhere else in the whole panoply of American industry. It is part of a shipment the toy manufacturer bought up from the Uruguayan War Assets Administration.

It is 11:45 by the time you manage to make the bolt hold with a piece of wire wrapped around it, and if the kid looks at that part, he will feel sure his toy is something the fireman repainted for the poor. Meanwhile the house has grown cold, three of the Christmas tree lights have winked at you by burning out, and your cigarette has fallen out of the ash tray and burned a six-dollar hole in the carpet. But the gun is starting to look like a weapon, and there can't be much more—only a couple of odd-looking metal pieces are left and a cardboard circle which is marked "Cosmic Ray Computer Dial."

One of the pieces of metal is easy enough to use. It's the missing plug, for lack of which the barrel has had that tendency to point to the floor like the tail of a whipped hound. The other is the crank with which the young gunner moves the barrel to keep on his target. You tackle the easiest job first—the computer is nothing more than two sections of light cardboard. "Bending

Tabs A, C, E and G," the directions say, "fit them into Slots B, D, F and H." The cardboard is a special kind which is as stiff as metal for a minute and then relaxes completely as you push, so that in twenty minutes you have four dog-eared tabs holding one crumpled dial marked with a little blood from the finger you cut trying to enlarge the slots.

Now you reach the part of the directions that tell you to fix on the telescopic sight. The diagram shows a handsome metal gadget coming to a square end, fitted into a ring fastened neatly around the end of the barrel. The only piece of metal you have left, outside of the crank, is a cotter pin. Even if you had missing part R, you still would have nothing like missing part Q which fits into it. You ransack the wrapping paper again, in what the novelists call cold fury, but with no luck. Finally, with great self-control, you smooth the wrinkled directions and read that jargon over again out loud. It is then that you come across Step 2. "In assembling Model A-100 Junior, our second-rate cheaper model for pikers, Step 1 may be disregarded." The directions continue: "No sight comes with this model. There is, however, a cotter pin. You can stick it on the barrel with adhesive tape and play like it's a sight. It ain't much, but then neither are you."

There is one final step—mounting the crank. "Slip Directional Crank 16 through Arm Y into Slot EE," the directions say. "When in position, give crank one quarter turn counterclockwise. Trigger should then fall sharply back into firing position." This is simplicity itself, and the only trouble is that if the crank goes through Arm Y, it misses Slot EE by a good quarter of an inch. The bitter thoughts that arise on Christmas Eve about the incompetent sleepwalker who bored that slot must visibly affect the temperature.

But the direction writer thought about this impasse, forehanded soul that he is. "It may be necessary, for best results"—meaning, to make the thing work at

all—"to enlarge aperture in Arm Y. This can be done quickly and easily by using a 16.3 metal file without tang, a 13-oz. dinging hammer and some Australian-canoe-builders' flux." This is equipment the ordinary household would be just as likely to have as a Javanese blowgun and a guroo bird, and you know, as your thoughts profane the early Christmas air, that the only 16.3 file in the world is one resting in the manufacturer's plant 850.3 miles away across the snowy landscape. So you gouge out a new Slot EE four times the proper size, the crank falls into place, wobbling foolishly, and the task is done. If it holds together until Christmas afternoon, you will be agreeably surprised, and a glance at the clock tells you that won't be long.

Yes, Virginia, there is a Santa Claus. If there weren't, ugly mobs of maddened parents would rove the streets Christmas Day armed with bolts, pins, wheels and axles, and some toy manufacturer would end up assembled on Movable Rail A wearing Feathers B and Tar C, after a slight going-over with No. 16 emery paper and a common hydraulic half-knurled center punch. (1947)

Robert M. Yoder

A Sure Sign That Christmas is Coming

In 1939, Irving Berlin completed a sheaf of songs for a movie to be called Holiday Inn and looked them over with an expert eye. Along with being a composer and the greatest source of musical accompaniment for America's festive occasions, Berlin is a publisher. It's his business to know how a song will go. Only two of these songs looked hopeful. In Berlin's estimation, "Be Careful, It's My Heart" had a chance of becoming a hit. He expected a modest success, but no more, for a song called "I'm Dreaming of a White Christmas."

Berlin has seldom been fooled by songs. This one fooled him completely. Of all his music—gay, sentimental or patriotic—it became "definitely the most successful," he says. That means topping such stand-bys as "God Bless America," which has earned well over $100,000 for the Boy Scouts and Girl Scouts, to whom Berlin assigned the royalties. White Christmas outsells even it.

What Berlin created, without in the least suspecting it, was a musical composition akin to Old Faithful, the geyser. It's a rare song hit that survives the brief, intense popularity of its first success and becomes a "standard," played year in and year out. White Christmas enjoys the rarest status of all—that of a perennial, automatic, ever-successful hit.

Every October for ten years now, as surely as the leaves begin to fall, it begins to sell anew like a fresh hit. In a day when sheet-music sales of 300,000 are considered very good, it runs to well over 3,000,000 copies. "It's a publishing business in itself," Berlin remarks, meaning that one such song alone would keep a publisher happy.

The radio stations start playing it on Thanksgiving Day—in very cautious amounts, actually, compared to the repetition of juke boxes. From Thanksgiving until midnight Christmas Day, there isn't a minute when the song isn't in the air somewhere. It is far more widespread than snow. In Vermont, a Christmas program would sound vaguely unofficial without it, though there may be eight inches of cold reality outside to make this dream a little bit unnecessary. But they sing it just as often in Louisiana and Florida and tropical places never touched by a snowflake.

Played "to death" in 1942, the year the song appeared, White Christmas has been played to death every year since, but doesn't die. For somewhere along the line it underwent a subtle transformation: It became a custom. A Gallup poll showed that of all the traditional Christmas music, only the classic "Silent Night, Holy Night" is a greater favorite. "Jingle Bells" and a dozen famous carols and hymns had to yield to Berlin's wistful air.

"The proof that I didn't expect this," the composer says, "is in the verse." For this is not, as thousands suppose, the expression of an American soldier honing for Christmas at home. According to the verse, the song is the lament of a Northerner stuck in California, and beefing about spending Christmas under the palms. When it was written, anyone with the price of a railroad ticket or a few gallons of gasoline could easily attain a White Christmas. But by the time the song appeared in 1942, millions of Americans were overseas. So in time it came to represent the longing for an old-fashioned Christmas in a world at peace.

A seasonal, topical song is born with two strikes on it. Christmas, furthermore, is perhaps the single occasion with which popular-song writers have had the least luck. Why should this prove such a resounding exception? Berlin explains its phenomenal success by saying he had thousands of collaborators. "People read a lot of things into that song," he remarks, "that I didn't put there." (1951)

Peg Bracken

Women Want the Oddest Things for Christmas

Women, as every woman knows, are gravely misunderstood. A major misconception about them, which men seem to cherish and even foster, concerns the gifts women like. It is based on the notion that women tend to focus on the price tag instead of the present.

It is time to set the record straight, and I must try. Lately I have been asking—of enough people to crowd the aisles of the annual Christmas church bazaar, including the Potholder and Penuche departments—a simple question: What is the best present anyone ever gave you?

My poll, I am glad to be able to report, proves that women are as sentimental as anyone else, and possibly more so. Indeed, women are starry-eyed and touchingly grateful for small favors; and right now, with the holiday season again charging us like a Miura bull, I think men should know this. Not only is it an interesting fact but it also can save them money.

A difference between the sexes became resoundingly clear long before I was done with my survey. A woman, for one thing, usually knows the answer right away. A man doesn't. A man must scratch his head and think. A woman's best present involves, nearly always, a man. But a man's best present is singularly uncluttered by romance. Dollars to doughnuts, he'll dredge it up out of the misty, many-layered, womanless past, out of the brave bright days when he was a boy. The pup he got when he was seven. The Fire Chief bike he got when he was ten. Or the dart board with real darts that went

"Thud!" Oh, boy! You'd think his girl or his wife never gave him a thing.

Now, perhaps there are sound reasons for this. Perhaps a man becomes so bemused after twenty or thirty adult Christmases, with their accompanying welter of sport shirts and camera attachments, that nothing comes very clear any more. As every woman knows, men are practically impossible to get presents for anyhow.

And perhaps a man figures, in some obscure but practical fashion, that it all comes out of his own hide anyway. He'll pay for it when the January bills roll in. Or else he figures he's paid for it already, in the number of casserole dishes he's eaten while she squeezed the price of it out of the grocery money. Or else, if she is a money-making working girl, he has likewise paid for it through a certain lack of dependable home comforts which he might otherwise be getting.

Whatever the reason, give a man a horse he can ride, a gun he can shoot, or a dart board with darts that go "Thud!" and give it to him when he's under twelve, and he will remember it, even though he probably won't remember that you gave it to him.

But women! Well, take my good friend Virginia, one of the first persons I questioned concerning her best gift ever. "The twelfth rose," she answered promptly. "But don't tell George!"

Well, the twelfth rose, it developed, was a rose which arrived on Christmas Eve—the final one of a dozen long-stemmed beauties given to her by a former suitor named Edward, delivered by a florist one at a time. He had told her that he'd always felt that a man should propose with a dozen long-stemmed roses, but he couldn't afford them all at once.

Observe, now, that Virginia didn't marry Edward. She married George; and this is probably a good thing. There is a certain pixies-in-the-bottom-of-my-garden touch to this gambit which doesn't augur too well as husband material. And if Edward couldn't afford even a dozen roses, how in the world did he think he could afford to get married?

Nevertheless, think of the gifts with which her husband has gifted Virginia! Carloads of heavy household equipment. Bushels of books, records, gadgets. Pecks of foamy lingerie, pearl earrings, candy. And yet, what flashes meteorlike through Virginia's little mind when you ask her about her best present? The twelfth rose.

Well, of course—a critic may carp—most women have a romantic memory or two tucked away, and how is a live husband to compete with a dead corsage? For that matter, why should he?

I can answer only that some of them do, and with excellent results. The best gift of another friend of mine is the small charm for her charm bracelet which her husband Joe gave her for Christmas. It is a little silver angel, the most impossibly angelic of all angels, and on the back of it is engraved, MOST OF THE TIME. LOVE, J.

Of course, this may not sound like much to a man, but it warms Amy's heart like a bonfire. Consider, too, its valuable side effects—what we might term the fallout. As any woman will perceive instantly, it gives Amy a most gratifying lead in the area of female friendsmanship. A friend notices the angel at luncheon, say, and asks to see it. Amy, co-operating gladly, hands it over. When friend reads that message of clearly

understated devotion, it sends her home in a state bordering on shock. *Her* husband never thought of giving any thing cute like that.

Now, this isn't to say that a woman always prefers that one perfect rose, or that one trinket, to that one perfect limousine. Nor is it to say that a woman can't feel sentimental about mink—a generic term here for any lavish object—if she gets it at the right time from the right person.

Unfortunately, though, it seldom works out like this. If her husband can easily afford it, then it is just another coat from daddy. And even though he can't easily afford it, still there's no escaping the fact that there's something in it for him. The caveman dragging that fur-covered carcass home was showing the world what a mighty hunter he was.

At any rate, none of the women I asked—including four minks, two beavers, and five of unknown but quite respectable ancestry—mentioned a fur. Or a jewel. Or, for that matter, the handsomely overpriced negligee-and-nightgown arrangement which harried husbands so often pick up at 5:29 on Christmas Eve. The simple fact seems to be that Presents and Possessions are filed in quite different compartments of the female brain.

Let's consider the case of my neighbor, Mary B. She is blessed, or hobbled, depending on where you sit, by having a husband who couldn't care less what he eats. But Mary, on the other hand, thinks it mightily important. Moreover she loves to cook.

For eight years, therefore, she has been doggedly cooking beautiful food—from Soufflé d'Écrevisses Florentine to Tournedos Nicoise, not to mention sauces Mornay, Bercy and Noisette—all the while knowing that her husband would be quite as happy with plain canned beans and store-bought cookies.

Then last Christmas her husband came through with the world's most beautiful gourmet cookbook, a superb, lavish, terribly expensive affair which she had wanted for years but had never felt, in all good conscience, that she could buy. This, Mary tells me, is her best present bar none, because—as she put it—it said more than it was.

Consider, too, the best present of my cousin Charlotte. Charlotte loves antiques or, more accurately, what she calls Cute Old Things, which she finds in Funny Old Shops or in obscure corners of the Salvation Army's collection depot. She has a special fondness for old bottles, old bootjacks and chipped stone pickling crocks; her husband, who doesn't share this enthusiasm, has been heard to complain that their living room is beginning to look like somebody's basement.

Nevertheless, one Christmas he gave her a twenty-five dollar receipt from one of the more disreputable of these places and told her to go buy some more.

There it is again—the lovely and warming affirmation that seems to be part and parcel of most best presents: simply, you're an odd duck, but I love you anyway.

And right here we have the reason why giving her The Gift She'd Never Buy Herself—unless she happens to be a teenager—can be an enormous booboo. Not that this isn't highly successful if the gift is what Billy Rose once called a Five-Dollar Cake of Soap, the very best-of-breed item in a category which the lady already likes. But when you choose a category you think she *should* like—say, a good big dollop of French perfume for a lady who never touches the stuff, or stout fishing waders for a Southern Camellia, you are walking on eggshells.

You see, gentlemen, most women past the age of consent cherish a notion, deluded though it may be, that they have achieved for themselves a rather satisfactory personal style. When you give

the out-and-out country-tweeds type a mad marabou trifle, you are implying, of course, "I can see the femme fatale peeping through that tailored exterior, and here is something to bring her out."

But how do you know she doesn't consider herself a tweedy-type femme fatale anyhow? Perhaps she has spent years perfecting this; and she wants and needs that marabou object like another eyebrow. She may misread the message as "Why don't you *do* something about yourself?"

You see, here you are verging perilously close to the Insult Gift—those holly-trimmed packets of toothpaste and other unlikely gift items which bloom like poinsettias in drugstores at this time of year. The merchants' enthusiasm is commendable but misguided; and anyone who gives one of these affairs to a lady of spirit is apt to get it back, right across the chops.

A variation on the Gift She'd Never Buy Herself theme, incidentally, is the Gift Unexpected, or, Let's Give Grandma a brace of falcons. A man I know, a rather philosophical type, does this frequently, in the fond hope that he is opening windows onto new vistas.

He once gave his wife an ant farm—one of those glass-enclosed ant universes, before which you are supposed to sit, hypnotized, watching the ants go around doing whatever it is ants do. But his wife was not hypnotized. She gave the ant farm to a little boy across the street who happens to be hot for bugs.

Actually, this window-opening theory reads prettier than it works out. Most of the people you know have plenty of windows open already; they just don't have the time to look out of them.

Now, with teen-agers, as I have indicated, the Gift She'd Never Buy Herself presents no problems. In the first place, it is hard to think of one. Teen-agers will buy *anything* for themselves, given the funds, and the farther out in left field, generally speaking, the better they like it. If your gift indicates that you have discerned the latent temptress beneath that pudgy or knobby-kneed exterior, you are a hero.

A friend of mine tells me that a lipstick, given to her at Age 12, was her best present. It was a brand widely advertised as kissproof, and although my friend never put it to the test, she says it was a glorious feeling just knowing that it was there in her school-going pocketbook, safe among her grubby handkerchiefs and her streetcar tokens.

Conversely, my friend Eloise suffered greatly in her formative years. One Christmastime her lad, of whom she had expected great things, gave her a sturdy, solemn, practical, navy-blue umbrella. To Eloise this was about as romantic a gift as a jar of peanut butter. That Christmas was curtains for him.

And I'll never forget my own traumatic experience back in my salad days—and very green salad days they were. I was going with an older, sophisticated man of eighteen, and I had stars in my eyes, but he had a gleam in his. His Christmas present to me was a bottle of French champagne, which somehow wiped the "Merry" off my Christmas like a wet sponge. I had wanted something to cherish, you see, and something that I could flaunt, ever so casually, in front of the girls. Champagne wasn't romantic; it was—well, just wicked.

The rule here would seem to be this: if you are a teen-ager's dashing, sophisticated uncle, a bottle of champagne might be a dashing, sophisticated gift. But if you are her true love—or she considers you so—she wants an Ever Thine bracelet, or an Arlene Francis-type heart.

You cannot pursue the matter of presents any distance without coming upon the subjects of toe covers and sidesaddles.

Toe covers—I don't know where they got the name—are those highly improbable widgits like left-handed *fettucine* cutters or a set of seven blue velvet bookmarks, each dedicated to a different day of the week, which provoke a really sincere "Oh, you shouldn't have!" from the recipient. They are usually rewrapped and redistributed the following Christmas, if you are certain you remember whom not to give them back to.

Only by a happy fluke does a toe cover ever turn out to be someone's best present. The only instance I know of which comes even close concerns a hand-embroidered, fluted, scalloped, starched linen liner for a breadbasket—truly a magnificent toe cover—which was given to a business girl. She had no breadbasket, of course, nor did she have a summer hat; and she needed a summer hat to wear to a wedding. So she wore this hand-embroidered, fluted, scalloped, starched linen breadbasket liner, and it was a vast success. While this doesn't make it a Best Present exactly, it's still getting remarkable mileage out of a toe cover.

Sidesaddles, too, are seldom "best presents." A sidesaddle is our family's name for that good book you give your husband because you want to read it yourself, or the croquet set which the croquet fan happily gives to a member of his immediate family for the whole family to enjoy.

These can be good presents, mind you, but not best presents. An illustration of this is the best present a friend of mine, named Constance, received from her husband, named Al.

It was their second Christmas and first baby. Al's original idea, for Connie's Christmas, was a smart nonmaternity suit, which he certainly would have enjoyed seeing her in after all those smocks. Next he thought of a decent record player, for they both wanted one. But he finally discarded both these sidesaddles in favor of a one-day-a-week baby sitter for a year.

This brought him no joy. He didn't look forward to having the lady around. But to Connie, who had heard the clank of the jail gates closing as she regarded the diaper-and-bottle-bound vista before her, it was the absolutely best present of her life.

Thus, the best present, it seems, isn't usually laden with side benefits to the giver, although it does bring its own subtle rewards.

Indeed, what the best present isn't can be quite as instructive as what it is. Item: a woman's best present isn't usually like anyone else's.

Many a fond husband and father has come a cropper here. Wandering dazedly through a department store, with his wife and daughter on his mind and the December 25 deadline breathing hot on his neck, a man may stumble into the Christmas crop of cashmeres and solve his problems in one fell swoop. Both his women like yellow, he knows, and anyway his feet hurt. So he settles for two identical yellow cardigans.

This he should not have done, as he will learn on the first shopping day after Christmas, when he finds that one or the other of the yellow cashmeres has been magically transmuted into a red pullover or an electric skillet.

Another point that it is well to keep in mind is that her best present isn't usually the one she ordered.

The huge exception here is little girls. If a little girl wants a doll buggy, expects a doll buggy and doesn't get a doll buggy, she won't even see all the hand-smocked dresses and doll houses and Teddy bears she *does* get, and you will be scouring the town in search of an open-for-business Doll Buggy Store on Christmas morning.

But adults are different, especially female adults. One woman whom I asked said that last Christmas she had pined for, and asked for, a certain marble-topped cigarette table, which her husband gave her. But the present she truly loved, the present she shows everyone, was an unexpected one. It was a little framed picture—a color snapshot of her azaleas that he had taken,

quite unknown to her, the previous spring.

It is true, too, that some of the best presents are bittersweet. My friend Phyllis had a beloved cat named Giddy, who died in her seventeenth summer, having had a rich full life and approximately 238 children. Phyllis has received some impressive gifts in her time, but the one she remembers was the exact, lively, kitten replica of Giddy, which her husband gave her the following Christmas.

Then there is Alicia, whose best present was the watch her mother gave her when she was twelve. She had wanted a watch badly; and her mother, a woman of sentiment and tradition, had her own mother's handsome heavy gold lapel watch checked over, beautifully polished and gift-wrapped.

But Alicia's idea had been something sporty—in white gold—a wrist watch, the kind the other girls had. When she saw the heirloom she was crushed; and then, when she saw her mother's face, she was doubly so, but the moment couldn't be undone. Alicia remembers it vividly—perhaps, as she says, because she did more growing up in that moment than in all her twelve years.

A woman's best present can be any one of many things, you see, depending on who she is and where she stands, and also who is standing beside her. Another friend of mine was given a gift which is hard to forget.

She and her husband had had a warm, happy marriage; he died suddenly in September. Christmas was a bleak time for her that year; but, for the sake of her two young sons, she trimmed the traditional tree in their traditional way.

Under the tree on Christmas morning she found a special gift for herself: a fifty-cent piece, wrapped as only a ten-year-old boy would wrap it, from Doug, the elder.

You see, it had been his father's custom to give his mother, among her other gifts, a small wrapped-up check. Now that Doug was the man of the family, he was keeping, as best he could, the old traditions alive. (1959)

Author Unknown

The First Merry Christmas

An English gentleman by the name of Henry Cole once found himself in something of a predicament. Actually, it was the sort of a pinch any chap could create for himself. Christmas of 1843 was drawing nigh, and he had fallen far behind in his correspondence to friends. His impulsive solution was the first Christmas card, an idea which traveled around the world and has solved similar problems for millions of tardy correspondents ever after.

But to get back to Mr. Cole, he was quite an imaginative fellow. After his initial inspiration, he contacted an acquaintance, John Calcott Horsley of the Royal Academy, and commissioned him to design some sort of a card which would reflect seasonal sentiments. He also wanted a card which could be printed in quantity and sent around to all the people to whom he owed letters. In the back of Cole's mind, no doubt, there was the recent English Postal Reform which had created penny postage. Cole's lively brain had seized the moment.

Horsley's first card, shown on this page, depicted a convivial family party in progress, the adults holding their glasses up in a toast to the recipient of the card. The side panels show two of the oldest traditions of Christmas, feeding the hungry and clothing the needy.

The greeting on the first Christmas card is as

The end of Henry Cole's correspondence problem, and the beginning of a custom: the first Christmas card.

The Christmas element was often obscure in early cards.

familiar as "Hello," and just as friendly. "A Merry Christmas and a Happy New Year to you" was the simple but heartfelt message it conveyed to the recipient.

At least 1,000 copies of the Cole-Horsley card were printed. Of that number, only a dozen are known to exist today. Two of them, including the only known unused copy, are on display; they may be seen in the Hallmark Historical Collection in Kansas City, Missouri, as may all the rare cards shown on these pages, and thousands of others.

Henry Cole's novel idea really caught on in the British empire. It was boosted considerably by the penny post which made a large-scale exchange of cards possible throughout the United

Children were popular subjects during the Victorian age.

Kingdom—upon which in those days the sun never set.

An established printer of playing cards, Goodall & Sons, issued in 1862 what is probably the first large selection of Christmas cards. Other English publishers, notably Marcus Ward and the De La Rue Company, added their own beautifully printed or engraved works to the market.

England's famous woman artist, Kate Greenaway, entered the Christmas Card competition at this point, contributing outstanding greeting-card designs to Marcus Ward. Over the years, her paintings of cute children dressed in high fashion drew many imitators.

Much can be learned of the tastes, manners and preoccupations of people of an earlier generation by a study of their Christmas cards. Their archaic notions amuse us.

The Victorians, for example, imagined their beloved children as miniature men and women and saw them as innocent and coy. This is reflected in the cards of that age. Also characteristic

The humor of a bygone era is often reflected in its cards.

of the Victorian age were a kind of gamey, masculine wit and, in contrast to this, an almost mawkish sort of sentimentality.

The most popular cards of the 1860s and 1870s showed little Christmas significance. They depicted a variety of subjects, such as children, landscapes, kittens, fairies and flowers, portraits, animals, fish and even reptiles.

Then Bostonian card-maker Louis Prang appeared on the scene. He wrought two big changes in the industry. Prang, who became known as "the father of the American Christmas card," perfected the lithographic process of multicolor printing in the 1870s, thus making possible a new level of artistic quality in Christmas cards.

Prang held contests in which artists competed with their finest works. Many of the winning pieces were of the Nativity and other religious scenes; thus Prang helped put religious significance into Christmas cards.

Nineteenth-century America was a rugged and sometimes harsh place; there was a longing for

Artwork has ranged from serious, religious topics. . .

. . .to not-so-serious, fanciful illustratons.

A single, well-designed Christmas card can convey the season's greetings and a feeling of peace on earth, as well.

fragility and beauty expressed in the Christmas cards of that era.

By 1881, Prang was already printing almost five million Christmas cards a year. As incentive, he offered prizes of as much as $4,000 to promising artists who submitted designs for his growing line of cards.

Near the turn of the century, however, Prang was forced into the background by a great influx of penny cards made in Germany. The entire Christmas-card industry from then until the World War I era was virtually monopolized by the Germans.

In the 1920s, major American greeting-card companies again emerged, and as before, their Christmas cards reflected the spirit of the times. During the Great Depression, cards spoofed being poor, and always hinted that tomorrow we'd all be better off.

Through World War II, Christmas-card Santas carried American flags, and there were "missing you" sentiments for the many servicemen who were separated from their families by the oceans. In the years that followed, the grimness of the Cold War brought about a demand for more humor in greeting cards. It was then that the studio card—with its odd Santas and dopey-looking reindeer—was born.

Nowadays, the Christmas cards received and sent each year number in the billions, their number multiplied by factors such as the affluence and mobility which disperse friends and families to far places.

Just to give you an idea, Hallmark Cards, Inc., the largest and best-known publisher of cards, prints its greetings in 21 languages and distributes them in more than 100 countries and, to keep the happy wishes rolling, turns out approximately eight million greeting cards *daily*! A staff of more than 300 artists creates more than 12,000 greeting-card designs annually.

Making his rounds on wheels in an earlier card—the jolly old elf.

The Hallmark people estimate that as many as 3,000 people, involved in up to 300 separate processes, actually combine their talents in the conception and publication of a single greeting card. Each card has to run the gauntlet of 30 testing stations before it is finally ready for the customer: About 95 working days (and possibly more, if there are over-heated discussions concerning the length of Santa Claus' beard) are needed to completely develop a greeting card from the first step to the final product.

All this emanated from the conviction of a young lad, Joyce C. Hall, in 1910, that what was needed on greeting cards—and lacking at that particular time—was a "from me to you" sentiment. It sounds almost too simple, perhaps, but that little bit of sentiment, according to recent estimates in the business press, brings in today annual sales of more than $300 million to Hallmark.

Christmas cards, those convenient conveyors of peace on earth and goodwill among men, are here to stay even though the penny post is now eight cents. (1971)

The range of characters and scenes depicting seasonal sentiments is limited only by designers' imaginations.

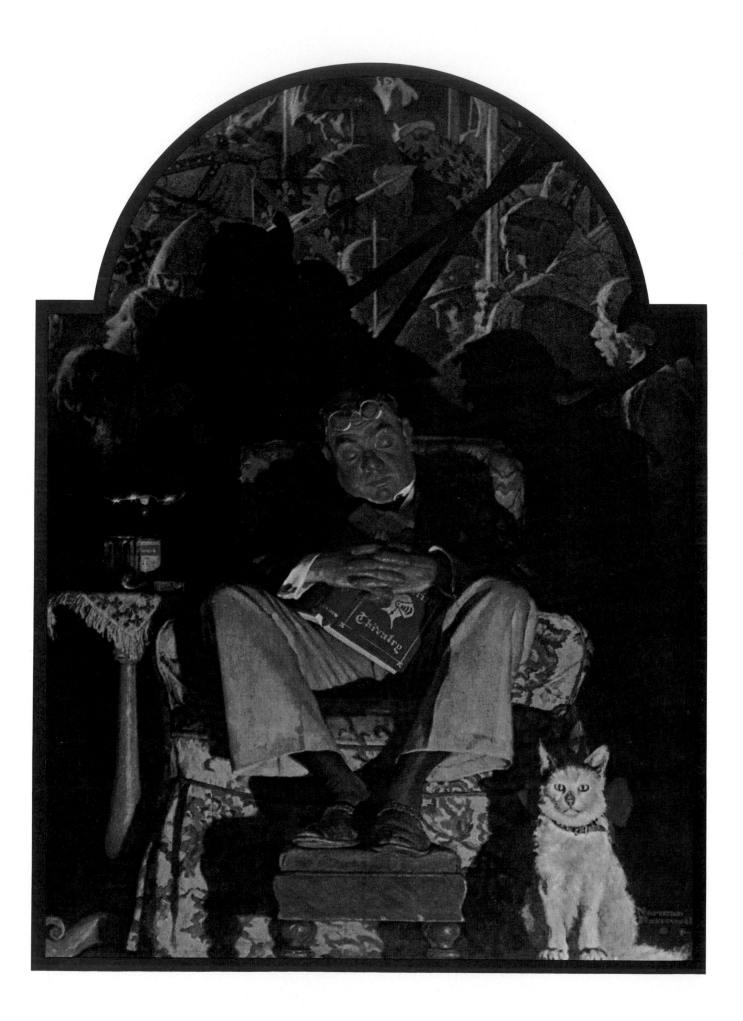

CHRISTMAS SCENES IN FACT AND FICTION

Mack Thomas

Hard-Rock Candy

It wasn't long after Thanksgiving until the getting ready for the Christmas Service at the Methodist Church began. First there was the swing of the Bible from Proverbs to Revelation. The rest of it happened almost automatically.

Miss Ruth started the first Sunday in December, giving out parts to the three-, four-, five-, six,- seven- and eight-year-olds in her Sunday-school class. Billy Dixon got to be Joseph in the Nativity scene. Mary Lou Gannaway got to be Virgin Mary. Pud got a rhyme that went

Little fairy snowflakes
Dancing in the flue . . .
Old Man Santy Claws
What is keeping you?

Toby got to hold up the pole with the bright star of Jerusalem because nobody else would do it. The others got thought into clusters to sing "Santy Claws Is Coming to Town" or one chorus of "Jingle Bells" because Miss Henrietta's nine-, ten-, eleven-, twelve- and thirteen-year-olds were doing "Silent Night."

Mamma and Celia got to make a red flannel fairy's costume for Pud and a pole-holder's costume for Toby. Papa got to supervise the learning of Pud's rhyme. Jenny got to drive everyone almost crazy trying to make herself able to sing "Away in a Manger" for her solo an octave too high.

Somehow everything and everyone was ready by Christmas Eve. Everyone set out about seven o'clock, coming up all the ways to Luke Street and the warm lights in the windows of Methodist Church shining through the winter dark and the winter cold.

Miss Ruth was grabbing kids as they came through the wooden front doors, getting her cast together. The grown-ups stood around in their coats feeling *different* than when they were in the churchhouse on Sunday or even Prayer Meeting Night.

Down front in the right-hand corner the fat tree that flattened two feet of its top on the ceiling was hung with all the fancy in Cottonmill. There were red ropes and green ropes of bristled paper twisted or sewn on backbones of string. There were bangles and balls, and crayoned and scissored angels, dangling at branchtips. There were pieces of colored glass shaped like lean fangs of ice that hang from eaves, and thousands of long shreds of tinfoil twisting and glittering in the light. Crisscrossing everything, binding it all, were interlocked bracelets of flourpasted pieces of red and orange and green and all other possible colors of paper.

Here and there and there in the branches were little packages, ribboned and bowed. There and there and here in the branches were cap pistols and dolls. Plain cap pistols, silvery and small, and Buck Jones pistols with pearly-looking handles. Rubber dolls you could drop and not break and dolls with clothes and hair and blinking eyes, dolls that could sleep like people.

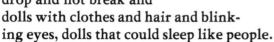

Under the tree, waiting for Santy Claws to come at the end of the program and give them out, were flat and thick and square packages wrapped in tissue and Christmas paper. And there were long presents that had to be baseball bats, and skates and scooters and even a Red Racer wagon or two. Then there were all the plain brown-paper sacks, like the kind at Tragers' Store for carrying home groceries. The top was twisted on all of them, but everyone knew they were from the Mill and had sometimes an apple and sometimes an orange and always six pecans and a four-inch piece of wiggledy hard-rock candy.

By seven-thirty all the Cottonmill Christians and some that weren't were gathered. The place was filled with Shepherds and snaggled-toothed Angels; Shepherds with Red Goose shoes and rolled-up overalls under their flowing, bed-sheet robes, Shepherds with handles from brooms and handles from mops to make-believe were things you could sit on and twist on and throw and play swords with and poke with and ride like a witch until it was time for them to be Shepherds' staffs. All the Angels had were wings and halos, and the wings felt funny and itched; the halos slipped. One of the Angels was cross-eyed, another had freckles and a sty on his eye. Another had one wing torn loose from its harness and another had a fat split lip. One Angel nicked a Shepherd's nose with his halo and screamed and cried at the top of his four-year-old lungs when the Shepherd poked him with a staff.

Finally, Brother Cartwright stood up and held up his arms like he knew how to do and settled his half of the problem by saying, "All right, now, if you grown Brothers and Sisters will find a seat, the children have their Christmas program to give us." With that he met Miss Ruth at the piano, and said, "I'll give a prayer, then the rest is up to you."

"Now, Brother Cartwright," she said, "you know good and well that I'm not able to do all this by myself. Ardell!" she said to the cross-eyed Shepherd, "you leave Bessie's halo alone!"

"But you know I've got to see that the tree doesn't catch on fire," Brother Cartwright said to Miss Ruth.

"I've got it all written down here on this piece of paper," said Miss Ruth. "Just read out what I've got as you come to it so everyone will know what the children are doing." She made him take the paper, then turned to seeing about the music and left him standing there. After a minute he quit looking at the back of her head and glanced down at the paper.

By now all the grown-ups were more or less settled on the benches. Brother Cartwright said a prayer, saying how grateful everyone was for coming through another year of joys and hardships to another birthday of Jesus the Savior, and asking blessings on the little children who were about to take part in the program, and on everything. He saw that the Shepherds and Angels were getting restless so he said Amen and cleared his throat while he tried to figure out the instructions Miss Ruth had written on the paper.

"Now why don't we all stand and start things off this evening with the first and last verses of. . .*O Little Town of Bethlehem how still we see thee lie. . .above the deep and dreamless. . .* well, I'm sure all of you know it."

Everyone stood, and Brother Cartwright said, "Would you start us off, Miss Ruth?"

Miss Ruth played the part that matches "*the silent stars go by,*" and everyone came in more or less together. Not many sang the last verse because not many knew it. When they got through it Brother Cartwright waited until everyone got settled again, then read, "Now the littlest ones in the Sunbeam Class will sing 'Jingle Bells.' "

Half the ones in Miss Ruth's class that didn't have a part in the Nativity came away from the wall beside the piano and lined up bed sheet to bed sheet in the space in front of the pulpit. Miss Ruth had to get up from the piano and straighten it out about who was to stand closest to the Christmas tree. When that was settled she went back to the piano and played the last line of the song, hunching her shoulders and elbows up and down, hoping some of the children would be watching her and get an idea of when to start singing from what she was doing. There was some trouble with "*Dashing thro' the snow in a one-horse open sleigh*," but once they were past that line everything went about as well as she had expected.

It had to be settled all over again from year to year about the clapping, but Brother Cartwright did it when "Jingle Bells" was finished so the rest of them started. The children being clapped at stood there too long or Brother Cartwright read the next thing on the list too soon, one or the other, but everything got all snarled up when the other Sunbeamers tried to start lining up to sing "Santy Claws Is Coming to Town." Miss Ruth was worrying with a sore finger she'd just hurt, thinking about how she should have let the little ones sing "Santy Claws Is Coming" and had the older ones do the one with the hard part about the one-horse open sleigh, and so Brother Cartwright quietly came down from the pulpit, and a couple of helpful women came up from their seats and got the little Sunbeamers all out of the way. When that was finally done, Brother Cartwright felt someone might have forgotten what was going to be sung so, to be on the safe side, he read it again before he got back up in the pulpit.

"Santy Claws Is Coming" sounded fine, even to Miss Ruth and she knew music. Even the Sunbeamers that sang joined in the clapping, but there's a limit to how long two hundred people can clap at six- and seven- and eight-year-old kids, even their own, so it ended, finally, and Brother Cartwright stood up and read, "Next is Pud—I guess I ought to say Alfred, it being Christmas and all—but anyhow he's going to say us a Christmas poem, called "Little Fairy Snowflakes.""

Pud edged out from the wall with the red tip of his fairy cap hanging wrong and tickling his nose, looking all sheepish and uncertain and neckless, his round cheeks and chin scrunched down into his shoulders. His eyes got big when he made it to where he was supposed to stand, and he started looking all around until he saw Papa and Mamma again sitting on the second bench. He looked at Papa and waited. Papa nodded at him, and so he started, "*Little Fairy Snowflakes dancing in the flue, Old Man Santy Claws, what is keeping you?*"

Then, before clapping could start, he looked at Papa again and Papa nodded at him again, so he went on with the rest of the poem, reciting it just like Papa had carefully taught it to him before, saying, "*. . .the Vinter Vind, whi. . .I mean vistling around the corner of the house.*"

Everyone in Cottonmill knew that last part wasn't in the regular poem because "Little Fairy Snowflakes" was in the program every year.

When they all started laughing with their clapping, Pud got all excited and not too sure about things but thinking it must be all right because the laughing about it sounded good and not *at* him, and he started laughing too. The ones that could looked away from Pud to where Mamma and Papa were sitting with Celia. Papa had his arms folded across his chest, and there was a big grin on his face. Celia looked like it didn't bother her at all, but Mamma almost died.

It took a while for all that to die down, but finally it was time for the Nativity. Miss Ruth had it worked out nice. There was hay down front, between the piano and the tree, and there was a manger. Burlap was scattered around and hanging from the rail where you knelt to take Communion. A doll was in the manger, wrapped good, and there was plenty of space around it for standing close.

Miss Henrietta's class lined up behind the Communion rail and waited. Toby got to stand in the pulpit and hold up the cane pole with the wire taped to it and the light at the top for the star. The three wise men got in place, and Mary Lou Gannaway came and stood looking into the manger. She was all wrapped in a bed sheet dyed a pale shade of blue.

Jenny went over by the piano and waited while Miss Ruth took the matches she'd brought from home and lit candles and handed them out to the Angels. She got them spread around the way she wanted them, then she lit a big one on a saucer and handed it to Joseph, telling him, "Now, you be careful with that, Billy, and don't set fire to anything." Billy went over and stood by Mary Lou, beside the manger. It was getting pretty crowded but the Shepherds were left to stand where they wanted to and finally everything was ready.

Brother Cartwright went back to the fuse box on the wall just inside the door and waited until Miss Ruth got back to the piano where Jenny was waiting, then he pulled the switch and Miss Ruth played the introduction to "Away in a Manger" and Jenny came in just at the right time, singing it clean and pure and making some of the notes like she was striking glass bells. When she finished there was a hush on the whole place, then Miss Ruth hit three notes, like that, do me so, and Miss Henrietta's class came in with the words, singing, "*Si-ilent Night. . .Ho-oly Night. . .All is calm. . .All is bright. . .*" and it

 was beautiful. Some of the Angels looked in love with their candles and some of the Shepherds couldn't keep from wiggling their staffs but it was beautiful, all the candles flickering in the Angels' hands and making soft shadows in the hollows and bends of faces and everything, the lights on the tree making dim branch-shadows on the walls and the ceiling, the presents all through and underneath, the star of Bethlehem dipping and bobbing just a little, silvery blue, looking far away up there above the manger, and the harmony working right in the singing, making you want to do it when the words of the song said, "*Sleep in Heavenly Pe-e-eace. . .Slee-eep in Heaven-ly Peace.*"

When it was over nobody thought about clapping. A few of the mammas got up and started hugging Shepherds and Angels, not knowing exactly why. Mary Lou Gannaway's mamma had tears in her eyes when she hugged Mary Lou. Some of the men cleared their throats and made a point of switching the way they had their legs crossed. All this couldn't have lasted over a minute because it wasn't any more than that between the end of the Nativity and the church-house doors banging open for Santy Claws. He came in just when Brother Cartwright turned on the lights, stomping down the aisle with a big sack on his back, saying, "Merrr-ry Christmas! Yo ho ho ho Merrr-ry Christmas!"

The little ones started squealing, and the bigger ones started jumping up and down and clapping their hands, yelling, "Santy Claws! Santy Claws! Ohhhh! It's Santy Claws, Mamma, it really is!" and one or two of the biggest medium ones said, "Heck!" and "Aw shoot! That ain't Santy Claws!" and some that didn't intend to stand for such awful things said, "It is *too* Santy Claws! It is!" and the doubters said, "Crazy, anybody can see it's just Homer Bates," but the faithful replied, "You're the one that's crazy, Crazy! It is too Santy Claws. . .ain't it, Mamma?" and all the time he kept coming down the aisle, saying, "Yo ho ho ho ho. . .it's old Santy! Merrr-ry Christmas! Yo ho ho ho ho!"

By the time he got down by the big tree there were so many kids pushing up around him it took Brother Cartwright's help to find a place to set the sack he swung off his back. "Now you little ones move back a little so Santy can get on with handing out the presents," said the preacher. "Come on now and get back out of Santy's way. . .that's right. . .My my! Isn't it exciting! Get on back, now."

Finally, Santy Claws had enough room for giving. He took a minute looking back and forth between the tree and the sack, making it look like he couldn't decide where to start. Even the ones that were willing to bet $50,000 to a doughnut hole that it was Homer Bates joined in the yelling for "The sack! The sack you had on your back, Santy!"

"What's that?" he said, "What's that you're wanting old Santy to do?" He held his hand to his ear rim and turned his head, pretending to do his best to make out what they were saying. "The sack!" they yelled. "Oh, Santy, the sack!"

"Ohh!" he said at last, "You've had all this time to look at the tree and now you want to see what's hid in the sack! Yo ho ho ho!" He opened the sack so his hand would go down its neck in a private way, and pulled out a tiny, shiny red purse and gave it to Emily Gregg for her Ohh and Ahh. His hand went back in the sack and pulled out a fishnet pocket of marbles. Billy Dixon that once had been Joseph said, "Boy! A whole bag of Zebras!" so then Santy gave them to him with a yo and a ho.

It went on like that. There were Yo-Yos and tops and bags of marbles, which went to the boys, and there were

patent-leathery purses and cards with a rubber ball and jacks and cards with curving yellow butterfly combs and butterfly hairclips, which went to the girls. When everyone had something from the bag, Santy Claws stuffed it under his coat and scratched his neck where the beard was beginning to itch. Then under the Christmas tree he went, making straight for one of the Red Racer wagons. He had some trouble reading the tag, or made it seem like he did, twisting his head from side to side, then his beard got caught on one of the catchy branches of the fir tree. It took some doing but he got it untangled and kept it on his face, then he went at the tag on the wagon's handle again. After a twist and a couple of squints, he said, "It looks like Pud and Toby Siler."

Toby had given it up way back in the middle of "Jingle Bells." While he was standing paralyzed, taking back the giving-up so the wagon could be his, Pud was under the tree and in the red bed and out and all over it and dragging and butting it out over barricades of presents and brown-paper bags. Toby thought, "Pud's," then Papa's voice said, "Toby, you'd better help him."

"You'd better. . .I'd better. . .I. . .mine!" ran through Toby's head, and then he thought, "OURS!" and he flew hands-first from the spring of belief to helping and touching and owning.

Finally, except for the decorations, the Christmas tree was clean as a wishbone stripped of wishes. There was nothing left but the brown-paper sacks, and a good thing, too, because by then Santy Claws was looking pretty tired. Some of the papas noticed there wasn't much ho anymore in his Yo ho, and started helping him see that every kid got his sack from the mill. Before it was through, Brother Cartwright and even Miss Ruth were lending a hand.

When it got down to the sacks that had no takers, Santy Claws stood for a minute with one in each hand, looking around. Then he said, "Well, I guess that's it," to no one in particular, and put them down. After a turn or two he found his big cloth sack and put it across his shoulder. Brother Cartwright said to him, "Here now, open that sack."

Santy Claws said, "What?" and watched the preacher put two brown-paper sacks in the cloth one. "Well, now," said Santy Claws.

And the preacher said, "That should help it carry better."

"I'm much obliged," said Santy Claws, and he went up the aisle and out of the church with one last Yo ho ho.

The preacher said, "Well," and the men said, "Well," and Miss Ruth closed the lid on the upright piano. The women said, "Oh, I hate to wake it up," and started inching coats and caps on sleeping Angels. The preacher took a step and said, "Wup!" and steadied himself and said, "Watch out for the marbles."

Widow and spinster and family by family, they went out the doors and left the warm lights in the windows of the Methodist Church. They went down Luke Street and down all the ways through the winter dark and the cold, humming hymns or hugging themselves or leading Shepherds or carrying snaggled-toothed sleeping Angels with tight hands locked on a purse or a pistol, and a piece of melting, wiggledly hard-rock candy. (1964)

Borden Deal

The Christmas Hunt

It should have been the best Christmas of them all, that year at Dog Run. It started out to be, anyway. I was so excited, watching my father talking on the telephone, that I couldn't stand still. For I was ten years old and I had never been on a quail shoot in my whole life. I wanted to go on the big Christmas Day hunt even more than I wanted that bicycle I was supposed to get. And I really needed the bicycle to cover with speed and ease the two miles I had to walk to school.

The Christmas Day hunt was always the biggest and best of the season. It was almost like a field trial; only the best hunters and the finest dogs were invited by my father. All my life I had been hearing great tales of past Christmas Day hunts. And now I knew with a great ten-year-old certainty that I was old enough to go.

My father hung up the phone and turned around, grinning. "That was Walter," he said. "There'll be ten of them this year. And Walter is bringing his new dog. If all he claims for that dog is true——"

"Papa," I said.

"Lord," my mother said. "That'll be a houseful to feed."

My father put his arm around her shoulders, hugging her. "Oh, you know you like it," he said. "They come as much for your cooking as they do for the hunting, I think."

My mother pursed her lips in the way she had, and then smiled. "Wild turkey," she said. "You think you could shoot me four or five nice fat wild turkeys?"

I wanted to jump up and down to attract attention. But that was kid stuff, a tactic for the five-year-olds, though I had to admit it was effective. But I was ten. So I said, "Papa."

My father laughed. "I think I can," he said. "I'll put in a couple of mornings trying."

"Papa," I said desperately.

"Wild turkey stuffed with wild rice," my mother said quickly, thoughtfully, in her planning voice. "Giblet gravy, mashed potatoes, maybe a nice potato salad——"

"If I don't fail on the turkeys," my father said.

"Papa!" I said.

My father turned to me. "Come on, Tom," he said. "We've got to feed those dogs."

That's the way parents are, even when you're ten years old. They can talk right on and never hear a word you say. I ran after my father as he left the kitchen, hoping for a chance to get my words in edgewise. But my father was walking fast and already the clamor of the bird dogs was rising up to cover any speech I might have in mind to make.

The dogs were standing on the wire fence in long dappled rows, their voices lifted in greeting. Even in my urgent need I had to stop and admire them. There's nothing prettier in the whole world than a good bird dog. There's a nobleness to its head, an intelligence in its eyes, that no other animal has. Just looking at them sent a shiver down my backbone; and the thought of shooting birds over them—well, the shiver just wasn't in my backbone now, I was shaking all over.

All of the dogs except one were in the same big run. But my father kept Calypso Baby in her own regal pen. I went to her and looked into her soft brown eyes. She stood up tall on the fence, her strong body stretched to its full height. Standing like that, she was as tall as I was.

"Hello, Baby," I whispered, and she wagged her tail. "Are you gonna find me some birds this Christmas, Baby? You gonna hunt for me like you do for papa?"

She lolled her tongue, laughing at me. We were old friends. Calypso Baby was the finest bird dog in that part of the country. My father owned a number of dogs and kept and trained others for his town friends. But Calypso Baby was his personal dog, the one that he took to the field trials, the one he shot over in the big Christmas Day hunt held at Dog Run.

My father was bringing the sack of feed from the shed. I put out my hand, holding it against the wire so Calypso Baby could lick my fingers.

"This year," I whispered to her. "This year I'm going." I left Calypso Baby, went with determination toward my father. "Papa," I said, in a voice not to be denied this time.

But my father was busy opening the sack of dog food.

"Papa," I said firmly. "I want to talk to you." It was the tone and the words my father used often toward me, so much of mimicry that my father looked down at me in surprise, at last giving me his attention.

"What is it?" he said. "What do you want?"

"Papa, I'm ten years old," I said.

My father laughed. "Well, what of it?" he said. "Next year you'll be eleven. And the next year twelve."

"I'm old enough to go on the Christmas hunt," I said.

Incredibly, my father laughed. "At ten?" he said. "I'm afraid not."

I stood, stricken. "But——" I said.

"No," my father said, in the voice that meant No, and no more talking about it. He hoisted the sack of feed and took it into the wire dog pen, the bird dogs crowding around him, rearing up on him in their eagerness.

"Well, come on and help me," my father said impatiently. "I've got a lot of things to do."

Usually I enjoyed the daily feeding of the dogs. But not today; I went through the motions

Kneeling for the shot ensures steady sighting, lessens the recoil.

dumbly, silently, not paying any attention to the fine bird dogs crowding around me. I cleaned the watering troughs with my usual care, but my heart was not in it.

After the feeding was over, I scuffed stubbornly about my other tasks and then went up to my room, not even coming down when my father came home at dusk excited with the two wild turkeys he had shot. I could hear him talking to my mother in the kitchen, and the ring of their voices had already the feel of Christmas, a hunting cheer that made them brighter, livelier, than usual. But none of the cheer and the pleasure came into me, even though Christmas was almost upon us and yesterday had been the last day of school.

That night I hunted. In my dreams I was out ahead of all the other men and dogs, Calypso Baby quartering the field in her busy way, doing it so beautifully I ached inside to watch her. All the men and dogs stopped their own hunting to watch us, as though it were a field trial. When Calypso Baby pointed, I raised the twelve-gauge shotgun, moved in on her on the ready, and Calypso Baby flushed the birds in her fine, steady way. They came up in an explosive whir, and I had the gun to my shoulder, squeezing off the shot just the way I'd been told to do. Three quail dropped like stones out of the covey and I swung the gun, following a single. I brought down the single with the second barrel, and Calypso Baby was already bringing the first bird to me in her soft, unbruising mouth. I knelt to pat her for a moment, and Baby whipped her tail to tell me how fine a shot I was, how much she liked for me to be the one shooting over her today.

Soon there was another covey, and I did even better on this one, and then another and another, and nobody was hunting at all, not even my father, who was laughing and grinning at the other men, knowing this was his boy, Tom, and his dog, Calypso Baby, and just full of pride with it all. When it was over, the men crowded around and patted me on the shoulder, hefting the full game bag in admiration, and then there was my father's face close before me, saying, "I was wrong, son, when I said that a ten-year-old boy isn't old enough to go bird hunting with the best of us."

Then I was awake and my father, dressed in his hunting clothes, was shaking me, and it was morning. I looked up dazedly into his face, unable to shake off the dream, and I knew what it was I had to do. I had to show my father. Only then would he believe.

"Are you awake?" my father said. "You'll have to change the water for the dogs. I'm going to see if I can get some more turkeys this morning."

"All right," I said. "I'm awake now."

My father left. I got up and ate breakfast in the kitchen, close to the warm stove. I didn't say anything to my mother about my plans. I went out and watered the dogs as soon as the sun was up, but I didn't take the time, as I usually did, to play with them.

"Me and you are going to go hunting today," I told Calypso Baby as I changed her water. She jumped and quivered all over, knowing the word as well as I did.

I went back into the house, listening for my mother. She was upstairs, making the beds. I went into the spare room where my father kept all the hunting gear. I was trembling, remembering the dream, as I went to the gun rack and touched the cold steel of the double-barreled twelve-gauge. But I knew it would be very heavy for me. I took the single-barrel instead, though I knew that pretty near ruined my chances for a second shot unless I could reload very quickly.

I picked up a full shell bag and hung it under my left arm. I found a game bag and hung it under my right arm. The strap was too long and the bag dangled emptily to my knees, banging against me as I walked. I tied a knot in the strap so the bag would rest comfortably on my right hip. The gun was heavy in my hands as I walked into the hallway, listening for my mother. She was still upstairs.

"Mamma, I'm gone," I shouted up to her. "I'll be back in a little while." That was so she wouldn't be looking for me.

"All right," she called. "Don't wander far off. Your father will be back in an hour or two and might have something for you to do."

I hurried out of the house, straight to Calypso Baby's pen. I did not look up, afraid that my mother might be watching out of the window. That was a danger I could do nothing about, so I just ignored it. I opened the gate to Baby's pen and she came out, circling and cavorting.

"Come on, Baby," I whispered. "Find me some birds now. Find me a whole lot of birds."

We started off, circling the barn so we would not be seen from the house and going straight away in its shadow as far as we could. Beyond the pasture we crossed a cornfield, Calypso Baby arrowing straight for the patch of sedgegrass beyond. Her tail was whiplike in its thrash, her head high as she plunged toward her work, and I had to hurry to keep up. The gun was clumsy in my hands and the two bags banged against my hips. But I remembered not to run with the gun, remembered to keep the breech open until I was ready to shoot. I knew all about hunting; I just hadn't had a chance to practice

Suiting up for the hunt denotes a coming of age.

what I knew. When I came home with a bag full of fine birds my father would have to admit that I knew how to hunt, that I was old enough for the big Christmas Day hunt when all the great hunters came out from town for the biggest day of the season.

When I ducked through the barbed-wire fence Calypso Baby was waiting for me, standing a few steps into the sedgegrass, her head up watching me alertly. Her whole body quivered with her eagerness to be off. I swept my arm in the gesture I had seen my father use so many times and Calypso Baby plunged instantly into the grass. She was a fast worker, quartering back and forth with an economical use of her energy. She could cover a field in half the time it took any other dog. The first field was empty, and we passed on to the second one. Somehow Calypso Baby knew

that birds were here. She steadied down, hunting slowly, more thoroughly.

Then, startling me though I had been expecting it, she froze into a point, one foot up, her tail straight back, her head flat with the line of her backbone. I froze too. I couldn't move, I couldn't even remember to breech the gun and raise it to my shoulder. I stood as still as the dog, all of my knowledge flown out of my head, and yet far back under the panic I knew that the birds weren't going to hold, they were going to rise in just a moment. Calypso Baby, surprised at my inaction, broke her point to look at me in inquiry. Her head turned toward me and she looked at me, puzzled. She asked the obvious question as plain as my father's voice: *Well, what are you going to do about these fine birds I found for you?*

I could move then. I took a step or two, fumblingly breeched the gun, raised it to my shoulder. The birds rose of their own accord in a sudden wild drum of sound. I yanked at the trigger, unconsciously bracing myself against the blast and the recoil. Nothing happened. Nothing at all happened. I tugged at the trigger wildly, furiously, but it was too late and the birds were gone.

I lowered the gun, looking down at it in bewilderment. I had forgotten to release the safety. I wanted to cry at my own stupidity, I could feel the tears standing in my eyes. This was not at all like my dream of last night, when I and the dog and the birds had all been so perfect.

Calypso Baby walked back to me and looked up into my face. I could read the puzzled contempt in her eyes. She lay down at my feet, putting her muzzle on her paws. I looked down at her, ashamed of myself and knowing that she was ashamed. She demanded perfection, just as my father did.

"It was my fault, Baby," I told her. I leaned over and patted her on the head. "You didn't do anything wrong. It was me."

I started off then, looking back at the bird dog. She did not follow me. "Come on," I told her. "Hunt."

She got up slowly and went out ahead of me again. But she worked in a puzzled manner, checking back to me frequently. She no longer had the joy, the confidence, with which she had started out.

"Come on, Baby," I tried to coax her. "Hunt, Baby. Hunt."

We crossed into another field, low grass this time, and when we found the covey there was very little time for settling myself. Calypso Baby pointed suddenly; I jerked the gun to my shoulder, remembering the safety this time, and then Calypso Baby flushed the birds. They rose up before me and I pulled the trigger, hearing the blast of the gun, feeling the shock of it into my shoulder knocking me back a step.

But not even one bird dropped like a fateful stone out of the covey. The covey had gone off low and hard on an angle to the left, and I had completely missed the shot, aiming straight ahead instead of swinging with the birds. Calypso Baby did not even attempt to point singles. She dropped her head and her tail and started away from me, going back toward the house.

I ran after her, calling her, crying now but with anger rather than hurt. Baby would never like me again, she would hold me in the indifference she felt toward any person who was not a bird hunter. She would tolerate me as she tolerated my mother, and the men who came out with shiny new hunting clothes and walked all over the land talking about how the dogs didn't hold the birds properly so you could get a decent shot.

I couldn't be one of those. I ran after the dog, calling her, until at last she suffered me to come near. I knelt, fondling her head, talking to her, begging her for another chance.

"I'll get some birds next time," I told her. "You just watch. You hear?"

At last, reluctantly, she consented to hunt again. I followed her, my hands gripping the heavy gun, determined this time. I knew it was my last chance; she would not give me another. I could not miss this time.

We hunted for an hour before we found another covey of birds. I was tired, the gun and the frustration heavier with every step. But, holding only last night's dream in my mind, I refused to quit. At last Calypso Baby froze into a beautiful point. I could feel myself sweating; my teeth were gritted hard. I just had to bring down a bird this time.

It seemed to be perfect. I had plenty of time but I hurried anyway, just to be sure. Then the birds were rising in a tight cluster and I was pulling the trigger before I had the heavy gun lined up—and in the midst of the thundering blast I heard Calypso Baby yell with pain as the random shot tore into her hip.

I threw down the gun and ran toward her, seeing the blood streaking down her leg as she staggered away from me, whimpering. I knelt, trying to coax her to me, but she was afraid. I was crying, feeling the full weight of the disaster. I had committed the worst crime of any bird hunter; I had shot my own dog.

Calypso Baby was trying to hide in a clump of bushes. She snapped at me in her fear when I reached in after her, but I did not feel the pain in my hand. I knelt over her, looking at the shredded hip. It was a terrible wound, I could see only blood and raw flesh. I snatched off the empty hunting bag I had donned so optimistically, the shell bag, and took off my coat. I wrapped her in the coat and picked her up in my arms. She was very heavy, hurting, whining with each jolting step as I ran toward the house.

I came into the yard doubled over with the catch in my side from the running, and my legs were trembling. My father was sitting on the back porch with three wild turkeys beside him, cleaning his gun. He jumped to his feet when he saw the wounded dog, and asked, "What happened? Did some fool hunter shoot her?" he continued.

I stopped, standing before my father and holding the wounded dog; I looked into his angry face. They were the

Frozen in time, a dog "points" to its quarry. A job well done.

most terrible words I had ever had to say, but I told him. "I shot her, papa," I said.

My father stood very still. I did not know what would happen. I had never done anything so bad in my whole life and I could not even guess how my father would react. The only thing justified would be to wipe me off the face of the earth with one irate gesture of his hand.

I gulped, trying to move the pain in my throat out of the way of the words. "I took her out bird hunting," I said. "I wanted to show you—if I got a full bag of birds, I thought you'd let me go on the Christmas Day hunt——"

"I'll talk to you later," my father said grimly, taking the dog from me and starting into the kitchen. "Right now I've got to try to save this dog's life."

I started into the kitchen behind my father. He turned. "Where's the gun you shot her with?"

"I—left it."

"Don't leave it lying out there in the field," my father said in a stern voice.

I wanted very badly to go into the kitchen, find out that the dog would live. But I turned, instead, and went back the way I had come, walking with my head down, feeling shrunken inside myself. I had overreached; I had risen up today full of pride beyond my ability, and in the stubbornness of the pride I had been blind until the terrible accident had opened my eyes so that I could see myself clearly—too clearly. I found the gun, the two bags, where I had dropped them. I picked them up without looking at the smear of blood where Calypso had lain. I went back to the house slowly, not wanting to face it, reluctant to see the damage I had wrought.

When I came into the kitchen, my father had the dog stretched out on the kitchen table. My mother stood by his side with bandages and ointment in her hands. The wound was cleaned of the bird shot and dirt and blood. Calypso Baby whined when she saw me and I felt my heart cringe with the rejection.

My father looked at me across the dog. The anger was gone out of him, his voice was slow and searching and not to be denied. "Now I want to know why you took my gun and my dog without permission," he said.

"David," my mother said to him.

My father ignored her, kept his eyes hard on my face. I knew it wouldn't do any good to look toward my mother. This was between me and my father, and there was no refuge for me anywhere in the world. I didn't want a refuge; I knew I had to face not only my father, but myself.

"I—I wanted to go on the Christmas Day hunt," I said again. "I thought if I——" I stopped. It was all that I had to say; it seemed pretty flimsy to me now.

My father looked down at the dog. I was surprised at the lack of anger in him. I could read only sadness in his voice. "She may be ruined for hunting," he said. "Even if the wound heals good, if she doesn't lose the use of her leg, she may be gun-shy for the rest of her life. At best, I'll never be able to show her in field trials again. You understand what you've done?"

"Yes, sir," I said. I wanted to cry. But that would not help, any more than anger from my father would help.

"You see now why I said you weren't old enough?" my father said. "You've got to be trained for hunting, just like a dog is trained. Suppose other men had been out there, suppose you had shot a human being?"

"David!" my mother said.

My father turned angrily toward her. "He's got to learn!" he said. "There's too many people in this world trying to do things without learning how to do them first. I don't want my boy to be one of them."

"Papa," I said. "I'm—I'm sorry. I wouldn't have hurt Calypso Baby for anything in the world."

"I'm not going to punish you," my father said. He looked down at the dog. "This is too bad for a whipping to settle. But I want you to think about today. I don't want you to put it out of your mind. You knew that when the time came ripe for it, I intended to teach you, take you out like I'd take a puppy, and hunt with you. After a while, you could hunt by yourself. Then if you were good enough—and only if you were good enough—you could go on the Christmas Day hunt. The Christmas Day hunt is the place you come to, not the place you start out from. Do you understand?"

"Yes, sir," I said. I would have been glad to settle for a whipping. But I knew that a mere dusting of the breeches would be inadequate for my brashness, my overconfidence, for the tremendous hurt I had given not only to the fine bird dog but also to my father—and to myself, as well.

"You've got to take special care of Calypso Baby," my father said. "Maybe if you take care of her yourself while she's hurt, she'll decide to be your friend again."

I looked at the dog and I could feel the need of her confidence and trust. "Yes, sir," I said. Then I said humbly, "I hope she will be friends with me again some day."

I went toward the hall, needing to be alone in my room. I stopped at the kitchen doorway, looked back at my father and mother watching me. I had to say it in a hurry if I was going to say it at all.

"Papa," I said, the words rushing softly in my throat, threatening to gag there before I could get them out. "I—I don't think I deserve that bicycle this Christmas. I don't deserve it at all."

My father nodded his head. "All right, son," he said gravely. "This is your own punishment for yourself."

"Yes," I said, forcing the word, the loss empty inside me and yet feeling better too. I turned and ran out of the room and up the stairs.

Christmas came, but without any help from me at all. I went to bed on Christmas Eve heavy with the knowledge that tomorrow morning there would be no shiny new bicycle under the tree, there would be no Christmas Day hunt for me. I couldn't prevent myself from waking up at the usual excited time, but I made myself turn over and go back to sleep. When I did, reluctantly, go downstairs, the Christmas tree did not excite me, nor the usual gifts I received every year, the heavy sweater, the gloves, the scarf, the two new pairs of blue jeans. I just wouldn't let myself think about the bicycle.

After my father had gone outside, my mother hugged me to her in a sudden rush of affection. "He would have given you the bicycle anyway," she said. "If you hadn't told him you didn't want it."

I looked up at her. "I didn't deserve it," I said. "Maybe next year I will."

She surprised me then by holding me and crying. I heard the first car arrive outside, the voices of men excited with the promise of hunting. My mother stood up and said briskly, "Well, this is not getting that big dinner cooked," and went into the kitchen without looking back.

I went out on the front porch. It was perfect quail-hunting weather, cold but not too cold, with a smoky haze lying over the earth. The dogs knew that today was for hunting; I could hear them from around behind the house, standing on the wire fence in broad-shouldered rows, their voices yelping and calling. All except Calypso Baby. All except me.

I stood aside, watching the men arrive in their cars, my father greeting them. Their breaths hung cloudy in the air and they moved with a sharp movement to their bodies. These were the best hunters in the whole countryside, and today would be a great comradeship and competition. Any man invited on this hunt could be proud of the invitation alone.

I felt almost remote as I watched, as I went with them around the side of the house to the dogs. They all went to examine Calypso Baby, and I felt a freezing inside; but my father only said, "She got shot by accident," and did not tell the whole terrible story.

Then my father looked at his watch and said, "Let's wait a few more minutes. Walter ought to be here soon. Hate to start without him."

One of the men called, "Here he comes now," and Walter drove up in his battered car.

"Come here, son," my father said, speaking to me for the first time this morning, and I went reluctantly to his side. I was afraid it was coming now, the whole story, and all the men would look at me in the same way that Calypso Baby had after I had shot her.

My father drew me to the side of Walter's car, reached in, and brought out a basket. "You wanted a bicycle," he said. "Then you decided yourself you should wait. Because you made the decision yourself, I decided you were old enough for this."

I looked at the bird-dog puppy in the basket. All of a sudden Christmas burst inside me like a sky rocket, out of the place where I had kept it suppressed all this time.

"Papa," I said. "Papa——"

"Take him," my father said.

I reached into the basket and took out the puppy. The puppy licked my chin with his harsh warm tongue. He was long, gangly, his feet and head too big for his body—but absolutely beautiful.

My father knelt beside me, one hand on the puppy. "I told Walter to bring me the finest bird-dog puppy he could find," he said. "He's kin to Calypso Baby; he's got good blood."

"Thank you, papa," I said in a choking voice. "I—I'd rather have him than the bicycle. I'll name him Calypso Boy, I'll——"

"When this puppy is ready for birds, we'll train him," my father said. "While we train the puppy, we'll train you too. When the time comes, you can both go on the Christmas Day hunt—if you're good enough."

"We'll be good enough," I said. "Both of us will be good enough."

"I hope so," my father said. He stood up and looked at the men standing around us, all of them smiling down at me and Calypso Boy. "Let's go," he said. "Those birds are going to get tired of waiting on us."

They laughed and hollered, and the dogs moiled and sounded in the excitement as they were let out of the pen. They fanned out across the pasture, each man or two men taking a dog. I

stood watching, holding the puppy warm in my arms. I looked at Calypso Baby, standing crippled in her pen looking longingly after the hunters. I went over and spoke to her. She whined; then for the first time since the accident she wagged her tail at me.

I looked down at the puppy in my arms. "We'll be going," I told him, as he licked at my chin. "One of these days, when you're a dog and I'm a man, we'll be right out there hunting with the best of them."

It was three years more before I got to go on my first Christmas hunt. Papa had been right, of course. In the time between I had learned a great deal myself while training Calypso Boy to hunt. With the good blood in him he turned out to be a great bird dog—second only, I guess, to Calypso Baby, who recovered well from her wound and was papa's dog the day Calypso Boy and I made our first Christmas hunt.

But of all the Christmases, before and since, I guess I remember best the one when Calypso Baby was hurt—and Calypso Boy first came to me. (1960)

The cycle of nature, of prey and predator, involves man and his dog at hunting time.

M.G. Chute

Johanna's Christmas Star

Johanna Olson turned over in bed to watch her husband struggling to get his boots off. He had put a handkerchief over his flashlight to dim it.

"I ain't to sleep," said Johanna. "You can turn the lights on."

"It's past two," said the sheriff.

Johanna obediently closed both eyes, but three seconds was about as long as she could keep them closed. "Things no good?" Johanna asked.

"Pretty good." The sheriff had one boot off and was hunting down in its depth for the three layers of socks that had come off with the jerk.

"Nothing much happened here," said Johanna. She kept the excitement out of her voice by not talking above a whisper. "Only Donna May brought a letter home from school."

Sheriff Olson grunted.

"What you say?" Johanna asked hopefully.

"Pretty cold out," said the sheriff.

"Miss Bates wrote it—Donna May's teacher." Johanna raised herself on her elbow and gave up trying to keep her voice down to a whisper. "Listen, they've got it planned all of a sudden for the first grade to be in the show on Friday. There's thirty-five kids in Miss Bates' class, and the play they're going to do, it only takes nine kids. That means all the rest don't get parts." She waited for this to sink in.

Sheriff Olson put his boots under the bed.

"And she wants," said Johanna, "for Donna May to be the Fairy Princess. It's all in the letter, how she's got to be dressed up."

The sheriff took off his pants, then his hat. "Yo, you ought to get started sleeping."

Johanna closed her eyes and snuggled deep into her pillow. When John Charles Olson was finally in bed, his wife opened her eyes.

"It's got most memorizing," said Johanna almost whispering again.

It was practically the last thing she had time to say quietly. In the morning it came over her all of a sudden: the day after tomorrow was Friday.

"Listen, Donna May; you eat up every scrap of that mush! Tell daddy about how you're going to have real wings and a crown, hon."

"Listen, ma; Betty Roberts don't have to wear shoes nor most nothing; that's on account of she's s'posed to be in bed right on the stage. Ain't that funny?...Ma-ma, Kristi's slapping at her milk with her spoon! Ma!"

"Donna May, don't you scream like that! Gosh, hon, ain't you got no sense? Want your voice like a crow's for the show?" With one hand Johanna filled the sheriff's plate with pancakes and with the other dealt with Kristi's new trick of leaving milk in the bottom of her bowl, so she could slap at it. "A real fairy with a wand and everything, tell daddy....Listen, John, I've got to have extra money on account of buying the stuff Miss Bates wrote I should buy for the costume. Maybe five dollars'll be enough."

"Look, Yo; can't you sit quiet to eat?"

"Gosh, I dunno what ma and Mabel are going to think, coming back to find Donna May's been a fairy while they was in St. Paul! We could maybe phone 'em, only they won't be at the hotel until tomorrow night, and that's too late almost. Ain't it the darndest luck they couldn't 've gone after Christmas 'stead of before?"

"Ma-ma, make Kristi stop slapping at me! Ma!"

"Donna May, you stop screaming! ...Listen, John, what you think; I should maybe try Merske's or Mr. Slabey for gilt paint?... 'Scuse me, I thought you was through drinking, the way you put down your cup. You yell when you're done with your plate, will you, hon, 'cause I gotta get started with the dishes?"

With John and Donna May out of the house, Johanna raced through what was left of her dishwashing. She thought some about changing sheets on the beds, but decided against it. They would last easy over another day.

She picked Kristi up from where the kid stood at the foot of her daddy's and mother's bed, patting in the bottom of the quilt like a real little housekeeper. She'd have to leave her next door and then come back to change her own clothes for shopping. The Franzens were new people, but real nice. Their own baby was a year younger than Kristi and only just beginning to walk, but Kristi got on fine with him, and Mrs. Franzen was awfully sweet about watching her good.

Johanna explained about the shopping she had to do. "It's for Donna May's costume for the show and tomorrow is dress rehearsal. She's Fairy Princess, so she's got to be fixed up pretty fancy."

Mrs. Franzen said, "My, ain't that something!" She helped Johanna pull Kristi out of her snow suit. "I didn't know there was going to be a show Friday. Can anybody go?"

"Everybody's supposed to go! Everyone in town always goes! People come from all over everywhere to go see it!"

"Ain't that something!" Mrs. Franzen again marveled. "How much are tickets?"

"Thir——Gee, I've forgot. John and I ain't been last three years. I'll find out for sure. Well, thanks for keeping watch on Kristi. Guess I better get going, so's Donna May won't be acting Fairy Princess in her play suit." She smiled at Mrs. Franzen's appreciative giggle. "Anyhow, all the mothers ain't got my troubles. The play's only got nine parts, and there's thirty-five kids in Miss Bates' class."

It was all right to talk like that to Mrs. Franzen. It wasn't like boasting, when her Donald was years off from being ready for the first grade anyhow.

After changing her stockings and her dress, Johanna found one of the children's crayons and ripped a tiny strip off a page of the telephone book. She wrote "needles" quickly, and "crown" and, after a little thought, "cherry pie." The pie could be for John's supper. With shopping and then the sewing she had to do, she wouldn't have time hardly even to cut bread for supper.

Then she got Miss Bates' letter out of the sugar canister. The first paragraph was all about why Donna May had been chosen for the Fairy Princess. Although she knew it practically by heart, she let herself read it through again. Maybe, if John fussed too much about the pie, she would read it through to him too.

The second paragraph was polite and interesting, but it wasn't quite so easy to read. Johanna leaned against the oven while she studied it.

I'm sure, with your skill and ingenuity, you'll have no difficulty in transforming Donna May into the loveliest of little fairies. I thought just the simplest of little white dresses—perhaps her own party frock—might be made the basis for rows of wee ruffles and flounces. Make them of organdy or stiffened gauze or even of crepe paper—but your own good sense will prescribe the best and easiest method! Tiny glass beads or bits of mica could be sewed on to give the sparkle of star dust to our little fairy's costume.

Johanna read the star-dust sentence through twice, but it didn't help. Then she sat down in a chair to finish the letter.

For the wand, any little rod, gilded and star-tipped, will be perfect. As for the crown, why don't we simply paint with gilt a little cardboard? The wings, of course, must be large and truly expressive. Wire and tarlatan make lovely wings, and—who knows?—perhaps they might be made to open and close like a butterfly's by means of narrow ribbons and wires, artfully concealed. But about this, as about the whole costume, you must use your own judgment, as I know you will—so ably! Hastily and gratefully,

LOUISE BATES.

Johanna sat limp. She was dumb, that was the trouble, and Donna May was going to suffer because her mother wasn't smart like the other ladies. She kept sitting, staring at "artfully," until suddenly she thought of the library.

The idea of going to the library was a good one, even if the fire station which held the library was six blocks out of the way of the stores, because a fairy costume was one thing you really could learn about in books. The crazy business was for the place to be closed just so the librarian could spend Christmas in Grand Rapids. With the show coming on, you would have thought the officials of Purgatory Springs would have realized that the library was more important now than at any other time of the year.

Shopping took quite a bit of running around, but it was well worth it, the bargains and the advice she got. Merske's Dry Goods had the tarlatan and the crepe paper, and the hardware store had wire for the wings and an old suit box she could cut down for a crown. Johanna got gilt paint at Janisky's Variety Shop and just looked at dancing slippers. They were sure real cute, but awful expensive for a kid. Mr. Janisky thought a lot about star dust, but couldn't think of anything better than lace. Mr. Slabey at the drugstore, where Johanna finally found the paintbrushes, said waxed paper crushed-up might look like glass, but you could never be sure.

Mrs. Joseph P. Reedy was buying Danish

Crowns and wands and ruffled gowns of Fairy Princesses are always noticed. Not so their mothers.

pastry at Dvorak's Bakery when Johanna got there for the cherry pie. Mrs. Reedy was president of the Parent-Teacher Association and general manager for the show, so Johanna left Dvorak's with twenty adult tickets to sell at thirty-five cents each and the same number for children at ten cents.

Johanna had only a dollar and fifteen cents left out of the five dollars John had given her; but when she had the stuff spread out on her bed after lunch, she felt pretty calm and contented about it all. She had bought quite a lot of each thing, but it was safer that way, and when she picked up Kristi and borrowed a package of needles which she had forgotten to buy, Mrs. Franzen was pretty nearly struck dumb by all that Mrs. Olson had accomplished in about two hours' time. Mrs. Franzen even took two tickets for the show; she couldn't pay for them until Tuesday, when her husband got home off the road, but that was all right.

The rest of the day wasn't Johanna's fault. Donna May got home from school acting real smart-alecky and wouldn't stand still for fittings. She cried, too, when Johanna cut the puff sleeves off the organdy dress. Johanna wasn't feeling any too good, anyhow, about having to use Donna May's best white dress, the way sewing crepe-paper ruffles on it was making big holes where the needle went in and out.

Then John, instead of being surprised and helpful over all the troubles she had been having with the sewing, started right in with fussing. He fussed about the cherry pie being bought and he sided with Kristi when she was naughty about not liking her rice and sardines. He said he sure hoped it didn't mean there was a shortage on potatoes in the United States. And he didn't like eating on the card table, because he claimed it rocked every time he tried to take a breath. But there was nothing Johanna could do about it; the wings had to lie flat on the dining-room table as long as the wire was only pinned to the tarlatan.

After supper the tarlatan took to unraveling itself; no matter how carefully Johanna sewed, it didn't want to twist around the wire right. The sheriff had found a chair that wasn't being used for sewing materials, and he looked good and lazy just sitting there doing nothing and reading.

When an inch of tarlatan had unraveled clear around the left wing, Johanna said, "You'd think I could have some of that lamp—my gosh!"

Sheriff Olson put down his paper. "Listen, Yo; don't you go getting worn out and crabby over a lot of nothingness."

"Nothingness!" said Johanna.

She talked the matter of nothingness over at intervals until ten o'clock, when the sheriff got up and went to bed.

Weeping gently, so as not to dampen the tarlatan out of shape, she worked on the wings until midnight. Messy was how they looked.

When she got into bed, John woke up. "Done with 'em?"

The sleepy smugness in his voice got her down. "No!" His awful calmness started her weeping again. "What you think? All the help I get!"

After a long time she quieted down to just sniffling. After another long time, John put his arm across her.

"Yo, listen. You asleep, Yo?"

"No."

"Yo, that star dust you was fussing about——"

"Uh?"

"Well, how'd Christmas-tree tinsel fix up?"

"Maybe," said Johanna. She couldn't say more than that, with the mean way he'd been acting, but she held his hand between the two of hers, so he'd know how sweet she thought he was.

In the morning, almost before John and Donna May were out of the house, Johanna got to work on the crown. It cut pretty easily out of the top of the suit box, and she used Kristi's head to fit it on, holding the kid still with cookies.

The gilt paint mixed to a sort of thin gray liquid with little shiny specks floating on its surface. Johanna gave up trying to use the gilt before the cardboard was all soaked through, and had a cookie herself. She couldn't feel terribly upset, because after the sheriff's idea about using tinsel for star dust, she had got to feeling that there was an answer for everything. Even the wings looked pretty good in the daylight, she thought.

Kristi, trying to finish off her cookie with a bite of crayon, didn't get a spanking for it like she maybe should have. Yellow crayon didn't color the gray cardboard so it looked exactly like gold, but it fixed it up pretty classy all the same.

By the time it had a jewel pasted straight in its middle and was lying down on the bed next to the wings, the crown was something really lovely to look at. The jewel was made by cutting a circle out of the hem of Johanna's red crepe dress. Almost you could have looked at the crown for an hour without getting tired.

When Johanna went downtown at eleven for the tinsel and to sell tickets, she took a curtain rod from the living room with her. Maybe a Christmas-tree star could be fastened to one end of it to make a wand. After the way the other things had turned out, anything was possible.

Mr. Slabey at the drugstore didn't carry Christmas-tree tinsel and he had already bought his tickets because he had two nieces in the sixth grade's part of the show, but he was real interested in the problem of the wand. After inspecting the curtain rod with his eyes squinted half shut, he suggested maybe it could be wired with a tiny battery and flashlight, so it would be something pretty snappy looking when Donna May waved it.

It was a lovely idea; it made a lump come into Johanna's throat just thinking about it.

"It'll twinkle real cute," said Mr. Slabey. He suggested trying the radio repairman at Nord-

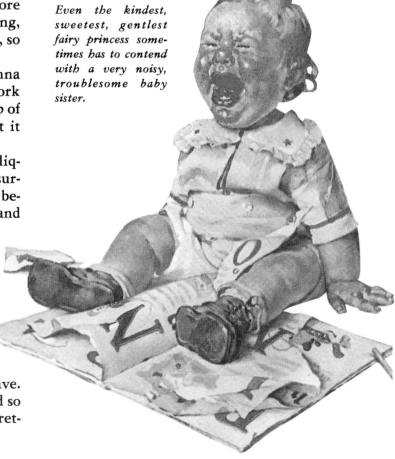

Even the kindest, sweetest, gentlest fairy princess sometimes has to contend with a very noisy, troublesome baby sister.

land's Insurance and Washing Machine Company to see about getting it wired right. "It's got to work good or you don't want it. . . .How about candy? Ever eat candy 'round your house, Mis' Olson?"

Johanna bought the special two pounds assorted for a dollar. It was the least she could do to thank Mr. Slabey, and Mrs. Franzen really had to have some sort of present, for the nice way she was taking care of Kristi practically all the time.

The radio repairman said he didn't like fooling around with small jobs, because they took as long as big jobs, only you couldn't ever charge what they were worth or customers raised hell. In the end he said he would have the wand ready by four o'clock, but that he wasn't guaranteeing nothing to nobody.

Fifteen cents wasn't enough even to buy the Christmas-tree tinsel, let alone paying for the curtain rod to be wired, but Johanna would almost have rather jumped down a well than have had to go to the courthouse, if jumping down the well would have got her the money.

In the courthouse, John Charles Olson dressed and looked the same as he did at home, but somehow he never was the same. It was almost like having to ask for money from a stranger.

When Johanna opened the door to the sheriff's office, there were about twenty men talking to the sheriff. Johanna backed out the two steps she had walked in. Her first feelings were to leave, but she opened the door again instead.

The man that was talking stopped talking. Johanna shut the door faster than the first time. She was halfway down the corridor when she remembered that Mrs. Franzen didn't have enough cash in her house even to pay for two tickets, let alone to lend Johanna money.

"Hi, Mrs. Olson!" Deputy Billy Christenson came running after her. They met halfway back to the office. "Sheriff's busy," said Billy. "Anything I can help at?"

She couldn't very well talk personal finances to one of John's deputies. "It's the furnace," Johanna said. "And—listen, if he could come out here just a second——It wouldn't take more'n a quarter of a second."

Billy went back into the office, and right away the sheriff came out.

Johanna tried to act calm, but it wasn't much use. "It was the candy, see? I had to buy it on account of

Mr. Slabey saying how the wand should be fixed; and anyway, with Mrs. Franzen keeping care of Kristi and——"

"Yo, Billy said how the furnace——"

"I had to tell him something, didn't I?" He kept staring at the candy box like it was part of the furnace that had blown off. "All I got is fifteen cents, and I ain't even got the tinsel or——"

"What you want, Yo?" He could easy stand there, acting superior, all the time and help he had! Johanna tried hard to get over sounding breathless.

"The tinsel maybe won't come to more'n fifty cents, but the man at Nordland's didn't know about the wand, and——"

"Listen, Yo, there's men waiting. Ten bucks see you right straight through everyt'ing?"

"Ten? Oh, gosh, yes! Maybe even I could bring back some if the wand——"

He didn't have to be so snappish about it. Donna May was as much his kid as she was hers.

The white ballet slippers at Janisky's were awfully expensive, five dollars and ninety-five cents, but Mr. Janisky said they were real French imports and practically the most elegant creations he had ever had the pleasure of stocking.

Johanna paid ninety-five cents for the Christmas-tree tinsel and promised to be back with Donna May on Friday to get the slippers fitted. She decided to wait until then before asking Mr. Janisky to buy tickets for the show, because he had all of a sudden started talking about taxes.

When she stopped to pick up Kristi, Johanna told Mrs. Franzen about the wand and gave her the candy. Mrs. Franzen was awfully excited over everything and offered to go across and help Johanna wash up her breakfast dishes. But Johanna was too ashamed of the way she had left the house to let Mrs. Franzen see it.

It was pretty unfair to Donna May, the way her mother had to keep thinking about housework when she ought all the time to be putting her mind on the costume. If it hadn't been for Mrs. Franzen being so nice with the kids, things would have been plain awful. After sewing some on the tinsel, Johanna took both kids next door.

For a wonder, the wand was finished at four o'clock. The radio repairman said it was one of the hardest jobs he had ever tackled and he wouldn't do it again for fifty dollars. He held the wand in the dark under the counter to show Johanna how it went on. Even in the half dark, you could see a real twinkle of light.

It was the loveliest thing Johanna ever saw.

It cost six dollars, but it was worth that much.

A wand showed up like everything on a fairy, and black patent-leather slippers were what kids always wore on the stage anyhow.

The radio man wouldn't buy a ticket, but Mr. Nordland himself took two after he had got Johanna to promise he could call around sometime next week, in case the sheriff might want to buy her a new washing machine.

While John and the kids ate supper, Johanna finished sewing the last row of Christmas-tree tinsel on Donna May's dress. After supper she curled Donna May's hair up on an iron. She hadn't planned curling it until Friday night, because dress rehearsals weren't really so important. But John had pretended like he thought the pale yellow crown going up so straight and Donna May's pale yellow hair going down so straight were all one piece, and had laughed about it until Johanna had to show him how nice the crown would look over curls.

It did look good, too, with the red crepe jewel in its front. And the tinsel on the dress sparkled like garlands of real stars. Even John was pretty interested and impressed when she turned out the lights so he could see how the wand twinkled. It was going to be sort of fun watching Miss

Women are always late when they've had to prepare a Fairy Princess for dress rehearsal.

Bates' expression when she first got a look at Donna May carrying a fairy's wand.

But when seven o'clock came and Donna May had to be driven to school for the rehearsal, her father had to do the driving. Johanna was still in her apron and bedroom slippers, and even John could see she was a good half hour from being ready to leave the house.

Johanna lay down on Donna May's cot after she had got Kristi to sleep. The excited way she was feeling, having Donna May's costume all finished and looking so awfully pretty, she hadn't expected to more than just be able to rest her feet. But she had been asleep three hours when the sheriff waked her.

"You home already yet?"

"It's on to eleven. Want I should go get her?"

"Eleven? Oh, gosh! No, I gotta get her. Listen, did Miss Bates say anything?"

Johanna put on her black taffeta dress with the cream-colored collar. Miss Bates had seen it once already at a P. T. A. meeting, but the new red crepe had to be fixed in the hem where the jewel for the crown had come out.

"I'll lock the car and the doors," Johanna said. "You get to bed. Kristi's sleeping real good."

It was funny, going out late to get Donna May. After a few years, Donna May would be going out almost every night. She was going to be the popular sort; you could always tell the kids that got picked to be in plays and things were the kind the boys always went for. She sure looked cute with the crown sitting on her curls as she danced around with her wings and wand.

The first graders were rehearsing in one of the classrooms. Johanna found that out from Mrs. Roberts. Mrs. Roberts acted sort of bored about having to get her Betty ready for the play. The way she talked gave Johanna a sort of depressed feeling, until she realized it was most likely sour grapes with Mrs. Roberts, because Betty had the part where she was dressed in just plain pajamas.

Donna May came running out of the classroom ahead of the other kids.

"Ma! Ma! Listen, I gotta have white shoes!"

"Sure, we'll get 'em, hon. Oh, gosh! Donna May, where's your wings? Tell mother, quick!"

"They got loose, and Miss Bates says I gotta have white shoes."

The wings were folded up over a desk at the back of the room. They looked sort of crumpled, but nothing seemed to have broken loose. Johanna picked the wand up off the floor.

"Oh, Donna May! Gee, hon, can't you be careful with your things?" But the wand worked all right; even in the lighted room you could see it flicker on just like a baby star.

"Mrs. Olson? So glad you could spare us a minute. . . .Gracious, you can hardly hear yourself think. . . .Children!"

"Donna May says you want she should wear white shoes."

"Yes, she'll have to wear white slippers—ballet preferably. And the wings must be tightened. And something else I wanted to——Oh, yes, the tinsel on her costume, it's rather—well, just a wee bit garish, don't you think? The simple little frock would seem better. And some sort of little sleeves, if you can manage. Small children do have such long arms and legs!"

"Sure, I planned——She'll be fixed real——"

"I'm sure she will!"

Johanna put Donna May to bed without making her wash. If the kid didn't get enough sleep, she'd be a plain wreck for the show, and she was naughty like anything already. Johanna couldn't even find out from her whether Miss Bates had said anything special about the wand. The way Donna May talked, you'd have thought Miss Bates hadn't even noticed it.

Sheriff Olson was asleep when his wife got into bed, but Johanna didn't dare wait until morning: "Listen, John, I need money for Donna May's—"

Sheriff Olson rolled over. "Car locked, Yo?"

"Listen, John. Miss Bates says she's gotta have them white, so I've gotta have money——"

John woke clear up. "I gave you ten bucks."

Johanna got out of bed. "The ones I gotta buy cost five dollars and ninety-five cents, and all I got left is three dollars and ninety cents." She showed him the money in her purse. "And seventy cents of it I shouldn't spend, because it's from Mr. Nordland for the tickets he bought. Anyway, Miss Bates says that she's gotta have 'em white, see?"

There was silence while she got back into bed.

"Where'd the six dollars and eighty cents go?"

"What six dollars and eighty cents?"

"Listen, Yo. Three dollars and twenty cents left from ten dollars means you spent——"

"Well, good gosh, I had to get the tinsel, didn't I? And some candy for Mrs.

Franzen for watching Kristi——"

"You had the candy 'fore you came to the office."

"Well, I know, but I only had fifteen cents left from yesterday. Listen, the way you talk——All I want is enough to make five dollars and ninety-five cents. Miss Bates says——"

"All I want is what you did with the ten."

"It wasn't ten! I've got three dollars and ninety cents left like I showed you, and only seventy cents has got to come off that. And, anyhow, you said your ownself how cute the wand looked. My gosh! Can I help it if Donna May's got to have white slippers?"

"Yesterday I gave you five bucks, and today ten, and now you want five more. What you got her fixed up in? Solid silver?"

"You ain't so funny! Listen, if you think I want my own kid to go out looking ragged in front of maybe a thousand people——Anyhow, I didn't say I wanted five dollars, I said enough so the three dollars and ninety cents I've got will make five dollars and ninety-five cents after the seventy cents is off. The trouble with you is you're plain stingy!"

"The trouble with you is you didn't eat no supper, Yo."

Two nights straight she had ended up by crying. And the way he could go off sleeping all at once

Whether it be "Fourscore and seven years ago," "Abou Ben Adhem," or "Twinkle, Twinkle, Little Star," the recitation rarely lacks critic or admirer.

like nothing was wrong, it was plain mean!

All night she seemed to be dreaming. It was mostly about a sort of basement place with long, dark halls that she was leading Donna May through to get to the play. And every time they were almost there, the hall would end in a sort of bank of green snow and Donna May wouldn't have anything on except a big pair of overshoes.

Then the lights went on with a lot of applause, and Johanna woke up.

There was sun on her nose and Kristi was lying on the bed beside her, talking to herself. The alarm clock showed fourteen minutes after nine.

Under the clock was a five-dollar bill. John was so dear. It hurt Johanna's throat even just thinking how sweet he was. Kristi began to cry with being hugged so tight and being hungry.

The housework and the beds had to wait another day to get fixed right. The wings alone took until eleven o'clock to get fastened to where they didn't droop when they were tied over the back of the kitchen chair. After that Johanna still had to get the tinsel off Donna May's dress and the sleeves back on. It was one lucky thing she had been too busy to make dolls' dresses for the kids out of the sleeves, like she had planned. But it was sad taking off the tinsel, after John had been so dear thinking it up in the first place and then getting his and Donna May's breakfast and everything.

Because of the play, Donna May got home an hour early from school, almost before Johanna had the lunch cleared away. The kid was so excited, Johanna didn't dare take her downtown to get the slippers fitted; matching an old pair would have to do. With the tickets she had left to sell, lugging Donna May around with her would just about finish the poor kid off.

Mrs. Franzen wasn't any too hopeful about getting Donna May and Kristi to take naps, because her Donald had been sleeping all morning and was acting pretty peppy, but she would sure be glad to do her best. She said it was a wonder Mrs. Olson wasn't dead on her feet. Mrs. Franzen was a nice, considerate person.

The slippers didn't take long to buy, and they had metal for tapping fixed in under the toes and real satin ribbons to lace around the ankles—worth more than five dollars and ninety-five

cents really. But Johanna fussed some about the price until Mr. Janisky had bought four tickets to the show.

After that, though, ticket selling didn't go so good. When it was half past four and she had gone down the whole of one side of the shopping street, Johanna added up how many tickets she had left. After three counts, when it still added up to twenty-one, she began to feel sort of desperate. Only just as many tickets had been printed as there were seats in the auditorium. Twenty-one tickets left unsold by Mrs. John Charles Olson, mother of the Fairy Princess, meant twenty-one vacant seats.

It was getting on toward six o'clock when Johanna got back to the Franzens'. Except for the three she was holding out for herself and John and Kristi, the tickets had all gone on exchanges.

On a few she had had to add cash to the exchanges, but she could always find uses for nails and dish mops; and when guests came, things like the cigars would come in handy if they happened to be guests that smoked cigars. And at Dvorak's Bakery she had been able to exchange three tickets for three pies.

Mrs. Franzen was all upset when Johanna got back. She had got Donna May to take a nap by promising her she could play coalman if she did. Playing coalman, Donna May had skinned her knee, and Mrs. Franzen had put iodine on it. The iodine had run down until her leg was a queer yellow, just where it would show most between the fairy's short skirt and her white socks.

A queer weak feeling came into Johanna's own knees, like she had been running too hard. She said "thank you" to Mrs. Franzen and grabbed Donna May's hand. Mrs. Franzen came running after her, carrying Kristi.

"Put her anywheres," Johanna said. "Quick, you gotta take these!" She shoved two of the pies at her. She didn't care whether Mrs. Franzen thought she was rude or crazy or what, banging the door. After the show was over, she had weeks and years she could explain things in.

John was home already and wandering about, not even dressed for the show. Johanna made him watch Kristi and set the table for bread and milk and pie while she got Donna May's hair curled. Donna May was acting like a little devil, and she couldn't even be yelled at to stand quiet and behave. You could sure feel sorry for the fellows that had to keep movie stars happy and behaving both at the same time.

"Listen, Donna May, hon; please eat like a sweet girl. . . .Daddy, you tell her she's gotta!

NORMAN ROCKWELL

Honest, she won't be able to stand up even, the way she keeps pecking. . . .Please, Donna May!"

"Eat somet'ing your ownself, Yo," John said.

"I can't. I don't feel so good. Listen, Donna May; mother ain't joking none. Show daddy how a real fairy princess eats. Oh, for gosh sakes, stop monkeying with your curls!"

At 7:15, Sheriff Olson drove Donna May over to school. Johanna had planned they should all go over together and then wait until eight for the show to start, but neither she nor Kristi was dressed in time.

John was back at half past seven. He didn't seem to know if the auditorium was filling up or not, and he guessed he had left Donna May in the right classroom.

"You guess! Oh, gosh, don't just stand around; put Kristi's coat on her or something! Listen, did the wings look all right? Did they wabble any?"

"Sure, they wabbled some. That don't hurt none. The teacher was there. Where's the kid's coat, hon?"

"Miss Bates was there? Why didn't you tell me first off? Honest, the way you don't tell things, you'd have me going crazy! Listen, John, did her curls look good under the crown, did Miss Bates say? Maybe I should maybe take a couple of big safety pins along to make sure with her wings. Did Miss Bates see the stuff on her knee? Honest, wouldn't you think Mrs. Franzen would have had sense enough to——Listen, you can't go wearing that old hat!"

She was wearing her formal herself. Maybe it was too dressy, but it was better than looking like she was just ordinary audience. And if the other mothers weren't dressed up, she had de-cided she could always just sit in her coat.

At ten minutes of eight, the Olsons were out of the house. The lights next door at the Franzens' were still on; they worried Johanna a lot, because people coming in late to a show made it hard to hear the actors, but John wouldn't let her stop to hurry Mrs. Franzen along. He was probably right, but it was sure a worry.

John stopped the car in front of the main entrance and took his ticket. He told Johanna to sit center toward the front, so he could find her when he got back from parking the car. It was exciting to see all the cars parked for blocks around.

It was going to be a real big crowd. The only trouble was that most of the audience stood around in the halls, just talking, when they should have been getting sat down and quiet. If someone could ring a bell or shout, it might help.

Johanna chose three seats in the middle section about twelve rows from the front. There were some vacant seats up nearer the stage, but she felt it might look sort of conceited if she acted like she wanted to sit extra close just because she was mother to the Fairy Princess.

Mr. and Mrs. Raddusky came in on Johanna's row. Mrs. Raddusky was in black satin, so tight she looked almost larger than she really was. Mr. Raddusky was small and smiling. He smiled at Johanna and wiggled a finger at Kristi.

Mrs. Raddusky felt of her seat before settling herself down into it. "Maybe she breaks, eh? No, she don't." She talked loud and laughed a lot, just like she was in her own home and not waiting for a play to begin.

Pretty soon Mrs. Raddusky started telling Johanna about the troubles she had been having making her Frankie look like a Chinese doll. But Johanna could only keep half of her mind on what Mrs. Raddusky was saying. If the show started before John got back, she would plain die.

At ten minutes after eight, a boy in white pants came out on the stage with a big card that he put up on a sort of easel. The card said: A CHRISTMAS TALE OF LONG AGO—FOURTH GRADE. Johanna tried to

In a school auditorium filled with anxious parents, a few late arrivals are a welcome distraction.

figure in her head whether the grades would most likely go up or down from there, but she couldn't keep her mind long enough off John to reason out anything that took arithmetic.

He could probably get a seat in back even if the play started, but not knowing whether he would be seeing Donna May or not was driving her pretty nearly crazy.

People were coming in the entrances in little bunches. It was funny, when the tickets and posters all said eight sharp, that they couldn't get to their seats on time. But it was different with John, because he was out parking the car and not just standing around talking and laughing.

If the committees had had real good sense, they would have marked off a parking place right in front for the cars that had brought the actors and actresses.

Even with John safely in his seat, Johanna couldn't somehow get to breathing easily. It was maybe the crowd or the way the place was heating up.

"John—listen, John; ain't Kristi cute the way she's looking all around? John, look; is there much of a crowd still outside? You'd think somebody'd tell 'em to come in. John, you spose maybe I ought to bring Miss Bates the two safety pins I got? Were they awful wabbly?"

"Listen, Yo, sit peaceful for once, huh?"

"Look around for Mrs. Swanson. Her Marian's the Dutch doll. Ain't it funny Mrs. Franzen don't get here?" She started to get up to look for Mrs. Franzen, but the lights went out. She sat down even before John told her to.

People went right on talking. Johanna sh-h-ed a couple of dozen times, but it didn't help any. The actors were going to have trouble getting heard right if people kept on being so rude. What they needed was a real big band playing one of

Complete with wooden shoes and tulips, Marian was the spittin' image of a little Dutch girl.

Sousa's marches. A piano and violin were real pretty and fairy-like sounding together, but they weren't loud enough to get all the people to shut up.

"John, listen; did Donna May's wings wabble just when you took her blanket off her or all the time?. . .Kristi, you want daddy to hold you?. . .Then stop your wriggling!"

The curtain went up. It didn't give any more warning than the lights had, but the people quieted down some.

The stage was empty when the curtain went up, but after a while three children came on, dressed like gypsies or something. They were talking to each other, but Johanna couldn't hear them. In a while some more came on, and pretty soon one of the Nielsen kids, dressed like a king with a crown and a purple cape. But the crown was real plain; it didn't even have a small jewel in front.

All of a sudden the audience began to laugh. The Nielsen kid's crown had dropped down over one ear, and he kept trying to push it back up. Every time it fell down again, a lot more people would start in laughing. Johanna wanted to scream at them to shut up laughing at the kid.

She was an awful bad mother, letting Donna May wear wings that maybe weren't fastened tight enough. It was because she was lazy and didn't take enough trouble with her sewing. If Donna May's wings didn't come loose tonight, she would never fuss again about having to sew, or about having to do anything for anybody ever.

"Listen, John, I'm going back to——"

"Sh-h-h!"

The curtain came down. Only the lights didn't

turn on. They'd have to pretty soon. Maybe if she could powder Donna May's knee some, the yellow wouldn't show so much.

The curtain went up without any lights having come on between scenes. The stage was a sort of gray blue; you could hardly see things on it.

Mrs. Raddusky stuck her elbow into Johanna's side. "*Ja*, now come our kids pretty quick out!"

Johanna stretched up to see better. She could hardly breathe, the place was so hot. There were two children in white lying on the floor.

"Betty Roberts," Mrs. Raddusky said, "and the Martinsons' kid."

"John, John, listen; this is Donna May's! Can you see good, John?"

The two kids stood up in their white pajamas. Johanna couldn't hear them. Maybe Miss Bates was making Donna May stay out of the play because of the wings coming loose. Maybe her knee was making her sick, or she was crying with being hungry because she hadn't been made to eat enough supper.

The piano started up again and something in bright green came galloping out on the stage. Mrs. Raddusky's elbow jabbed into Johanna's stomach.

Some things in life can be best appreciated in silence and Donna May's theatrical debut was one of those things.

"There's my Frankie! *Ja!* There he is!"

Mrs. Raddusky started making clucking noises to herself. Frankie was jumping up and down on the stage and shouting things.

The stage wasn't so awfully light. If it didn't get brighter pretty quick, it was going to be awfully hard to see the star actors real well. The only thing was that the wand showed up better when the lights weren't too bright.

After a long time there were more children on the stage. "Donna May," Johanna said softly way under her breath, "Donna May, mother loves you, darling; you're all right."

In the morning it would all be over. School plays weren't so much anyway; just a lot of kids trying to act smart. Two hours and it would all be over. Maybe in two minutes.

"Listen, John——" He was sitting still, and his breath was coming heavy and even. If Mrs. Raddusky would stop clucking, Johanna's own breath would be easier maybe.

One of the kids came forward and bowed. Then nothing happened for a long time, except that the music changed. It was light, pretty music, sounding like raindrops.

Donna May Olson skipped in to the music. Her mother didn't see her until she was almost center. She was all white and gold. You couldn't see much how she was dressed because she was moving so quick.

" 'S morning!" Donna May shouted. "Stop dancing, little dollies!"

Donna May skipped straight on across the stage, until the curtains hid her.

Some children sang or danced or something, and then, after a long time, the curtain came down and the lights went on.

Johanna put her arm through her husband's.

"She wasn't so awful bad, huh?" said Johanna. She couldn't more than whisper, her throat was so dry and funny feeling. She wanted to go home now and put the kids to bed and then maybe sit with John and just not talk. Or perhaps what she wanted was to hang around after the show was over, listening to what people said.

"Not too awful bad, huh?" said Johanna.

She gave a little sigh. You just couldn't talk much about some things.

She was glad, though, that there had been such absolute beauty and perfection in it all. Even John could see now that the money had been worth it. He was wiping Kristi's nose, pretending like he wasn't feeling funny inside him like Johanna was feeling. Men were cute. Johanna touched his shoulder gently with her fingertips. A hundred dollars would have been awful cheap. Ten times as much work, trouble and money would have been awful cheap. (1937)

Jim and Allan Bosworth

The Christmas Racket

After everybody but the janitor had gone home, Johnny Greer sat at his typewriter and smoked four cigarettes without punching a key. Outside was San Francisco, softened by a thin drifting fog that blurred the street lamps. The bells of St. Patrick's chimed "Silent Night, Holy Night," but Johnny heard only the surly undertone of traffic beneath the windows, where drivers forgot that Christmas Eve is a time of good will even toward other drivers. Inside was the *Evening Gazette* city room, a long and cluttered space permeated by that odor which is popularly supposed to get into a man's blood—the smell of printer's ink.

Johnny's nostrils failed to quiver at the scent, because he was an old and disillusioned hand. Six evenings a week, tongue in cheek, he turned out a column called "A Line of Cheer From Johnny Greer." It was full of corn and platitudes and Pollyanna philosophy. Thousands who read it pictured Johnny Greer as rotund and jovial, benevolent and wise—a "right jolly old elf."

They were very wrong. He was a lean and cadaverous man, grown cynical in a profession noted for cynicism, and given to grouches. What wisdom he had was a shrewd, hard kind, learned in a hard way. The column, therefore, was intellectually dishonest. It was a living, but Johnny hated it. Tonight he could afford to dislike it more than ever. He had just come from a barroom meeting with Big Bill Carnahan, a building contractor with political aspirations. Over three highballs, Carnahan had offered Johnny the job of handling his mayoralty campaign, and there was to be further discussion that evening at Carnahan's home.

Drinks made Johnny garrulous, but a man can't be garrulous alone. He saw Dominick wheel a cleaning truck into the far end of the room and begin sweeping briskly; and he speculated idly on Dominick's way of life, and how many voters like the little man it would take to put Carnahan into office. Then he sighed and rolled paper into his typewriter.

Tomorrow's piece had to be written. A Christmas column. He could look back on seven Christmas columns, and, before that, on twice seven years on rewrite desks. Working every Christmas to grind out pap about Yuletide cheer and jolly old St. Nick. Writing salivary salutes to roast turkey, chestnut stuffing and plum pudding, and yelling, "Hey, boy! Run over to Dinty's and get me a hot dog with mustard and onions!"

He stared at the unsullied paper, and took time out to examine a stack of mail. It was mainly Christmas cards. He pitched them unopened at the nearest wastebasket. "A damned commercial racket!" he muttered, and then sat up straight. Why not? For once, why not drop the Pollyanna role, and write what he thought? The managing editor would see it in galley proofs tomorrow. If he didn't like it, he knew what he could do.

Readers conjured up a pleasant picture of columnist Johnny Greer that bore little resemblance to the man himself.

He bent over the typewriter and was oblivious of Dominick, who moved nearer industriously. The lead took shape:

'Twas the night before Christmas, and up from the pressroom came three ink-stained retches—Burp, Burp and Burp. Those succinct sentiments, translated into what a lot of solid citizens REALLY think about Christmas, would——

"Happy Christmas Eve!" a voice said.

Johnny looked up. Dominick had a thin, dark face, and eyes that reminded him of a spaniel's.

"Dominick," Johnny said, "did you ever hear of Old Scrooge?"

"No," Dominick said respectfully.

"Well, he had something. I am about to write a column advocating organization of the OSS—Old Scrooge Society. All you have to do to join is to be sick and tired of Christmas. Just admit that it is a pagan custom, fast degenerating into a com-

At the end of a long day, a columnist has time to reflect on his demanding job—providing the public with inspiration, the managing editor with copy.

mercial racket, and you're in our lodge."

Dominick did not understand all the words, but he leaned on his broom and shook his head. "Oh, no, Mr. Greer!" he said earnestly. "Christmas is a fine, good, happy time. Last year was bad, yes. But now, it's justa fine!"

"Name one good reason," Johnny said.

"I gotta work," Dominick said simply. "Last Christmas I was very sick for a long time. No work, no money. No presents." His eyes showed how bad that was, and then he smiled. "What'sa matter, Mr. Greer? You gotta good job too!"

Johnny laughed. "Dominick, you've been seeing movies. You don't realize that newspaper business is monotonous drudgery, and that only once in five or ten years does a good story—a really good story—come along. And you will be shocked to learn that the once-vaunted power of the press is no more. Look at the last election!"

"Yes," Dominick said, bewildered.

"Take my advice," said Johnny. "Don't work for a newspaper. Quit, like I'm going to do." He opened a drawer and produced a bottle that had been sent him by a press agent. "We'll drink, Dominick. Not to Christmas, which is a day I ignore, but to a new job. I'm leaving this shabby, ill-ventilated house of journalistic prostitution."

"I justa drink wine, Mr. Greer."

"This calls for stronger brew. Drink to next November and the race for mayor. Remember, the Man with the Plan is Carnahan!"

Dominick took a token taste. "He's a good man?" he asked. "He's honest?"

"Let us be frank," Johnny said. "With me to help him, Carnahan can win. How'd you like a job sweeping out City Hall?"

"I like this job," Dominick said, emptying a wastebasket. "Mr. Greer, I got a big hurry. Excusa me. Giannina, she's waiting for to see her Christmas."

"If she's your wife, Dominick, don't let her give you a necktie."

"My wife, she'sa dead," Dominick said. "Giannina, she's my little girl."

"That's different," Johnny said hastily. "Well, I have to hurry, too, so let's get to work. Here, Dominick, put this dollar into Giannina's piggy bank for me. Now, let's see....If half the Christmas ties were used to garrote the people who gave them, it would be justifiable homicide. Got to put that down."

At eight o'clock sharp, the bells of St. Patrick's

chimed again. Johnny pushed back his chair and read the column. If he said so himself, it was a masterpiece of sharp, satirical wit—a surprise for thousands of readers expecting sugarplum prose. Best of all, it was the kind of stuff that makes people write letters. The managing editor was too smart not to see that.

He covered his typewriter, and heard a "Merry Christmas, Mr. Greer!" from Dominick. Johnny looked up, and saw him with his hat on, at the far end of the room. He was staggering under the awkward burden of a large sheet of plate glass.

"What's that for?" Johnny demanded, staring.

Dominick laughed happily. "It'sa Giannina's Christmas!" he said, and maneuvered the glass riskily through the door. "Gooda night!"

Johnny cleared his desk, hearing the elevator whine up to get Dominick, thinking the season was even sillier than he had dreamed. Plate glass for a child's Christmas! Then he shrugged and went for his hat and coat. He'd take a cab to Big Bill Carnahan's big house in Sea Cliff, and talk business. Then back to his bachelor apartment, and tomorrow he could sleep until the managing editor called to ask if he had gone crazy.

"Merry Christmas, Johnny," said the elevator man, who had been around a long time. "You got another column like you had last year? My wife clipped that column and sent it to a dozen folks back East."

"She won't like the one tomorrow, then," Johnny said. "I just shot Santa. Good night."

He went outside. The fog was lifting. The thin wail of a siren lifted above the mutter of traffic, coming nearer. He started across the intersection and stopped short.

A big car was angled desperately toward the street's center line, with a knot of people caught in its headlights like moths drawn to a lamp. Jigsaw fragments of shattered glass lay flat along the pavement, reflecting light in irregular pools.

By the time Johnny Greer could get into the crowd, the ambulance had rolled up. He saw a tall policeman, and a hatless, white-faced man who was talking excitedly. And then he saw Dominick, lying on his back with his crumpled hat for a pillow, his face twisted with pain.

"The glass reflected my lights, officer!" the driver was saying. "It threw my lights back at me. I thought it was another car—a car on the wrong side of the street. If he had to take that glass somewhere, why didn't he use a truck?"

"You can tell that at Harbor Station," the officer said, and shouted for the crowd to make room. Johnny went in with the hospital stewards, and showed the policeman his press card.

"He works for the *Gazette*," Johnny told him. "How bad is it?"

"A busted leg, poor fellow. A fine Christmas present."

"I'll ride to Harbor Emergency with him," Johnny said. He bent over Dominick, thinking how much worse it could have been. "Take it easy," he said. "Everything will be all right."

"No," Dominick said. He closed his eyes, and when he opened them again they were wide and tragic. "No present for Giannina. No fine, happy Christmas this time for her."

"What does she like?" asked the man who didn't believe in Christmas. "Dolls? Candy? I'll find a drugstore, Dominick——"

"It'sa no good, Mr. Greer. Giannina wants a Christmas window. For a long time I tell her she'sa going to have a window. Justa the big glass. And now it'sa broke!"

He began to cry, and Johnny knew it wasn't because of the pain. They put him in the ambulance, and Johnny sat with him. "The Christmas window," he said over and over. "It'sa broke!"

"I don't understand, Dominick," Johnny said. "You mean you promised Giannina a window like in the stores, with toys and lights?"

"Oh, no, justa the big glass. So she can see Christmas."

"Give me the address. I'll see what I can do."

"It'sa too late, Mr. Greer. The stores—they're all close. And I got no more money."

"Who was going to fix this window?"

"Me, I could fix. But now——" He closed his eyes and groaned.

They put him on a table at Harbor Emergency, and Johnny left as they gave him an anesthetic. The address on the accident report was a street number in that shabby but colorful section where Chinatown and North Beach come together. Johnny went outside, cursing himself for a softhearted fool, and called a cab. It was nearly nine; the Christmas Giannina had been promised she would see was only three hours away. . . .

The cab stopped before a dingy three-story flat. Johnny struck matches until he found the name of D. Cardoni on a mailbox; then he climbed two sets of rickety stairs and went down a dim and evil-smelling hall. Downstairs, a radio made noise. He found a door.

A gray-haired, plump woman answered his knock. She had a shawl around her head, as if ready to go out on the street, and when she saw him her wrinkled face showed disappointment.

"Oh, not Dominick!" she exclaimed.

"No," said Johnny. "He's—he's late. Are you Dominick's mother?"

She shook her head. "No. Mrs. Latta. I watch Giannina while he'sa work."

"Is that you, papa?" a child's thin voice called. "Did you bring my Christmas present?"

Johnny hesitated, and Mrs. Latta opened the door wider, bowing and fussing with her apron. He went in awkwardly, and saw a big, old-fashioned, white-enameled bed in a poorly furnished but clean room. Propped high on pillows was a tiny, thin-faced girl. She had a festive red ribbon on her black braids, and wore plain gold earrings to make her look like some diminutive gypsy, and Dominick's large eyes were hauntingly eager in her small dark face.

"I'm Johnny, Giannina," he said gravely, turning his hat in both hands. "Your papa sent me. He can't get home tonight."

She studied him a moment. "But it is Christmas Eve," she said slowly. "And he is bringing me a Christmas present. Of course he will be home!"

"Oh, of course," Johnny echoed. "But he will be late. You see——" And then she shifted in her bed, and he saw the braces. He thought, *Oh, Lord; polio*, and a feeling like shame swept over him.

Mrs. Latta turned, whispering pityingly, "For three years she not walk. Maybe never walk."

Giannina trusted in Christmas.

But Giannina was smiling. "I will go to sleep!" she announced with the bright faith of the very young. She lifted one thin arm and covered her eyes. "I will go to sleep, and when I wake up it will be Christmas. And papa will be here with my present. You wait and see."

"Yes, Giannina," Johnny nodded. "You go to sleep." Then he took Mrs. Latta by the arm and led her into the next room. It was unfurnished, except for a big easy chair that stood facing the wall—and suddenly things were clear to Johnny. At one time there had been two windows in the wall. Now sash and glass were gone, and ugly boards covered the space, as if alterations had been long delayed. The room was blind.

"The Christmas window?" he asked, pointing.

Mrs. Latta nodded agreement, and her wrinkled face softened. "The big glass," she said.

He understood it all but one thing, and that made him ashamed too. For nearly a year he had worked in the same place with Dominick, seeing the tragedy in the little man's eyes, and never trying to learn why it was there. Dominick's life would be like this—a blank wall of low income and doctor bills and worry. Out there, fast approaching, was Christmas; out there would be something for a child to see every day. Blue sky and sunshine and silver fog curtains. Rooftops in the rain, and clothes dancing on the line in the wind. Cars moving over the hilly streets, and other children who could walk and run.

"Look, Mrs. Latta," he said. "Dominick's leg is broken. Can you stay with Giannina, if I pay you?" He pulled a bill from his pocket.

Mrs. Latta motioned it away. "No money," she said, "It'sa Christmas."

"Johnny!" Giannina called. "I'm nearly asleep!"

That would be the bells of Old St. Mary's taking up the carols now, and it was nine o'clock. He tried to swallow a lump in his throat.

"It'll take a lot of doing," he said. "Is there a phone here?"

There wasn't, but Mrs. Latta directed him to a drugstore on the corner. When he tiptoed through the other room, Giannina was still, her lips parted slightly, and her long, dark curling eyelashes lying on her small cheeks.

He sat in the stuffy telephone booth with the classified directory on his lap, and wrote down the numbers of a large building-supply house and a glass company. Time was getting short. That section between the two windows would have to be sawed out, and some sort of sash put in before the glass could be put into place. The whole affair became urgent. Midnight was a deadline.

He dialed the first number, and heard the phone ring a dozen times. If there was a night watchman at the building-supply company, it apparently wasn't his job to answer telephones. The same lack of response greeted his attempt to rouse the glass company. It was, after all, Christmas Eve.

Then he remembered the party which he was supposed to be attending, and Big Bill Carnahan, the builder. He dialed again, and the receiver went up on merry sounds and a jovial and hearty voice answered, "Bill Carnahan speaking."

"This is Johnny Greer. Look, I need your——"

"Where've you been, boy?" boomed the man who wanted to be mayor. "What's holding you up? I've got two county supervisors and some other important people out here, and we're whipping up an organization and waiting to see Santa fall off the Christmas tree. Come on out!"

"Sorry," Johnny said. "I can't make it tonight. Could you get a store to open and sell me a sheet of plate glass, eight by five?"

"Tonight? What the devil, Johnny, it's Christmas Eve! Come on out and have a drink!"

"I've got to have a big window put in before midnight," Johnny said.

Carnahan laughed. "Oh, been out busting windows already, eh? Tell 'em I'll bail you out, and tell 'em they'll have to wait."

"It's for a little crippled girl, Mr. Carnahan," Johnny said. "A Christmas present for her. How about lending a hand?"

"Well, now you know I'd like to help, Johnny, but I've got guests here, and it's Christmas Eve, and——Well, the thing is impossible tonight, anyway. You couldn't get it done."

"The hell I can't!" Johnny flared, and hung up.

He looked at his watch. Somebody ought to know the people who owned those stores where they sold glass. Members of the building trades, perhaps. And who would know the right person to contact in the building trades? He sat up with a flash of inspiration—the *Gazette's* labor editor, Wade Mason!

He looked up Mason's home telephone, smiling to himself, thinking how wrong a man can be. Hardly two hours before, he had told Dominick that the power of the press no longer existed. He had said that only once in five or ten years did a really good story come along. Now that story was in his hands, to be shaped and built and made complete, and a curious, warming pride filled him as he knew he had found the way to do it. The power of the press.

Wade Mason answered, and Johnny quickly outlined the problem, beginning with Dominick and the glass. He told it as an experienced leg man would tell a story to the rewrite desk, and Mason grunted now and then to show that he understood the problem. Mason had been in the business a long time too. He didn't say much, but Johnny knew the contagion had caught.

And now both of them were pretending,

as newspapermen have done for years, that they were doing all this for the story. Mason said, "Okay, I'll call Joe Gallagher. He's the head of the Carpenters Local, and he'll be able to get the glass and round up a crew. You go on back and stand by. What about pictures?"

"I'll get a photographer," said Johnny, who had forgotten about pictures. "But are you sure Gallagher and his men will do the job?"

"It's Christmas, isn't it?" asked Mason. Then, as if ashamed of having put it on that sentimental basis, he added, "Besides, they want their names in your column now and then, don't they?"

Giannina was still sleeping when the truck and three cars parked at the curb below, and if she didn't sleep through the sawing and hammering that went on behind the closed door of the front room, she did a very good job of pretending, even when a couple of flash bulbs went off.

But she heard the bells. All over the city the

Big Bill Carnahan, the builder, dreamed of being the big man of the town. As the Man with the Plan, he was designing to win the mayoralty of San Francisco in the next election.

bells began at midnight, and those of Old St. Mary's sounded very near as they chimed "Adeste Fideles." She sat up in bed, her big eyes shining.

"It is Christmas, Johnny!" she said. "And papa has come home with my present."

"Yes," Johnny said, watching the closed door. "It is Christmas, Giannina. Your papa will be late, like I told you, but the present is here, and in just a minute——"

Wade Mason opened the door. He said, "Okay, Johnny, it's ready."

Johnny held out his arms, and the child put hers around his neck. He lifted her, thinking how tiny and fragile she was; he carried her into the front room and put her into the big chair.

"Merry Christmas, Giannina!" he said then, and everybody joined in a chorus.

"Merry Christmas, Giannina!" said burly Joe Gallagher, the workmen and Wade Mason.

She clapped her hands. "I want to see my present!" she said excitedly.

Joe Gallagher reached up and pulled aside the blanket that had been hung over the window. Wade Mason turned out the light. The bells were chiming "Oh, Little Town of Bethlehem."

A lump caught in Johnny Greer's throat. There was the big window, framing darkened rooftops and the glow from the street lamps, and a clear midnight sky. Almost centered in it was the lighted cross on Old St. Mary's, and farther on, above the brilliant symbol of everything that Christmas stands for, was a single bright light on the top of some tall building.

Giannina pointed to this. "It is beautiful," she whispered through the silence that held the room. "It is like the star the Wise Men followed."

Johnny remembered that quote an hour later when he sat down at his desk and picked up the telephone. The first number he dialed was that of the city's most famous orthopedic surgeon, and the conversation with him was most satisfactory. The second number was one he had called earlier, and the voice answering was annoyed.

"Carnahan," Johnny said, "I've been thinking it over. I've decided that, with the proper help, you can be defeated. Good night."

He hung up and rolled a sheet of paper into his typewriter. At the top he typed A Line of Cheer From Johnny Greer. Then he lighted a cigarette and began to write steadily. (1949)

John Collins Harvey

The Christmas Gift

Christmastime at our hospital is one of the best times of the whole year. The usually busy and bustling corridors are quieter. The wards are almost empty of patients, for most, who can be, have been discharged. Few new patients come in; only those who are really sick. One half of the resident staff of doctors and nurses is given a three-day holiday. Those remaining can take a breather and relax somewhat from the grueling daily routines followed during the rest of the year. Best of all, though, the spirit of Christmas invades the place.

During the week preceding Christmas the corridors and wards are decorated. Patients, doctors, nurses, aids and orderlies all give a hand. Hidden talents come to light. Christmas scenes are painted on the omnipresent glass partitions and windows. Camels, Wise Men, sheep and shepherds are marching ceaselessly around the wards. Sometimes they are hard to identify, but then everyone is kind to those whose spirit is willing, but whose hand and eye aren't. Wreaths of pine, holly and mistletoe are hung over doorways and in the halls. A Christmas tree, gay with dyed bits of cotton and gauze and other hospital-made decorations, is put up in the center of each ward.

To my mind the most beautiful effect of this face lifting is achieved by the Administration Building, a hideous old Victorian structure of rather ugly proportions with marble floors and heavy oak woodwork. The building, four stories in height, has a central, octagonal-shaped rotunda extending upward from the ground floor to the large glass dome. The main entrance to the hospital opens into this rotunda. In the center, facing the door, is a larger-than-life-sized statue of Christ, with its cold white marble arms warmly lifted in an embrace. Appropriately at the base is this inscription, "Come unto me, all ye that are weary and heavy laden, and I will give you rest." The main stairway to the upper floors is opposite the front entrance. The four floors form four inner balconies about this central rotunda.

On the walls of the main stairway are hung huge wreaths of pine and holly. On the old heavily ornamented and multi-branched brass candelabra at the foot of the stairs are placed two huge pine wreaths with red-ribbon bows. The heavy oak bannisters and posters which give a feeling of solidarity to the balconies about the rotunda are wrapped in pine-and-holly garlands. The simplicity of these decorations adds even more grandeur to the awe-inspiring figure of the "Merciful Comforter."

Since the opening of the hospital in 1889 the choir of Brown's Memorial Baptist Church has come each Christmas Eve to sing carols for the staff and the patients. Many of the choir members are employees of the hospital, but almost all have been patients in the hospital at some time or other. By now some of the members who came originally as youngsters are grandparents; yet each year they return on Christmas Eve to give their present to their beloved hospital.

The choir always begins caroling in the rotunda. There, grouped about the figure of Christ, after brief prayer, they sing the best-loved carols and Negro spirituals. They finish with the "Hallelujah Chorus" from "The Messiah."

The doctors and nurses who can slip away for a few brief minutes from the wards, some patients in wheel chairs or on stretchers, and many friends of the hospital arrange themselves on the

The only life Irene had ever known was the hard and humble life of a farm on the Eastern Shore.

balconies to listen to the carols. It is a glorious occasion and one not easily forgotten. I know, for I have been part of the group listening each Christmas Eve for many years.

The most memorable Christmas Eve for me, however, was my first one, when I was a house officer in the hospital. This year, known as the internship, is the first year of practice for a newly graduated doctor. The theories of medicine have been learned in the long hard years of medical school; the practical experience in medicine has now begun.

It is only in the practice of medicine that the full realization dawns of the tremendous responsibility for human life placed in the hands of the physician. Believe me, this is quite frightening for the young physician. Many grave doubts arise in an intern's mind about his own knowledge, ability and worthiness for such a sacred trust. Wise and gentle guidance from more experienced physicians, coupled with the appreciation and affection shown him by the patients whom he has helped care for, builds self-confidence in the intern. However, the process is a slow and sometimes seemingly endless one.

Certainly I was no exception as an intern in having grave doubts about my abilities and worthiness for a medical career. These doubts were so great in the fall of my internship year that I had just about decided to leave medicine and enter another field. I figured I just could never be a good doctor. But Fate has a way of intervening in the affairs of most people, and it did with me in the person of Irene "S."

One Saturday morning in early September I was "covering" for a few hours in the Accident Room for another intern who was sick. I was at the time assigned to the female ward, but found time to spare to give a hand in the Accident Room. A thirty-nine-year-old Negro woman was brought in by her family. They had brought her to Baltimore from their small farm on the Eastern Shore of Maryland. They had driven the long way around the bay in their twenty-year-old truck because they didn't have the money to pay the ferry toll. They started about five o'clock that morning and reached the hospital about ten o'clock. A twenty-year-old broken-down farm truck doesn't make a fast ambulance.

Irene's brother, sister, eldest daughter and cousin were with her. They were obviously very poor, simple farm people who were turning to the hospital for help as a last resort. They had been told that Irene was crazy and should be put away, but they decided to bring her to Baltimore to see if she couldn't be helped.

She was a pitiful creature, emaciated, woebegone, and looking twice her age. She was talking irrationally at times and, when she could muster the strength, would struggle feebly with those supporting her. She fidgeted with the bedclothes and pulled at her hair. Her family reported that she had been getting "peculiar" for some time. She had been losing weight, for she didn't eat, complaining that food made her sick. She vomited what she ate, and retched frequently when she didn't eat. She had become so weak that she had taken to her bed and showed no interest in her surroundings. A doctor had been called to see her, and told her family that she was mentally ill and should be committed to the state mental hospital.

I proceeded to examine her. She was extremely pale. She was quite emaciated and she had great muscle weakness. Her facial expression was dull and listless. She was short-winded and had signs of dropsy. I didn't know what was wrong with her, but I did think she was seriously ill. I made arrangements to admit her to the hospital; she was brought to the ward where I was assigned as intern. Thus the responsibility for her care in the hospital fell partly on me.

That afternoon the resident physician and I examined her more closely and performed some laboratory tests. We found she was bleeding from her bowels and that this blood loss had caused a profound anemia. It became obvious that her nausea, vomiting and refusal to eat were associated with abdominal pain. The muscle weakness and nervousness seemed to be linked to severe overactivity of the thyroid gland. A basal metabolism test was performed which showed a result consistent with that diagnosis. She was started on iodine drops, the proper medication for Graves' disease, or hyperthyroidism. Digitalis was given for her heart condition. The X ray of her stomach, taken the next day, showed a large ulcer. Proper anti-ulcer treatment was instituted. She was given blood transfusions and was fed intravenously for a

few days until the medicine could take effect.

Gradually Irene began to respond to our therapy. She became quiet and subdued, so that sedation could be discontinued. She began to eat. Her heart began to function more efficiently. The abdominal pain disappeared. Her anemia disappeared. She became quite a different person.

All of this treatment necessitated long and close observation. I got to know her well during this time. She had little formal schooling, but she was endowed with a great deal of common sense and she was rich in her love for other people. This began to show immediately as improvement occurred.

I enjoyed talking with her and would spend spare moments at her bedside, listening to her talk about life on the farm, crops, cooking or her family. She dearly loved flowers, and since she could not use the little land the family had for growing anything other than food, she would pick wild flowers and tree blossoms in the fields. One of her favorites was holly, which grew in profusion around her home. She knew little of current events and virtually nothing about the world beyond the Eastern Shore. She had never been to Baltimore before the time she was brought to the hospital by her family.

She improved steadily, and finally the day came for her to be discharged. She said good-by to the nurses, to the other patients with whom she had

A large dose of Christmas cheer—a likely prescription for every patient.

become friendly during the time she had spent on the ward, and to the doctors. She shook hands with me and said simply, "Thank you, Doc."

We arranged for her to be cared for by a physician in a town on the Eastern Shore, since she had no money to come back for periodic checkups at our hospital. She thought traveling from her home and getting about in Baltimore would be too confusing for her anyway. The physician sent word on several occasions that she was doing well. I did not think much about Irene in the press of work.

Then Christmas approached with all its excitement. The wards were decorated. Patients had been discharged. The doctors and nurses who had Christmas holiday were gone. The quiet of Christmas Eve descended. In the dining room that night there were lighted candles on the tables. They furnished the only light in the room except for the twinkling lights on the gaily decorated Christmas tree in the center of the room. It was pleasant and cozy, and the usual hospital meal actually tasted good!

Soon the time came to go over to the rotunda for the carols. The choir assembled. The group of listeners became quiet. There was the sparkle of anticipation in the air. Here most of the people away from home and loved ones, each quite alone with his own problems, yet bound together in the common work of treating and caring for the sick, stood or sat on the balconies waiting for the music. Below, the choir, gowned in cassocks, prayed softly around the statue of Christ and then burst into song. The singing was magnificent. The whole situation was more beautiful than I had been led to believe by those who had told me about it.

Yet I was terribly sad. This was my first Christmas away from home. Always before, during school, college and medical-school days, I had managed to get home for Christmas. Now I seemed to be terribly alone even in the midst of friends! Doubts in my own ability, dissatisfaction with my own efforts, and a feeling of unworthiness overcame me. Self-pity is inexcusable and terribly destructive. I tried to concentrate on the singing, so as to drown my sadness. Soon the choir was singing the "Hallelujah"—a final burst

of heartfelt song, and it was over. The choir was now moving behind the stairs and on into the main corridors to the wards. I still felt depressed.

I turned to go downstairs and back to my ward when I caught sight of the porter at the front door, beckoning to me. I walked down the stairs and across the floor to him. He handed me a box wrapped up in brown paper tied with a knotted piece of red string. He said that during the caroling a Negro woman had slipped in the front door and asked him if he would find me. He told her he thought I was up on one of the balconies listening to the caroling, and that when it was finished he would call me, but he couldn't do it while the caroling was on. She said she couldn't wait, and asked him to give me the box she was carrying. He said she told him she had only twenty minutes before the last bus left for home, and since he couldn't call me she would have to hurry along. He said he tried to explain to her that a bus left from in front of the hospital about every fifteen minutes. He couldn't understand her worry over missing the bus.

I took the package up to my room and opened it. Over the old brown paper were pasted Christmas decorations cut from newspapers. On one of the flaps of the box was pasted one half of an old Christmas card which had a printed name lined through with red crayon and my name printed crudely on it instead.

I opened the box, and inside were pieces of holly branches obviously freshly picked. I knew immediately who the donor was and what the hurry was. She had a four-hour trip back to the Eastern Shore to get home for Christmas!

Freshly picked holly in a crudely decorated carton tied with a knotted piece of red string. A simple present from a poor, uneducated woman? Not at all—the greatest gift I have ever received!

I looked out the window into the dark sky with its shining stars. And I thought of that night some nineteen hundred years ago. From another part of the hospital I heard the choir singing, ". . .bearing gifts we traverse afar. . . ."

I knew then what I had wanted to know for some time. (1958)

Lt. Col. Melvin Russell Blair

A Christmas Story from Korea

On the south bank of the Imjin River, Korea, the 25th (Tropic Lightning) Infantry Division was dug in, waiting for the Chinese Army to attack. Three battle-hardened regiments —the 24th (Eagles), the 27th (Wolfhounds) and 35th (Cacti)—were holding the sector near the confluence of the Imjin and Han rivers where the Chinese were expected to strike. As the soldiers listened to the peculiar, high-pitched wail of the wind that came in from the Yellow Sea, whipping up little twisters of snow as it bit into the north bank where thousands of North Korean refugees were huddled, one GI mirthlessly commented, "Wind's singing us a carol." It was December 24, 1950.

Our biggest nightmare was the refugees. Between the 25th Division and the Chinese were some 40,000 North Korean civilians. It was an ironic paradox that these people feared the Chinese communists—their "allies" —more than death itself, and fled from their approach. They were mostly women, children and very old men—for the North Korean Army had conscripted all of the able-bodied males.

There we were—an outnumbered army in a tactically indefensible position, with thousands of refugees in our line of fire.

What we saw across the river was hard to take. The refugees were starving, and we had no food to give them. They were dressed in cotton rags in weather that dropped to five degrees below zero; yet, if they lit a fire, our patrols were forced to put it out, for fires would attract the enemy.

The meager roads became choked with refugees who crossed the Imjin, creating a security hazard. Finally, 8th Army headquarters ordered that no more North Koreans be permitted to cross the river.

The men of the 25th were confused about these people. They had no love for them, for they knew of the savageries perpetrated by North Korean civilians upon our wounded and captured soldiers. Yet, as they silently watched the ragged, starving women and children pass through their lines before the embargo was clamped on, they were reminded of their own women and children back home. They wanted somehow to help. But they didn't know exactly how.

The answer came on this day before Christmas.

It had been a rather special day. We had expected the Chinese attack to come on Christmas Day, so headquarters had ordered that we feed our men Christmas dinner a day early. The quartermaster worked a minor miracle and brought a hot turkey dinner right up to the front-line troops. Turkey and all the trimmings—including stuffing, cranberries, sweet potatoes, rolls and real butter—even candy and mince and pumpkin pie.

What really tickled the men, though, was that packages from home came through, just in time for Christmas. Expecting the Chinese to strike, no one heeded "Do Not Open Until Christmas" instructions. Front-line foxholes bulged with cakes, tinned delicacies, socks, mittens and the like.

I happened to be at the front lines that afternoon in connection with my duties as Division G-2 (Intelligence officer). I stopped in the area held by the 35th Infantry, leaned over a foxhole and asked the soldier occupying it who he was and how he was doing. He hopped out and told me he was Pfc. Stanley Crowley, of Birmingham, Alabama, and that he was doing all right. He was a red-haired, freckle-faced rifleman, nineteen years old. He was not particularly chunky, but he looked enormous because of the six layers of clothing he was wearing in the subzero weather.

"Let me show you what I got for Christmas, colonel," Crowley drawled. First, he produced a wool scarf; then, commencing an odd sort of strip-tease, he pulled back layer after layer of clothing, finally coming to the object he had next to his skin. It was a fruit cake. "Got it here to keep it from freezing," he explained.

Just at that moment there was a diversion. A band of refugees, utterly desperate, decided—orders or no orders—to cross the river.

The stampede—and hundreds came across before we could stop it—was led by a woman with three children. It was low tide. She waded through the ice-clogged water that came above her waist. With one arm, she carried a child of about three; with her other arm, she supported a second child of about five so his head was above water. The third—a boy of about seven—had to make out for himself.

These four were the first to reach the south bank, and they started running right through the 35th's position. When they reached Private First Class Crowley's foxhole, they stopped, for Crowley was standing in their path.

He looked at the woman. She returned the gaze from black, sunken sockets. He looked at the children. Their lips were cracked and bleeding; their fingers bluish with frostbite. The oldest boy had slipped and gone in over his head in crossing; his hair was frozen into icy wisps.

Slowly, from around his neck, the red-haired boy from Alabama unwound his Christmas scarf. "Here, take it," he said to the woman.

She drew back in fear. Crowley kept holding it out, and finally she took it. She looked at her children to see which needed it worst. She settled on the oldest boy, who was shaking so violently he hardly could stand.

Then Crowley again began his curious strip-tease with the six layers of clothing. He brought out his fruit cake and handed it to her. Again she hesitated. Then she took it.

She broke off three small pieces and handed a piece to each of her children. None for herself. She handed the cake back to Crowley. By gestures, he conveyed that she was to keep it all. She stood expressionless, then bowed to Crowley, and motioned for each of her children to bow.

While this was going on, other refugees were watching. So were the men of Private First Class Crowley's company. Silently, spontaneously, a sort of spiritual chain reaction began. Crowley had shown what to do about the refugees.

Out of their foxholes came the soldiers, bearing gifts for the North Koreans. They gave gloves, mufflers, food from their own rations, cakes and delicacies from the U.S.A. Some of the soldiers made second trips and came back with blankets and shoe-pacs; others peeled off jackets and draped them around wet, shivering children.

The whole thing was done almost in dead silence, though some of the boys said things like "Merry Christmas, Joe," or "Happy New Year, little girl," as they passed out their presents.

In the middle of it all, up raced the battalion commander in an open car, ready to chop off heads for the flagrant security breach. What the hell was going on, he wanted to know. He found out. Before he left, he passed out a pocketful of hard candy to Korean kids. He also turned his head when his driver gave away the blankets they had been swathed in when they drove up.

"Sure cold today, colonel," said the driver cheerfully.

"Drive on," said the colonel.

Slowly, Operation Santa Claus subsided. South Korean police stopped the refugee flow. Those who had come over were directed to a railroad track and told to start walking south—fast.

Then the soldiers returned to their foxholes. Materially, they were poorer; militarily, they had done a risky thing. The only thing about it was that the men of the 35th, holding their sector of the 25th Division's battle line, all felt so good that evening. There was no peace, but there was considerable good will, on the south bank of the Imjin on that Christmas Eve, 1950.

(P.S.: In April, 1951, Pfc. Stanley Crowley was reported killed in action.) (1951)

Olaf Ruben

Christmas on the Island

A little grinning lad came up the track as MacGregor began to climb the tall, upthrust boulder they called the Fishermen's Rock, his bare toes digging into the ancient footholds. In one hand the boy carried three hen eggs carefully wrapped in a lily leaf; in the other a mud crab, its claws pinioned with a strip of palm frond.

"Where are you going?" he wanted to know.

MacGregor stopped and looked at him. The boy's grin was from ear to ear.

"I'm going to the top of the rock," MacGregor said carefully.

"Just to see about?" asked the boy.

"Just to see."

"All right. You see plenty."

From the top of the rock, MacGregor saw plenty, indeed. He saw the whole beautiful world, and in the middle of it, in the water almost directly beneath him, a ketch setting sail, ice-white, immaculate and curiously remote in spite of the muted rattle of blocks, the groaning of the anchor winch which came as an undercurrent to the screaming of the parrots in the trees. The departure of the little ship disturbed him—the setting out of someone he had never known for a destiny he could not guess at. It was like his own farewell to civilization six months before—it was emotionally cold. Like himself, for that matter. Or at least that was what Kathleen had told him.

"Underneath, you're as cold as a fish," she had said when she gave him back the ring. "Nothing ever warms you. You're too good, Mac. You're clinically exact. And it isn't good for you. It won't get you anywhere."

"I don't make mistakes, anyway," he said.

"Perhaps that's what I mean," she told him.

He had regretted Kathleen, but it was the pursuit of his painting career rather than her dismissal which had brought him to this island of

Owelaka, an outlyer of the Trobriand group which is itself an archipelago set in the Coral Sea. And he stayed, though the island is not of itself beautiful. It is simply a coral plain, a little tip tilted by forgotten earthquakes, with a vegetation that differs hardly at all from that of any coral island. But from his perch on the Fishermen's Rock, where traditionally the canoemen climbed to shout their successes to the expectant village, he could see the ocean's loveliest waters, studded at a little distance by islands that are dead volcanoes; and islands beyond islands, mountainous, symmetrical, tinted with the shades of sea distance.

He had been induced to stay by some furious necessity to master the problems presented by his art. He had found a home with old Frank Richards, the trader, in a great cool barn of four chicken-wire walls and a sago-leaf roof which served as storehouse, living quarters and trading post in the village of Lamari, on the east coast; and here he kept himself firmly applied to painting when he was not looking after Frank's interests during the trader's frequent absences. He was looking after them now, paying his weekly call at the district office in Papatalu, where a safe anchorage and adjacent copra plantations constituted Owelaka's sole commerical assets.

He was barefoot, because that was the best way to negotiate the three ragged ridges of abruptly upthrust coral that, under heavy forest, divided Lamari's lovely coral beaches, its populated villages and fertile garden land, from Papatalu. In four places he had had to balance on slippery peeled trunks of trees no more than six inches in diameter. Once he had crossed a rock bridge.

Perhaps beneath Mac's cool exterior ran warm currents.

There were two cliff faces, not high, but rugged, that had to be climbed with handholds; and everywhere except directly on the foot-wide, smooth-worn trail, the rock was jagged with razor edges. But he had all the time in the world, and the way was beautiful with flowers and butterflies and water-flecked green ferns.

The weather was hot. It was ten days before Christmas in the northwest monsoon, and MacGregor stayed on top of the rock resting and watching until the ketch had beaten northeast round the coral, heading, as he guessed now, for the main Trobriand group, which was in the north. He scrambled down to the track again and headed for the district office.

Stevens, the patrol officer, saw him coming, and threw a yellow envelope on the counter.

"Radiogram for you," he said.

MacGregor tore it open. "Three days old?" he complained. He wasn't really surprised.

"Yes. Well, there was no hurry," Stevens said. "You can't get a message out in reply. The radio's broken down."

"When are you going to have something urgent of your own so you'll fix it?" MacGregor inquired nastily, but Stevens only grunted and turned his back. He threw a bundle of letters—mostly for Richards—on the counter. The radiogram was from Richards too. It read:

DELAYED THREE WEEKS BROKEN PROPELLOR SHAFT STOP SOME DAMAGE STOP SLIPPING SAMARAI STOP PLEASE MEET LAYONI AND EXPLAIN WHY NO CHRISTMAS STOP LOOK AFTER HER STOP SORRY TO TROUBLE YOU. FRANK

Well, that was Frank all over, MacGregor thought. He had the ends all tied up, but, somehow or other, nothing went right for him. He had made a special trip to get Christmas stock for his store, and now he wasn't going to be home for Christmas. Layoni was his ten-year-old half-caste daughter and the apple of his eye, and Layoni's mother had died at her birth. MacGregor had never seen the child. He felt, at any rate, that he had no special affinity for small children. They bored him.

One of the letters, he saw, had the name of Layoni's mission school on the envelope, so he tore it open. It contained Layoni's school report and the news that the mission schooner would land her at Papatalu on Owelaka on December twenty-first. He looked up, reminded of something.

"Beautiful ketch just left the bay," he said. "Whose is it? No trader, I bet."

"You're safe," Stevens told him. "That was Innstrom's Tanagra. If I had his money I wouldn't be bucketing round these waters in a wind ship, that's for sure. Even though it's got everything that opens and shuts."

"Sir Gordon Innstrom?" MacGregor asked.

Stevens nodded. "The same," he said.

Sir Gordon was the one man above all others MacGregor would have liked to meet. He was the only one of the Australian millionaires, as far as he knew, who took any interest in painting. More than that, in MacGregor's view, it was an informed interest. Innstrom knew his subject.

"I'd have liked to meet him," MacGregor said.

"You'll get your chance," said Stevens. "He's coming back. He spent a few days with the Allisons, and they've asked him back for their Christmas party."

The Allisons had the biggest copra plantation. There were only a dozen Europeans on the island, and the Allisons comprised the self-appointed aristocracy. MacGregor avoided them whenever he could. Mrs. Allison got on his nerves more than just a little.

"So charmed to welcome an artist to our little community," she said when she met him first. "I paint myself, of course. But in my first year here I painted everything, absolutely everything paintable. One can't go on painting the same coconut palm." None of her efforts hung upon her walls, and the few prints there, while they were good, seemed to bear no relationship to one another.

MacGregor himself was engaged in a period of searching introspection. When he got home he went through his paintings again, stacking them up three or four at a time in the best light. They were not what he wanted.

He had left Sydney with no very impressive reputation, but in all honesty he did not know why. His work was modern. It had flow and rhythm; and in particular, a series of portraits that almost approached caricature had deserved, he felt, a public recognition. His techniques were good. He was a young man going places, and he had undertaken the visit to the Trobriands for publicity purposes as much as anything; it was a vivid place where no other artist had been. And then the islands had intrigued him, entangled him, and finally, he had to admit, defeated him. For the exaggerated color and the exotic forms of the tropics mated badly with his exaggerated technique.

He sorted out the portraits of Doraima, a Lamari village adolescent who, on a whim, had her head shaved entirely bald. The girl's figure was exquisite. The dainty conformation of her completely naked head mated wonderfully with her fine-cut features and her regal bearing. She painted designs of happiness on her face—eye-encircling curves of shining black and enameled white in pigments of charcoal and lime and coconut oil.

MacGregor's first painting of her, in his usual style, was so bad he destroyed it. The others now faced him: two or three representational treatments in assorted surroundings that offered a flat and clinical result, and a slightly better version, with an almost Egyptian flavor. This one had drawn praise from Mrs. Allison, but he felt it lacked something.

Over-all, he was very disappointed. His work

seemed alien to the land and to himself. The more immediate reason for his inspection, however, was to decide whether the quality of his work was sufficient to intrigue such a patron as Innstrom. If he could achieve Sir Gordon's patronage, his fame and future would be assured.

Several days later, when a native boy arrived at Lamari with an invitation to the Allison Christmas party, he was delighted to accept. He put the latest Doraima portrait back on the easel and added a few finishing touches, planning to present it to his hostess. Brought to the party, it would inevitably form a topic for conversation among the guests — conversation into which Sir Gordon must be drawn. Thus he would make his chance.

The Allison children and four or five others— the patrol officer's two and a Sanderson and two Emmets—were on the mission schooner with Layoni when he came to meet her. She was a slim child, primly dressed, with pipestem legs and neat polished shoes, and she stood a little behind the others, ignored by them, clutching her case in both hands, with her head downcast.

Her voice, when she spoke, was tiny but musical.

Mrs. Allison, having gathered her brood about her, nodded a bright farewell. She was a big, heavy woman, briskly pleasant.

"We'll expect to see you on Christmas Day then, Mr. MacGregor," she said. "Come in the afternoon. The children will be having their party then, and we'll expect you to stay for ours in the evening." She looked at Layoni. "Someone at Lamari can look after Frank's child," she added. "I doubt that she'd get on too well with our lot."

The little girl dropped her chin on her chest again and looked at the ground. MacGregor felt her register the snub, brutal and direct. He took her absurdly small case, made his farewells, and they started up the track. When they paused at the summit and sat in the sun by the Fishermen's Rock, Layoni waited awhile before she asked, "Will my daddy be home for Christmas?"

"I'm afraid he won't be," MacGregor said absently. "He'll have to stay in Samarai until his boat is fixed. A couple of weeks, maybe."

He suddenly sensed Layoni's disappointment, and looked at her closely. For the first time he noticed the dusky glory of dark hair, the smooth olive complexion, the incredibly beautiful liquid brown eyes. There was something a little pathetic, he thought, in the way she looked down at her toes. Suddenly realizing she was at home, on her own ground, away from the disciplined days of mission school, she reached forward, undid her shoe fastenings and stripped off her shoes and socks. MacGregor thought, uncomfortably, of another disappointment.

"I'm afraid there won't be any Christmas presents either," he said. "And no party. Your daddy was going to bring all the things back with him, and now he can't."

There was a long pause this time, while the movements of her hands were arrested, and then she said gently, "Oh, it doesn't matter." She looked up. "We did have a party at the mis-sion, and it was nearly Christmas," she said. "Some of the girls there don't have any parties but the mission parties." Later on, when they were walking down the track, she said, "The girls that have parties will tell us all about them when school starts."

"I thought Mrs. Allison might have asked you to come to her party," MacGregor said, and Layoni shook her head.

"She never does." She had the utmost composure and poise. "Maybe daddy will bring a party back with him," she said. "It won't be very far from Christmas, will it?"

She looked up at him, and her beautiful eyes belied these Pollyanna sentiments, for they were close to tears. He began to feel a real interest in this little scrap of humanity. Suddenly he made a resolve that she should have her party.

At night, after he had sent Layoni to bed, MacGregor sat and smoked his pipe. *What on earth does one do*, he thought, *to please a child at Christmas?* Most of his memories came from the commercial art work he had done in student days for city stores. There would have to be a tree—well, that was simple. He could manage that. But there were no toys, no ornaments, no strings of lights. Playmates would be no problem. And he could keep the party a surprise—last-minute invitations would not worry the native children of the village. There should be an angel for the top of the tree. He tried to remember what else.

The village of Paladau, in the south of the island, was renowned for its wood carvers. They were simple artisans who cheerfully tackled the job of making, say, a three-legged table; chopping it with most intricate design out of a heavy solid tree trunk, using tiny adzes of their own manufacture, smoothing the cuts with the sand-paper skin of a stingray, and adding the final polish with a boar's tusk. Their main products were beautiful wooden bowls, simply and hand-somely carved, but when a Paladau villager had nothing else to do he carved little fish or pigs, and instruments for the daily work of the people. None of the island natives cared to use any ar-tifact that had not been given some ornamentation of beauty, but a Paladau man would neglect his gardens for his carving, with the enthusiastic approval of his wife and family.

Timothy, the old village councilor, was sharpening an adz in front of his hut, and looked up, smiling, when MacGregor walked in. The artist came straight to the point.

"I want you to carve me an angel, Timothy. You know this something, an angel?"

"No, sir."

"A woman then—a woman that has wings on her back like a bird's wings; a woman this high"—he gestured with his hands about fifteen inches apart—"and in her right hand she holds a stick that has a star, like this, on the end of it." With the point of a knife he scratched a star-tipped scepter on the ground.

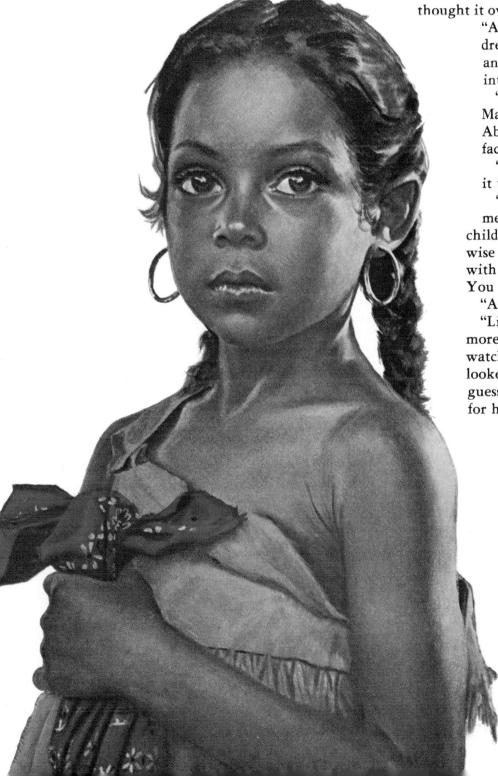

"A woman with wings and a stick?" asked Timothy. "This is an angel?" He pronounced the word three times over, trying to get it right.

MacGregor caught himself quickly. "Why, no," he said. "An angel is like a woman, truly, but she must be something more. She is the meaning of all giving, the cause of all happiness; she makes your heart light."

"Like a new bride?" asked Timothy.

MacGregor searched his mind. It seemed urgent that Timothy should have exactly the right idea.

"Like a new bride and a new mother," he said. "Like the bride and the mother of all the world." He wondered whence the image came, and thought it over. It did not sound ridiculous at all.

"And she looks like this," he added. He drew three quick little sketches of the angel while the councilor watched him intently, his curiosity growing.

"I want it quickly," warned MacGregor. "The day after tomorrow." Absently he added a halo to the front-face figure.

"All right," Timothy said. "I'll bring it to Lamari."

"Something else," MacGregor remembered. "I want some things for a child to play with. There should be three wise men with camels, and shepherds with their sheep, and a crib for a Baby. You know sheep? Or camels?"

"Are they like pigs?" asked Timothy.

"Like pigs," MacGregor said. "Only more like this." He drew a sheep and watched the old man's eyes when he looked at it. "Never mind," he said. "I guess pigs will do. They are for Layoni, for her Christmas presents."

The old man nodded. "I know this Christmas," he said. "That is when the government holds the sports at Losuia."

MacGregor drew a deep breath. "Christmas is more than that, Timothy," he tried to explain. "Christmas is when everybody thinks of other people, to make them happy. At Christmas the white man thinks of God, and pleases Him by making His children happy."

I sound like a preacher, he thought. *I have never thought these things before.*

Timothy smiled. "I have heard of these things, but not seen them," he said. "I will be glad to help. But Mr. Richards will bring toys."

"Not this Christmas, Timothy," MacGregor said. "His boat has broken down. That's why I want you to make these things. And not you only. Tell the others that I need toys for the children and that I will pay them well."

"The day after tomorrow I will bring them to Lamari," the councilor promised.

Once he had committed himself to give Layoni the party, MacGregor went about it enthusiastically. Layoni had renewed friendships amongst the children of the village, though in the year she had been gone she had almost forgotten the Boyowan language of the island; and most of the day she spent on the beach or in the water, and was never underfoot. MacGregor saw her only for meals, which he sometimes got himself, but oftener left to the hired boys Richards kept in the store. At night Layoni would look briefly at her books, which were few; then go to bed to sleep dreamlessly. MacGregor's affection for her grew with each meeting, and in the two days of preparations she was much in his thoughts.

It was easy, without her knowledge, to find a she-oak tree with the necessary symmetry and the desired size, and to install it in a corner of the store, concealed by burlap sheets and cartons of goods. He was also able to recruit a few of the village women to help him by making strings of shell beads and raucous trumpets made from the coiled leaves of the coconut palms. They caught his enthusiasm and by Christmas Eve other villagers to whom he had not spoken were bringing in gifts—a beautiful little canoe with mast, butterfly-wing sail, and tiny paddles; a set of tops made from coconut shells doweled with wooden pegs; a cord carrying bag in five colors.

Timothy and three men from Paladau came late on Christmas Eve with their carvings. The angel was a triumph, queerly modern in design, with a long body and short, thick legs; and, in place of the halo that MacGregor had drawn, she carried a cooking pot on her head. She had long almond eyes and a straight, unsmiling mouth. But she was nevertheless beautiful, with an air of proud kindliness most suitable for an angel. MacGregor handled the carving for a long time, turning it over and over. Then he looked at the other things, spread about him on the ground.

There were at least twenty little pigs, each round and fat, and standing stockily on four absurd short legs. There were three little figures of men. There was a short trough, shaped like a Phoenician galley—"Something for the baby," Timothy said. MacGregor recognized it. It was an ancient baby bath, just big enough to admit a mother's fingers, holding just enough water to clean a baby. It was the only Trobriand article made for babies. MacGregor set it down carefully. Then he saw the thing.

It was a big carving a foot long. It was cut from some golden timber, and it had a long body, six short legs and a tail that was a dragon's tail, except that it curved upward and back, its frill of broad spines soaring like a banner, and joined in two places to the thing's back. The neck balanced the tail, but carried an enormous head with two pointed ears, four round eyes and rows and rows of bared teeth. MacGregor picked it up.

"What is it?" he asked.

"It is a camel," said Timothy, and MacGregor put back his head and laughed.

"I think it is a camel. I have never seen a camel," Timothy added. He seemed affronted, and MacGregor stopped laughing.

"It is not quite a camel," he said. "But it is a very good something. I am truly pleased with it."

"Yes, it is a very good something," Timothy said complacently.

MacGregor paid the men well in tobacco and goods from the store, and they left. He looked at the angel a long time; then he took his paints and, with some compunction at hiding the beautiful grain of the wood, painted it in the colors of life. He painted the pigs, too, and the little men who represented shepherds; and when that was done, he turned to the decoration of the tree, tying in place the brilliant crimson globes of fruits and golden oranges, and all the colorful things he could think of. He could not add the angel or the painted toys until the morning, when the colors would be dry, but even so it was long past midnight when he went to take a final look at the sleeping Layoni.

She was lying quietly, an olive-skinned doll, her dark hair spread about the pillow, her thin arms carelessly outside the single sheet that covered her. In her sleep she looked a little sad and a little lonely, and he felt a great rush of affection for the child.

He took a long time to go to sleep himself, thinking not of Layoni but of the Allison party. He was excited about it, and in a way disgusted with himself for being excited, because he certainly condemned Mrs. Allison for her rejection of Layoni. It would have been easy for her to be kind to the child, who was, after all, the only person on the island alien to both the natives and the whites. At least on Christmas Day she could have given her the companionship of the other English-speaking children, MacGregor felt. On the other hand, he felt the prospects of the Innstrom contact to be enormously important. Sir Gordon's was an acquaintance which MacGregor could develop with, he felt, the happiest of results when he returned to civilization. From the starting point of the Doraima painting, which Mrs. Allison would certainly have in a place of prominence, he might even secure Sir Gordon as a kind of patron, and that, combined with his own abilities as an artist, would be quite sufficient to insure the success of his whole career.

So his thoughts went, on and on into the night, and it was quite late when he awoke.

"Where will you go this morning?" he asked Layoni at breakfast.

"Just swimming, I think," she said, and he nodded. He would be able to find her when he wanted her. So he said nothing about the waiting Christmas tree. Better to keep it really a surprise. In an hour or two it would be ready.

It took even less than that to set the painted angel at the top of the tree, to wrap in concealing leaves the painted pigs that should have been sheep and the funny little men that should have been shepherds, and the toys—the tops decorated now with bands of bright red and blue—and to arrange them all in their places. But when that was done, Layoni and her friends were nowhere to be seen.

It would be a four-hour walk to the Allisons—maybe three if he hurried—but MacGregor did not particularly worry about his schedule. A little later never mattered in the islands. The children would turn up by lunch; he could start the party and still get to the Allisons' in plenty of time. But it was early afternoon when Layoni appeared, and he felt aggrieved.

"We've had a lovely day, Uncle Mac!" she cried. "We found a cave——"

"Well, go and find all the other kids again," he said. "Bring them here just as fast as you can."

He looked at his watch as she ran off. It was one. He pulled down the burlap barriers and the pile of crates, and revealed the Christmas tree. Even in his impatience he was pleased with the result. The tree was beautiful, its branches gracious under the offerings. From the top twig the angel, proud and lovely, looked indeed as though she offered her benediction.

When the little girl came again to the doorway of the store, she just stood still and stared. Behind her, children pushed their way in, until they, too, could see the tree and the angel.

"Merry Christmas, Layoni," greeted MacGregor. She didn't hear him until he had said it twice more. Then she ran, not to the tree, but to him, clutching his legs and looking up at his face; and he felt the strong unselfish love of a man for a child welling up in him. It was new to him and took him by the throat and left him weak.

"Thank you, thank you, thank you," she cried.

"Just for you," he said, "and your friends."

She walked slowly over to the tree, picked her way daintily, and there was that in her eyes that dimmed the radiance of the angel enthroned there. It was a look of beauty, of complete adoration, reflecting the kind of sheer happiness that can bring tears. MacGregor watched her for long minutes; he sat there watching while she called the others; he sat on and on. And suddenly it was urgent that he should keep forever the memory of that look and that happiness; and almost

unconsciously he reached for his sketch pad.

Working swiftly, he captured the moment. Quickly he made sketch after sketch—the face, the uplifted eye, a hand outstretched—not coldly and clinically, but in a fever of excitement that somehow intertwined with his other emotions.

Suddenly she was lifting up the animal that Timothy had carved—the six-legged monster.

"What is it?" she asked.

"It's a something," he told her. "Timothy said it's a camel." She dissolved into laughter.

From there it went on as a children's party does, except that the creator of the party sat there amongst them, his pencil flying, stabilizing and holding forever the moments in which a fat brown baby sat in ecstasy, fingering a spotty painted pig; or the whirl of movement with which a lucky lad raced to the water with a toy canoe. And when, at last, MacGregor retrieved the angel from the top of the tree and Layoni took it and sat with it in her arms, with her face molded into a pure testimony of love and happiness, he sat and drew that, too; his lines swiftly conspiring to produce, not merely the features, the waving black hair, the liquid brown eyes, but the configuration of love itself—of love and happiness and the true recipient spirit of Christmas.

When he had finished he realized that the afternoon was gone, and that the Allisons would see neither him nor the portrait of Doraima. There was no time to go, and no excuse. He could never explain such a late arrival.

Instead he stayed with Layoni, and when the village children went, read to her a little while, and watched her sleep at last; the painted wooden angel clutched in her arms, its cooking-pot halo against her shoulder. He realized he had probably made an enemy of the Allisons—his explanation about Layoni's party would certainly not be acceptable to the woman who had refused to invite the girl herself. The Allisons didn't matter, but he regretted missing Innstrom.

The day after Christmas was like any day after Christmas, MacGregor thought moodily as he cleared away the tree and the debris. He worked slowly, absorbed in thought, and was surprised by a stranger at the door, a tall gray man, a little red in the face from walking, dressed in correct tropical whites and carrying an ebony stick. The stranger held out his hand.

"My name's Innstrom," he said. "You're MacGregor. I heard some talk about you last night, and I wanted to see for myself how an artist would treat all this magnificent material."

MacGregor could hardly believe his luck. They talked for a while, and he showed his paintings; some of the lesser ones first. But as Sir Gordon looked at painting after painting, MacGregor's spirits sank. The visitor was politely appreciative, no more. When at last the Doraima portrait was shown, MacGregor knew with certainty that his work hadn't passed the test.

"Interesting," said Sir Gordon, fingering a gray mustache. "A really interesting solution, and I can see the problems you're up against here."

MacGregor made tea, and managed with difficulty to keep up a conversation. Whatever it was the millionaire had come hoping to see, he had not found it, and the artist reacted with disappointment almost to the point of despair. But as he turned to go, Sir Gordon idly picked up the sketch pad with the drawings of the children at the party. Carefully he went through them, then, with the pad, seated himself at the table.

"Now these?" he asked. "They're recent?"

"Yesterday's." MacGregor laughed. "They're the reason I didn't meet you at the Allisons'."

"Obviously," said Sir Gordon, "you found something better to do." He pointed to the Doraima portrait against the wall. "You see the difference? That one's good—good technique, good balance, a fine subject—but it's cold. It lacks emotion. You felt nothing. You had nothing to feel. These"—he took up the drawings again—"these are different. They have feeling. They are alive. Here your hands were directed through eyes altered by your own emotions. You were emotionally involved, you see. You are forever involved. And I think you will never be the same as you were before." He reached in his pocket and found a card. "I must go, young man. I'm glad I came. I'd like to see more of your later work. Look me up when you come to Sydney."

MacGregor walked with him to the Fishermen's Rock at the top of the hill. He had a feeling he might never see Sir Gordon again, for suddenly he knew with certainty that he didn't need him. When he returned, Layoni came racing from the beach and threw herself into his arms. The angel hit him on the head, but he didn't care.

"Thank you! Thank you, Uncle Mac!" cried Layoni. "Thank you for the party!"

"Thank you, little girl," he said. "Thank you for everything." She didn't really understand him, but he didn't bother to explain it. (1956)

Rupert Hughes

Mrs. Budlong's Christmas Gifts

The morning after Christmas Eve is the worst morning-after there is. The very house suffers the headache that follows a prolonged spree. Remorse stalks at large—remorse for the things one gave—and did not give—and got.

Everybody must act a general glee which can be felt only specifically if at all. Everybody must exclaim about everything: Oh! and Ah! and How sweet of you! Isn't it perfectly dear? The Very Thing I wanted! How did you EVER guess it?

Christmas morning in the town of Carthage is a day when most of the people keep close at home, for Christmas is another passover. It is Santa Claus that passes over.

People in Carthage are not rich and the shops are not grandiose, and interfamily presents are apt to be trivial and futile—or, worse yet, utile.

The Carthaginian mother generally finds that father has credited the hat she got last fall to this Christmas; the elder brothers receive warm underthings and the young ones brasstoed boots, mits and mufflers. The girls may get something ornamental in their stockings, and their stockings may be silk or nearly; but then girls have to be foolishly diked up anyway, or they will never be married off. Dressing up daughters comes under the head of window-display or coupons and is charged off to publicity.

Nearly everybody in Carthage—except Mrs. Ulysses S. G. Budlong—celebrates Christmas behind closed doors. People find it easier to rhapsodize when the collateral is not shown. It is amazing how far a Carthaginian can go on the most meager donation. The formula is usually: "We had a lovely Christmas at our house! What did I get? Oh, so much I can't remember!"

Mrs. Ulysses S. G. Budlong, however, does not celebrate her Christmases behind closed doors—or, rather, she did not;

for a strange change came over her last Christmas. She used to open her doors wide—metaphorically, that is; for there was a stormdoor, with a spring on it, to keep the cold draft out of the hall.

As regular as Christmas itself was the oh-quite-informal reception Mrs. Budlong gave to mitigate the ineffable stupidity of Christmas afternoon—that dolorous period when one meditates the ancient platitude that anticipation is better than realization.

On Christmas Day Mrs. U. S. G. Budlong took all the gifts she had gleaned and piled them on and around the baby-grand piano in the back parlor. There was a piano lamp there, and it was about as large and as useful as a date palm tree. Then she invited the neighbors in. It looked like hospitality, but it felt like hostility. She passed her neighbors under the yoke, gloated over her guests, and seemed to overgloat her gifts.

She got the gifts though, no question about it. By hook or by crook she saw to it that the bazar under the piano lamp always gleamed.

One of the chief engines for keeping up the display was the display itself. Everybody who knew Mrs. Budlong—and not to know Mrs. Budlong was to argue oneself unknown—knew that he or she would be invited to this Christmas triumph. And being invited rather implied being represented in the loot.

Hence ensued a curious rivalry in Carthage. People vied with each other in giving Mrs. Budlong presents. Not that they loved Mrs. Budlong more, but they loved comparisons less.

The rivalry grew to quite ridiculous proportions, but of course Mrs. Budlong did not care how ridiculous it grew; for it could hardly have escaped her shrewd eyes that people gave her presents in order to show other people that some people needn't think they could show off before other people without having other people show that they could show off too, as well as other people could—or something like that. The psychology must be correct, for it is incoherent.

Mrs. Budlong herself was never known to break any of the commmandments; but in her home her neighbors made flitters of the tenth—against coveting thy neighbor's son and so on.

As Mr. and Mrs. County Road Supervisor Detwiller were walking home from one of these occasions Mr. Detwiller was saying: "Well, ain't Mizzes Budlong the niftiest little gift-getter that ever held up a train? How on earth did we happen to get stung?"

"I don't know, Roscoe. It's one of those things you can't get out of without getting out of town too. We've gone and skimped our own children to buy something that would show up good in Mrs. Budlong's back parlor; and when I laid eyes on it in all that clutter—

why, if it didn't look like something the cat brought in I'll eat it!"

Mr. Detwiller's one and only consolation—and he grinned over it—was:

"Well, there's no use cryin' over spilt gifts; but did you see how she stuck old Widower Clute for that Japanese porcelain vase? She called it vahs!"

"Porcelain?" sniffed Mrs. Detwiller. "Paper-musshay!"

"Well, getting even a paper-what-you-said from old Clute is equal to extracting solid gold from anybody else. He's the stingiest man in seven states. He doesn't care any more for a two-dollar bill than he does for his right eye. I bet she gave him ether before

Mrs. Ulysses S.G. Budlong—the busybody of Carthage, creator and champion of Carthage Christmases.

he would let go."

"Oh, she works all the old bachelors and widowers that way," said Mrs. Detwiller with a mixture of contempt and awe—"invites 'em to a dinner party or two round Christmas marketing time, and begins to talk about how pretty the shops are and how tempting everything she wants is; says she saw an imitation bronze clock at Strouther & Streckfuss that it

to the bone and never got any thanks—other women keepin' two and three hired girls—and after him denyin' his children things to get expensive presents for a shameless creature like that Budlong woman——"

All over Carthage on Christmas afternoon couples were similarly celebrating Mrs. Budlong's annual triumph.

almost broke her heart to leave there. But of course she couldn't afford to buy anything for herself now when she's got to remember all her dear friends; and she runs on and on. And the old bach growls, 'Stung again!' and goes to the store and tells Mr. Streckfuss to send Mrs. Budlong that blamed bronze clock she was admiring. That's how she gets things. I could do it myself if I'd a mind to!"

Mr. Detwiller felt that there was more envy than truth in this last remark, and he was rash enough to speak up for justice.

"You could if you'd a mind to? Yep!—if you'd a mind to. That's what somebody said about Shakespeare's plays—'I could 'a' wrote 'em myself if I'd a mind to!' says he; and somebody else said, 'Yes—if you'd a mind to,' he says. And that's about it. Anybody could do what Mizzes Budlong does if they had the mind to; but the thing is, she's got the mind to. She goes after the gifts—and gits 'em! She don't almost git 'em and she ain't just agoin' to git 'em—she gits 'em! And what gits me is how she gits 'em!"

"Roscoe Detwiller, if you're goin' to praise that woman in the presence of your own lawful wife I'll never speak to you the longest day I live!"

"Who's praisin' her? I was just sayin'——"

"Why, Roscoe Detwiller, you did too!"

"Did what? Why, I was roastin' that woman to beat the band!"

"And to think that on Christmas Day, of all days, I should live to hear my own husband, that I've loved and cherished and worked my fingers

Now, of course Mrs. Budlong did not get all these presents without giving presents—not in Carthage! It might have been possible to bamboozle these people one Christmas, but never another. Mrs. Budlong gave lots of presents. Christmas was an industry with her—an ambition. It had long ago lost its religious significance for her as for nearly everybody else in Carthage.

Even Mr. Frankenstein, the Pantatorium magnate, is one of the most ardent advertisers of Yuletide bargains, while Isidore Strouther and Esau Streckfuss are almost persuaded every December. They might be entirely persuaded if it were not for the scenes they witness in their aisles during the last weeks of shopping and the aftermath of trying to collect from the Carthage husbands.

Mrs. Budlong's Christmas presents were of two sorts—those she made herself and those she made her husband pay for. He was the typical husband who never fails to settle his wife's bills so long as he may raise a row about them until his wife cries and looks like an expensive luxury which only a really successful man could afford. Then he subsides until the first of the next month.

II

Mrs. Budlong's Christmas campaign was undertaken with the same farsightedness as a magazine editor's. Along about the Fourth of July she began to worry and plan. By the second week in August she had her tatting well under way. By the middle of September she was getting in her embroidered doilies. The earliest frost rarely surprised her with her quilts untufted. And when the first snow flew her sachet bags were all stuffed and smelly.

She was very feminine in her sense of the value of her own time. At missionary meetings she would shed tears over the pathetic pictures of oriental women who spent a year weaving a rug that would sell for a paltry hundred dollars and last a mere century or two. Then she would happily devote fifteen days of incessant stitching at something she toted in a sort of drumhead.

In the end she would have compiled a more or less intolerable piece of colored fabric which she called a "bureau cover" or a "drape" or a "throw." It could not be duplicated at a shop for less than one dollar and seventy-five cents, and it would wash, perhaps three times.

Mr. Budlong once figured that if sweatshop proprietors paid wages at the scale Mrs. Budlong established for herself all the seamsters and seamstresses would curl up round their machines and die of starvation the first week—but he never told Mrs. Budlong this. Fancy stitching did not earn much, but it did not cost much and it mysteriously contented her. She was stitching herself to her own home all the time.

The Christmas presents Mrs. Budlong made herself were not all a matter of needle and thread. Not at all! One year she turned her sewing room into a smithy. She gave Mr. and Mrs. Colonel Tisnower the loveliest hand-hammered brass coal-scuttle that ever was seen—and with a purple ribbon tied to it. They kept flowers in it several summers until one cruel winter a new servant put coal in it and completely scuttled it.

The same year she gave Mrs. ex-Mayor Cinnamon a hammered-brass version of a C. D. Gibson drawing. The lady and gentleman looked as if they had broken out with a combination of yellow fever and smallpox, or suffered from enlarged pores or something. And the plum-colored plush frame didn't sit very well on the vermilion wallpaper; but Mrs. Cinnamon hung it over the sofa in the expectation of changing the paper some day. It stayed there until the fateful evening when Mr. Nelson Chur called on Miss Editha Cinnamon and was just warming up a proposal that had been held over almost as long as the wallpaper, when bang! down came the overhanging brass drawing and bent itself hopelessly on Mr. Chur's cranium! Mr. Chur said something that may have been Damocles—but he did not propose. Mrs. Budlong was weeks wondering why Mrs. Cinnamon was so snippy to her.

The hammered-brass era gave way to the opposite extreme of painted velvet. They say it is a difficult art; and it must be. Mrs. Budlong's first landscape might as well have been painted on the side of her Scotch collie.

Her most finished roses had something of the look of shaggy tarantulas that have fallen into a paintpot and emerged in a towering rage. It was in that velvetocene stratum that she painted for the

Christmas according to Mrs. Budlong meant presents made by her own hand.

church a tasseled pulpit cloth that hung down a yard below the Bible. Doctor Torpadie was a very soothing preacher, but no one slept o' sermons during the reign of that pulpit cloth. Mrs. Budlong was so elated over the success of it, however, that she announced her intention of going in for stained glass. She planned a series of the sweetest windows to replace those already in the church; but she never got nearer to that than painted china.

The painted-china era was a dire era. The cups would break, the colors would run; they never came out what she expected after they were fired. She knew the pigments must suffer alteration in the furnace—but such alteration!

She soon became accustomed to getting green roses with crimson leaves, and deep blue apple blossoms against a pure-white sky; but when she finished one complete set of table china in fifty pieces, each cup and saucer with a flower on it, the result looked so startlingly like something from a medical museum that she never dared give the set away. She lent it to the cook to eat her meals on.

During this epoch, Master Ulysses Budlong, Junior, was studying, at school, a physiology ornamented with a few color pictures representing the stomachs of alcohol specialists. They were meant, perhaps, to frighten children from frequenting saloons during recess or to warn them not to put whisky on their porridge.

It was at this time that Mrs. Budlong spent two weeks' hard labor painting Easter lilies on an umbrella jug. When it came home from the furnace her husband stared at it and mumbled:

"It's artistic—but what is it?"

Little Ulysses shrieked: "Oh, I know!" And darting away he returned with his physiology opened at one of those gastric sunsets; and—well, it was this that impelled Mrs. Budlong to a solemn pledge never to paint china again—a pledge she has nobly kept.

From smeared china she went to that art in which a woman buys something at a store, pulls out half of it and calls the remnant drawnwork. A season of this was succeeded by a mania for sofa cushions. It fairly snowed sofa cushions all over Carthage that Christmas; and Yale, Harvard and Princeton pillows appeared in homes that had never known even a nightschool alumnus.

There ensued a sober period of burnt wood and a period of burnt leather, during which excited neighbors with a keen sense of smell called the fire department out three times and the board of health once. And now Indian heads broke out all over town; the walls looked as if a shoemaker's apron had been chosen for the pennant.

There were other varied spasms of manufacture, each of them fashionable at its time and foolish at any time. But, foolish soever, Mrs. Budlong was fair. A keen sense of sportsmanship led her to give full notice to such people as she planned to honor with her gifts. She knew how embarrassing it is to receive presents from one to whom no present has been sent; and she made it a point of

Somewhere between firing and final product, Mrs. Budlong's china underwent drastic changes.

Calls returned promptly meant "be prepared" at all times to those being called upon.

honor somehow to forewarn her prospective beneficiaries betimes. Her favorite method was the
classic device of pretending to let slip a secret. For
instance:

"Yesterday morning, my dear, I had the
strangest experience. It was just ten o'clock. I
remember the hour so exactly because for the last
few days I have made it a rule to begin work on your
Christmas present just at ten——Oh! but I didn't
mean to tell you! It was to be a surprise. No; don't
ask me—I won't give you an inkling; but I really
think it will please you. It's something you've
needed for such a long time."

And she left the victim hopelessly to writhe from
then on to Christmas, trying alternately to imagine what gift was impending and what would be

an appropriate countergift to give Mrs. Budlong.

III

In more ways than one Mrs. Budlong kept Carthage on the writhe. Christmas was merely the
climax of a ceaseless activity. All the year round she
was at work like yeast alert in a soggy dough.

She was forever getting up things. She was one of
those women who return calls on time—a little
ahead, in fact. That made it necessary for you to
return hers earlier. If you didn't she called you up
on the telephone and asked you why you hadn't.
You had to promise to come over at once, or she'd
talk to you until your ear was welded to the telephone. Then, if you broke your promise, she called

you up about that. She got in from fifty-two to one hundred and four calls a year, where one or two would have amply sufficed for all she had to say.

It was due to her that Carthage had such a lively social existence— for its size. Once she fell ill and the people felt as passengers might feel when a street car is suddenly braked back on its haunches—all Carthage found itself wavering and poised on tiptoe and clinging to straps; and then it sagged back on its heels and waited. Mrs. Budlong was the town's motorman—or "motorneer" as they say in Carthage. Before she was up she had invitations out for a convalescent tea; and everybody said: "Here we go again!"

If strangers visited Carthage Mrs. Budlong counted them her clients from the moment they arrived. Of course the merely commercial visitors she left to the hackmen at the station, but friends or relatives of prominent people could not escape Mrs. Budlong's well-meant attentions. It was sometimes embarrassing when relatives appeared—for everybody has somewhere concealed some relatives he is perfectly willing to leave forever in concealment.

Mrs. Alex—pronounced Ellick—Stubblebine never forgave Mrs. Budlong for dragging into the limelight some obscure cousins of her husband's who had drifted into Carthage to borrow money on their farm. Mrs. Stubblebine was always bragging about her people—her own people, that is. Her husband's people, of course, after all, were only Stubblebines, while her maiden name was Dilatush— and the Dilatushes, as everybody knew, were related by marriage to the Tatums.

These were Stubblebines that came to town, however. Mrs. Stubblebine could hardly slam the door in their faces, of course, but she would fain have locked the doors after them. She would not even invite them out on the front porch. She told them the back porch was cozier and less conspicuous. Then Mrs. Budlong had to call up on the phone and sing out in her telephoniest cheer:

"Oh, my dear, I've just this minute heard you have guests—some of your dear husband's relatives. Now they must come to me to dinner tomorrow. Oh, it isn't the slightest trouble, I assure you! I'm giving a little party anyway. I won't take no for an answer."

And she wouldn't. Mrs. Stubblebine fairly perspired excuses; but Mrs. Budlong finally grew so suspicious that she had to accept or leave the impression that the relatives were burglars or coun-

terfeiters in concealment. And they were not—they were pitifully honest.

The result was worse than she expected. Mr. Stubblebine's cousin was so shy that he never said a word except when it was pulled out of him, and then he said: "Yes, ma'am!" And not another syllable.

In Carthage when you are at a dinner party and you don't quite catch the last remark, you don't snap "What?" or "How?" or "Wha' jew say?" Whatever your home habits may be, at a dinner party or before company you raise your eyebrows gracefully and murmur: "I beg your pardon?"

Mr. Stubblebine's rural cousin, however, said "Huh?"—like an Indian chief trying to scare a white general. And he was perfectly frank about the intimate process of mastication.

And when he dropped a batch of scalloped oysters into his watchpocket he solemnly fished them out with a souvenir after-dinner coffee spoon having the Statue of Liberty for a handle and Brooklyn Bridge in the bowl.

The wretch's wife was so nervous she talked all the time about people the others had never seen or heard of. And she wasn't ashamed of what she was chewing either. And she said she "never used tomattus."

Mrs. Stubblebine would have felt much obliged to Fate if she had been presented with an apoplectic stroke, but she had to sit the dinner out. And from what she said to her poor husband afterward you would have thought he picked out those relatives just to spite her, when, as a matter of fact, he had always loathed them and regretted them; and the next day he borrowed money to lend them and send them back to the soil.

Mrs. Budlong had constituted herself an entertainment committee for all sorts of visitors. If a young girl came home from boarding school with a classmate the real hostess had hardly time to show her to the spareroom and say, "This is the bathroom round here; watch out for the steps—and if the water don't run just wait——" when the telephone would go br-r-r-r! And there would be Mrs. Budlong brandishing an invitation to a dinner party that evening.

When the supply of guests ran low she would visit the sick. If a worn-out housewife slept late some morning to catch up, Mrs. Budlong would hear of it and rush over with a broth or something. It is said that old Miss Malkin got out of bed in spite of the doctor's orders, just to keep from eating more of Mrs. Budlong's renowned wine jellies.

In Carthage one pays for the telephone by the year. The company lost money on Mrs. Budlong's wire. She was an indefatigable telephonist. She would spend a week-end at the instrument while the prisoner at the other extreme of the wire shifted from ear to ear, sagged along the wall, postponed household duties, made signals of distress to other members of the family and generally cursed Mr. Alexander Graham Bell.

Three wall telephones were changed to table 'phones on Mrs. Budlong's account, and Mrs. Talbot had hers put by the bed. She used to nap while Mrs. Budlong talked, and trained herself to murmur "Yes, dear!" at intervals in her sleep.

By means like these, Mrs. Budlong kept Carthage more or less under her thumb. Carthage squirmed, but it could not crawl out from under. This, then, is the history of how the thumb was removed for good and all. It was Mrs. Budlong that removed it. Carthage could never have pried it up.

And the thumb came off because it grew popular.

Hitherto Mrs. Budlong had never been truly popular. People were afraid of her. She was a whipper-in, a true social bush-beater—driving the populace from cover like partridges. She would not let the town rest. The merchants alone admired her, for she was the cause of much buying of new shoes, new hats, new clothes, fine groceries, olives, Malaga grapes, salted almonds, raisins, English walnuts and other things one eats only at parties. She was the first woman in Carthage who ever gave a luncheon and called it breakfast as, years before, she had been the first hostess to give a dinner at any time except in the middle of the day. She was also the first to say "Come to me" when she meant "Come to our house." It had a Scriptural sound

and it was thought shocking till Carthage grew used to it.

It was due to her that several elderly men were forced into their first evening dress. They had thought to escape through life without that ordeal. Old Clute would have preferred to be fitted for a pine box and would have felt about as comfortable in it. He tried to compromise with the tailor on a garment that would serve as a "Prince Albert" by day and a "swaller-tail" by night; but Mr. Kweskin could not manage it, even though he struggled valiantly.

So Mr. Clute blamed Mrs. Budlong for yet another expense. Husbands all over town were blaming Mrs. Budlong for running their families into fool extravagances. Mothers were blaming her for dragging them round by the nose and never letting them rest. They never dared trust themselves about the house in a wrapper, for Mrs. Budlong might happen in as like as not—rather liker than not. Everybody in town resentfully obeyed Mrs. Budlong. Roscoe Detwiller, for his part, wanted to organize a Homekeepers' Union, and strike.

And then, just as the town was fermenting for revolt, Mrs.

Another gown, another Budlong affair.

Budlong came into a lot of money.

IV

That is, Mr. Budlong came into a lot of money. Which meant that Mr. Budlong would be permitted to take care of it while his wife got rid of it. One of those relatives very common in fiction, and not altogether unknown in real life, finally let go of her money at the behest of her impatient undertaker; and the Budlongs had the pleasure of seeing the glorious news of their good fortune in big headlines in the Carthage paper. It was the only display Mr. Budlong ever received in that paper without paying for it—except for the time when he also ran for mayor on the opposition ticket and was referred to in letters an inch high as "Candidate Nipped-in-the-Budlong."

Now the cornucopia of plenty had burst wide open on the front porch. It seemed as if they would have to wade through gold dollars to get to their front gate *when* the money was collected.

And now it was Mrs. Budlong's telephone that rang and rang. It was she who was called up and called up. It was she who sagged along the wall and shifted from foot to foot, from elbow to elbow and ear to ear.

After living in Carthage all her life she was suddenly, as it were, welcomed to the city as a distinguished visiting stranger. And now she had no need to invite people to return her calls. They came spontaneously. Sometimes there were a dozen calling at once. It was a reception every day. There were overflow meetings in the room that Mrs. Budlong called Mr. Budlong's "den." It was a place where she kept the furniture she did not dare keep in the parlor.

People who had never come to see her in spite of her prehensile telephone dropped in to pay up some musty old call that had lain unreturned for years. People who had always come formally, even funereally, rushed in as informally and with as devouring an enthusiasm as old chums. People who used to run in informally now drove up in vehicles from MacMulkin's livery stable; or if they came in their own turnouts they had the tops washed and the harness polished, while the gardener and furnaceman who drove had his hat well-brushed, was not allowed to smoke, and was also urged to sit up straight and keep his foot on the dashboard.

People who had been in the habit of devoting a day or two to cleaning up a year's social debts, and walked down the streets dropping doleful calls like wreaths on headstones, walked in unannounced of mornings. It was now Mrs. Budlong that had to keep dressed up all day. Everybody accepted the inevitable invitation to have a cup of tea, until the cook struck. Cook said she had "conthracted to cuke for a small family, not to run a continurous bairbecue!" Besides, she had to answer the doorbell so much she couldn't get her hands into the dough before they were out again. And dinner was never ready. The amount of tea consumed, and bakery cake, and the butter, began to alarm Mrs. Budlong. And Carthage people were so nervous at taking tea with a millionairess that they kept dropping cups or setting them down hard.

Mrs. Budlong had never a moment, the whole day long, to leave the house; and she suddenly found herself without a call returned. She had so many invitations to dinners and luncheons that her life became a hop, skip and jump.

During the first ecstasy of the good news Mrs. Budlong had raved over the places she was going to travel to—Paris—now pronounced Paree—Westminister Rabbi, Vienna, St. Mark's, the Lion of Lucerne! She talked like a handbook of Cook's Tours. To successive callers she told the story over and over until the rhapsody finally palled on her tongue. She began to hate Paree, St. Mark's and the Lion of Lucerne. All she wanted to do was to get out of town to some quiet retreat—for Carthage was no longer quiet. It simmered to the boiling-over point.

Once it had been Mrs. Budlong's pride to be the social leader of Carthage. Now that her husband was worth—or to be worth—a hundred thousand dollars, Carthage seemed a very petty parish to be the social leader of. She began to read New York society notes with expectancy, as one cons the Baedeker of a town one is approaching.

She lay awake nights wondering what she should wear at Mrs. Stuyvesant Square's next party and at Mrs. Astor House's sociable. She fretted over the choice between taking a letter from her church to St. Bartholomew's, or to Grace, or St. John the Divine's. And all the while she was pouring tea for the wives of harnessmakers and druggists, dentists and grocers! All the more reason for not appearing before them in the same clothes incessantly. With a dinner or a reception or a tea or a ball every night, her two dressy-up dresses became so familiar that she could hardly afford to trot them round much more. And she could hardly afford to get new ones; for, after all, she had not come into the money. She had just come at it or toward it or, as her husband began to say, "up against it."

Mr. Budlong was kept on such tenterhooks by lawyers with papers to sign, titles to clear, executors and executrices to consult, and waivers, deeds, indentures and things, that he had no time for his business.

Like housemaids' knee and painters' colic is millionaires' melancholia. And the Budlongs were enduring the illness without entertaining the microbe.

It is almost as much trouble to inherit money nowadays as to earn it in the first place. Mr. Budlong was confronted with such a list of postmortem debts that must be prepaid for his deceased Aunt Ida that he almost begrudged her her bit of very real estate in Woodlawn. And they began to think that funeral monuments were in bad taste if ostentatious.

They had always accounted Aunt Ida a hard-fisted miser before, but now she began to look like a slippery-palmed spendthrift. They began almost to suspect the probity of the poor old maid. Worse yet,

The changes brought about by the money-yet-to-come caused Mr. Budlong to despair that it ever would.

they feared that some later will might turn up, bequeathing all her money to some abominable charity. She had been addicted to occasional subscriptions during her lifetime.

The Budlongs themselves were beginning, even at this distance from their money-to-be, to suffer its infection, its inevitable reaction on the character. Those who live beyond their means joyously when their means are small become small themselves when their means get beyond living beyond. The Budlongs began to figure percentages on sums left in the bank or put out on mortgage. They began to think money—and money is money, large or small. Mrs. Budlong began to feel that she had been unjust to Aunt Ida. What she had called miserliness was evidently prudence and thrift, and some other pleasant sounding virtues.

When it came to the point of deciding that she must give a large dinner to wipe off a number of social obligations all at once, and she found that the olives, the turkey, the Malaga grapes, the English walnuts and a man from the hotel to wait on table would total up twenty-five dollars or so, she found herself figuring how much twenty-five dollars would amount to in twenty-five years at compound interest.

She grew frantic to be quit of Carthage—to rub it off her visiting list. Unconsciously her motto became Cato's ruthless *Delenda est Carthago*; but she could neither wipe Carthage off her map nor free her feet from its dust. Her husband's business required him yet a while. Even to close it up took time; and he would not and could not borrow on Aunt Ida's estate until he was sure it was his.

All the while, however, the festival reveled on. People in Carthage, to whom New York was an inaccessible Carcassonne, were now planning to visit Mrs. Budlong there at the palatial home she had described. Some frankly told her they were coming. Wealth took on a new discomfort.

Mrs. Sally Swezey afflicted the telephone with gossip: "Mrs. Talbot was saying yesterday, my dear, so many people have threatened to visit you in your home on Fifth Av'noo, that you'll have to hang hammocks in your yard."

That was the discomfort of the morrow, however. Today was busy enough. One morning she was called to the telephone by the merciless Sally Swezey with a new infliction. There was something almost ghoulish in Mrs. Swezey's cackling glee as she sang out across the wire:

"We're all so glad that the next meeting of the progressive euchre club is to be at your house."

Mrs. Budlong's chin dropped. She had quite forgotten this. Sally chortled on:

"And, say, do you know what?"

"What?"

"Everybody says you're going to give solid gold prizes, and that even the booby prize will be handsomer than the first prize was at Mrs. Detwiller's."

"Ha-ha!" laughed Mrs. Budlong in a tone that sounded just like the spelling.

Mrs. Budlong's wealth seemed to be accepted as a sort of general legacy. All Carthage assumed to own it and to enjoy it with her. Her walls rang with the hilarity of her neighbors; but her laughter took on more and more the sound of icicles snapping from the eaves of a shed.

She became the logical candidate for all the chief offices in clubs and societies and circles. She suddenly found herself seven or eight presidents and at least eleven chairwomen. The richest woman in town heretofore was Mrs. Foster Herpers, wife of the pole-and-shaft manufacturer. He owned about half of the real estate in the county, but his wife had to distill money out of him in pennies. With a profound sigh of relief she resigned all her honors and privileges in Mrs. Budlong's favor.

Being president chiefly meant lending one's house for meetings, as well as one's china and tea and sandwiches, and being five dollars ahead of everybody else in every subscription. Mrs. Budlong was panicstricken with her own success, for there is nothing harder to handle than a dam-break of prosperity.

Worse yet, Mr. Budlong was ceasing to be the meek thing of yore. Every day was beginning to be the first of the month with him.

It was well into November when he flung himself into a chair one evening and groaned aloud:

"I don't believe Aunt Ida ever left any money! If she did I don't believe we'll ever get any of it. And if we do I know we'll not have a sniff at it before January. One of the lawyers has been called abroad on another case. We've got to stay in Carthage—at least over Christmas."

"Christmas!" The word crackled and sputtered in Mrs. Budlong's brain like a fuse in the dark. The past month had been so packed with other excitements that she had forgotten the very word. Now it blew up and came down as if one of her own unstable Christmas trees had toppled over on her, with all its ropes of tinsel, its eggshell splendors and its lambent tapers.

V

First, Mrs. Budlong felt amazement that she could have so ignored the very focus of her former ambition. Then she felt shame at her unpreparedness. She caught the evening paper out of her husband's lap to find the date. November ninth and not a Christmas thing begun! Yet a few days and the news-stands would apprise her that Christmas was coming; for in the middle of November all the magazines put on their holly and their Santa Clauses, as women put on summer straw hats at Easter. Mrs. Budlong's hands sought and wrung each other as if in mutual reproach. They had been pouring tea and passing wafers when they should have been Dorcasing at their Christmas tasks. And now, at the eleventh hour, she found herself without a single present tatted or painted or hammered or fired. It had been left for her husband—of all people—to warn her that Christmas was imminently approaching!

If he had been a day later the neighbors would have anticipated him as well as the magazines. The Christmas idea seemed to strike the whole town at once. Mrs. Budlong became the victim of her own classic device of pretending to let slip a secret. The townswomen shamelessly turned her own formula against her.

Mrs. Detwiller met her at church one Sunday and said:

"Yesterday morning I had the most curious presentiment! I remember the hour exactly because I've been making it a rule to begin work on your Christmas present every morning at——Oh, but I didn't intend to let you know. No, I won't tell you what it is. But I can't help believing it's just what you'll need in New York."

Myra Eppley, with whom Mrs. Budlong had never exchanged Christmas presents at all, but with whom an intimacy had sprung up since Mrs. Budlong came into the reputation of her money, had the effrontery to call her up on the telephone one morning and say:

"Would you mind telling me, my dear, the shade of wallpaper you're going to have in your New York parlor, because I'm making a——Oh—but will you tell me?"

Poor Mrs. Budlong almost swooned from the telephone. She did not know what the color of her wallpaper would be in New York. She did not know that she would ever have wallpaper in New York. She only knew that Myra Eppley, too, was calling her "My dear!" Myra Eppley also was going to give her a Christmas present—and would have to be given one.

Mrs. Budlong had received fair warning, but she

felt just about as grateful as a wayfarer feels to the rattlesnake that whizzes: "Make ready for the coroner!"

Next, Mrs. Chur—Editha Cinnamon that was, for she had finally landed Mr. Chur in spite of the accident, or because of it—called up to say:

"Oh, my dear, my husband wants to know what brand of cigars your husband smokes; also, deary, what size bath-slippers do you wear?"

When Sally Swezey came to the progressive euchre fight at Mrs. Budlong's she noted with joy that her hint had borne fruit. The prizes were, indeed, of solid gold. Mr. Budlong did not learn it until the first of the following month, when the bill came in from the jewelry store.

As if she had not done enough in forcing solid gold prizes on Mrs. Budlong, Sally had to say:

"I'm just dying to see your back parlor, my dear, this next Christmas afternoon! It has always been a sight for sore eyes; but this Christmas it will be a perfect wonder, for I do declare everybody in town is going to send you something nice."

This conviction was already chilling Mrs. Budlong's marrow. Of old she would have rejoiced at the golden triumph; but now she could only realize that if everybody in Carthage sent her something nice it was because everybody in Carthage expected something nicer. And she had not tatted or smeared or hammered a thing! As usual, too, the excess of work on hand had a paralyzing effect. At a time when she should be half done she could not even begin!

The realization that Christmas was near shocked the normally over-active Mrs. Budlong into in-action.

VI

Days and days went by in a stupor of hopelessness. Thanksgiving came and the Budlong turkey might as well have been a crow. In desperation she decided to make a tentative exploration of the shops now burgeoning with Christmas.

The length of the list sent her to the cheaper counters, but she was not permitted to browse among them. At Strouther & Streckfuss' Mr. Strouther said with reeking unctuousness:

"Vat makes Mees Bootlonk down here amonkst all this tresh? Come see our importet novelties."

And he led her to a region where the minimum price was MBBA-BDJA, which meant that it cost twelve dollars and twenty-five cents and could be safely marked down to twenty three dollars and seventy-five cents.

She eluded him and got back to the 25¢ realm, only to be apprehended by Mr. Streckfuss, who beamed:

"Ah, nothink is here for a lady like you are! Only fine kvality suits, such a taste you got!"

By almost superfeminine strength she evaded purchasing anything there. She went to other shops, only to be haled to the expensive counters. Storekeepers simply would not discuss cheap things with the millionairess-elect.

Sympathy was last on Mr. Budlong's list.

She crept home and threw herself on her husband's mercy. He had none and she lighted hard. It was the first of December; and, in addition to his periodical rage, Mr. Budlong was working himself up to his regular pre-Christmas frenzy, when he felt poor and talked poorer in order to keep the family in check.

His face was a study when he heard his wife's state of mind. He delivered the annual address on Christmas folly, that one hears from fathers of families all round the world at this time.

"Christmas has quit being a sign of people's affections!" Mr. Budlong thundered. "It has become a public menace. It's worse than Wall Street. Wall Street is supposed to have started as the thermometer of the country's business, and now it's gone and got so goldurn big that the thermometer is makin' the weather! When Wall Street feels muggy it's got to rain; and the sun don't dare shine without takin' a peek at the thermometer first off.

"Christmas ain't any longer an opportunity to show good will to your neighbors. It's a time when you got to show off before your neighbors. You women make yourselves and us men sick the way you carry on all through December! And the childern!—they're worse'n the grown-ups!

"Old-fashioned Christmas was like old-fashioned circuses—mostly meant for the childern. Nowadays circuses have growed so big and so improper that nobody would dast take a child to one—or, if you do, they get crazy notions.

"When I was a boy, if I got a drum and a tin horn I was so happy I couldn't keep quiet; but last Christmas little Ulie cried all day because he got a 'leven-dollar car when he wanted an areoplane big enough to carry the cat over the barn.

"This Christmas Trust business ought to be investigated by the Gov'ment and dissolved! Talk about your tariff schedules! What we need is somebody to pare down this Christmas gouge. It's the one kind of tax you can't swear off.

"And as for you—why, you're goin' daffy! Other years I didn't mind so much. You spent a lot of time and some money on your annual splurge; but I will say you took in better'n you gave. But now you're on the other side of the fence. These Carthage women have got you on the run. You'll have to give 'em twice as good as they send or you're gone. You're gone anyway! If you gave each one of 'em a gold platter, full of diamonds, they'd say you'd inherited Aunt Ida's stinginess as well as her money!"

Mrs. Budlong went on twisting her fingers.

"Oh, of course you're right, Ulie. But what's the use of being right when it's so hateful? All I can think of is that everybody in town is going to give me a present! Everybody!"

"Can't you take your last year's presents and pass 'em along to other folks?"

"Everybody would recognize them and I'd be the talk of the town!"

"You're that anyway, so what difference would that make?"

"I'd rather die!"

"You'd save a lot of money and trouble if you did just that."

"Just look at the list of presents I must give!" She handed him a bundle of papers. He pushed up his spectacles, put on his reading glasses and snorted:

"Say! What is this—the town directory?" He had not read far down the list when he missed one important name. "You've over-looked Mrs. Alsop."

"Oh, her! I've quarreled with her. We don't speak—thank Heaven!"

"It would be money in your pocket if you didn't speak to anybody. Gosh!" he slapped his knee. "I have an idea! Stop speaking to everybody."

"Oh, don't be silly. This is serious."

"But I'm not being silly. I'm quite serious."

VII

Ulysses S.G. Budlong was a man fertile in resources and unbending in their execution. Otherwise he would never have attained his supremacy as the town's leading hay-and-feed merchant.

"It's as easy as falling off a log!" he urged her. "You women are always spatting about something. Now's your chance to capitalize on your spats."

"Men are such im-boo-hoo-ciles!" was Mrs. Budlong's comment as she began to weep.

Her husband patted her with a timid awkwardness, as if she were the nose of a strange horse.

"There! there! We'll fix this up fine! What did you quarrel with Mrs. Alsop about?"

"She told Sally Swezey—and Sally Swezey told me—that I used my Carthage presents to send to relatives in other towns."

"She flattered you at that," said Mr. Budlong unconsolingly. "But don't you ever dream of forgiving her until after Christmas."

Mrs. Budlong was having such a good cry and enjoying the optical bath so heartily that her grief became very precious to her. It suggested what a beautiful thing grief is to those who make a fine art of it. She smiled wet-liddedly.

"There is nothing in your idea, Ulie; but I have a good one. I'll announce that I can't celebrate Christmas due to our great grief for Aunt Ida!"

"Great grief!" Mr. Budlong exclaimed. "Why, you couldn't have celebrated Aunt Ida's finish more joyous without you'd serenaded her in Wood-lawn with a brass band!"

"Ulysses Budlong! You ought to be ashamed of yourself for saying such a thing!" But she suddenly heard—in fancy—the laugh that would go up if she sprung such a pretext. She gave in.

"We'll have to quarrel with somebody, then; but what excuse is there?"

"Women don't need any real excuse. You simply telephone Sally Swezey that a certain person told you—and you won't name any names—that she had been making fun of you, and you'd be much obliged if she never spoke to you again!"

"But how do I know Sally Swezey has been making fun of me?"

"Oh there ain't any doubt but what everybody in the town of Carthage is doing exactly that!"

"Ulysses Budlong! Why, how can you talk so?"

"If people without money couldn't make fun of people with, what consolation would they have? Anyway, it's not me but the other folks you're supposed to quarrel with. You spend an hour at that telephone and you can get the whole town by the ears."

"But I can't use the same excuse for everybody."

"You'll think up plenty, once you put your mind to it." And with that a perfect excuse came in pat—came in howling and flagrant.

Ulysses, Junior, burst into the room as if he had forgotten the presence of the door. He was yelping like a coyote and from his tiny nose an astonishing amount of blood was spouting.

"What on earth is the matter?" the startled mother gasped. "Come here to me, you poor child —and be careful not to bleed on the new rug."

Ulysses' articulation was impeded with sobs and the oscillations of three semi-detached teeth that waved in the breeze as he screamed:

"Little Clarence Detwiller licked me. And I on'y p-pushed him off his sled into a puddle of ice-wa-wa-water; and he attackted me and kicked my f-f-fa-face off!"

Mr. and Mrs. Budlong were so elated with the same idea that they forgot to console their heart-broken offspring with more than Mr. Budlong's curt: "First teeth anyway—saves you a trip to the dentist." He nodded to his wife. "Just the excuse we were looking for."

"Sent direct from Heaven!" nodded Mrs. Budlong. "You call up Roscoe Detwiller this minute and say his son has criminal tendencies, ought to be in jail, and will undoubtedly die on the gallows. Then he won't speak to you tomorrow."

"You bet he won't! He'll just quietly do to me what his boy did to Ulie. No, my dear; you tell all ly!—Boys will be——Oh, I'm sorry you punished him. He's such a sweet child!——Oh, don't think of it! I'm sure it was all Ulie's fault. It will teach him next time. He's so rough! ——Oh, how awfully sweet of you! Good night, dear."

She stuck the receiver on the hook and then looked for a hook to hang herself on. Her eyes were shifty with shame as she mumbled: "I couldn't get a word in edgeways. She apologized."

"She apologized!" Mr. Budlong roared. "And you ate out of her hand! And you were going to show me what a coward I——Butter wouldn't have melted ——Say, why didn't you kiss her?"

Mrs. Budlong was suffering a greater dismay than remorse.

"What d'you suppose that cat of a Clara Detwiller's going to do?" she moaned. "She's going to make her boy send Ulie a nice Christmas present! And now we shall be obliged to buy one for Ulie to give to him!"

"Well, of all the——Oh, you're a great manager, you are! You call up a woman to get rid of giving one Christmas present and now you've got to give two! Here! Where you going?"

"I'm going to that 'phone and tell Mrs. Detwiller what I think of her."

"You keep away from that 'phone. Before you could ring off again her husband would have a Christmas present wished on to me!"

that to Mrs. Detwiller yourself."

Mrs. Budlong tossed her head with an air of fine contempt.

"What cowards men are!—always shielding themselves behind women's skirts! Well, if you're afraid, I'm not. I'll give her the biggest talking to she ever had in her born days!"

She rose with fortitude and started to the telephone—sneered at it and glared at it. Her husband stood by her to support her in the hour of need. He watched her ask for the number and snap ferociously at the central. Then she felt panicky again and held the transmitter to him appealingly. He waved her away scornfully. She set her teeth hard and there was grimness in her tone as she said: "Is this you, Mrs. Detwiller? Oh, yes, thank you; I'm very well. I wanted to tell you——Oh, yes, he's well too. But what I started to say was——Yes; so Ulie says! Yes, right in the face!—Oh, of course——Natural-

VIII

The next morning Mrs. Budlong arose from dreams of finding bargains after all. She felt a spirit in her feet that led her to the Christmas-window street; but the crowds and the prices and the servility of the salesfolk drove her out again.

On her laggard way home she saw Sally Swezey, lean and lanky, and reminding her of a flamingo. Mrs. Budlong remembered her husband's suggestion. She made a quick resolution to do or die. Her cheek was cold and white, and her heart beat loud and fast; but she tried to set her chin into a square jaw, and she passed Sally Swezey as if Sally Swezey were a lamp-post by the curb—just a common lamp-post by the curb, and nothing more.

She heard Sally's gush of greeting stop short, as if someone had turned a faucet in her throat; she heard a gulp; then she heard a strangled silence. Then she heard Sally call her name tentatively, tenderly, reproachfully. Then she heard no more.

And she knew no more until her feet somehow carried her home; but she had hardly time to flop into a rocker and utter a prayer of gratitude and pride for having been vouchsafed the courage to snub a Carthaginian before—br-r-rr!—the terrible telephone was rattling at her. She knew just who it was and she braced herself to meet one of Sally's sharp-tongued assaults. Sally said, in part:

"Oh, you poor darling dear, is that you? And how are you now? I was so alarmed for you. You looked so ill and worn; and——Aren't the Christmas crowds awful this year? And nothing fit to buy, and such prices! And——You must be just worn out! You really must spare yourself; for do you know what you did, dearest? You went right by me without seeing me or answering me. Yes, you did. I was so startled that I didn't have brains enough to run after you and assist you home. I'm so glad you got there alive. I do hope you're feeling better; and I'm so ashamed of myself for letting you go all that way alone in that condition. Can you ever forgive me?"

When Mr. Budlong came home for luncheon Mrs. Budlong told him the whole story. He glared at her with an I-give-you-up expression and growled:

"And when she said all that what did you say?"

"I don't know," Mrs. Budlong faltered. "All I know is she's coming over this afternoon with a lot of that wine jelly I gave her the recipe for."

"Well, what do you intend to do this time?" Mr. Budlong demanded. The skeptic in his tone stung her to revolt. She could usually be strong in the presence of her husband. She looked at least like Mrs. Boadicea as she said:

"I intend to tell her what you told me to. And I will accept no apologies—none whatever."

When Mr. Budlong came home to dinner she avoided his gaze. She confessed that she had changed her program. She hadn't the heart to insult Sally, she had admitted she was a bit dizzy and qualmish, and she had—Well, she—

Mr. Budlong finished for her fiercely:

"I know! You ate a lot of her wine jelly, told her she was a love and kissed her goodby; and would she excuse you from coming to the door, because you were still a little wobbly!"

Mrs. Budlong looked at him in surprise. "She told you."

"Nah! I haven't seen her."

"Then how on earth did you ever guess?"

"It was my womanly intuition!" he snarled; and that evening he went downtown and sat in the hotel lobby for a couple of hours. He usually did this anyway—in summer he sat on the sidewalk; but this evening he did it with a certain implication of escape. On the way home Mr. Budlong was busy with schemes. His mind turned again to his son.

In a smallish town a growing boy is an unfailing source of *casus belli*. As an inciter of feuds there was something almost Balkan or Moroccan about Ulysses Budlong, Junior. Nearly every day he had come charging into the house with bad news in some form or other. Some rock or snowball he had cast,

Made of snips and snails and puppy dog tails, full of the devil, all boy—such was Mrs. Budlong's darling little Ulie.

Carthage, no longer subjugated, was overwhelming.

with the most innocent of intentions, had gone through a window or a milk wagon or somebody's silk hat. Or he had pulled a small girl's hair or taken the skates away from a helpless urchin. He had bad luck, too, in picking victims with belligerent big brothers.

Mr. Budlong recognized these desperado traits and he fully expected Ulysses, Junior, to make him the father of a convict. Suddenly now despair became hope. Let Mrs. Budlong capitalize her spats; he would promote Ulie's. The Affair Detwiller had turned out badly, but Mr. Budlong would not yield to one defeat. He watched eagerly for the next misdemeanor of his young hopeless. He relied on him to embroil, as it were, all Europe in an international conflict.

The dove of peace, however, seemed to have alighted on Ulysses' shoulder. He even began to go to Sunday-school—the Methodist this year, because they had given the largest cornucopias in town the Christmas before. He talked nothing but golden texts; Mr. Budlong began to think he would one day be the father of a clergyman.

Meanwhile Mrs. Budlong grew belligerent again. She snubbed people right and left, and they imputed it to absent-mindedness. She failed to go to the dinner party the Teeples gave in her honor, and she sent no excuse. This was the unpardonable sin

in Carthage and the Budlong chairs sat vacant through the dinner.

Mrs. Teeple, however, assumed that she was ill and sent her cut flowers. And she hoped Mrs. Budlong would feel better soon.

A few days later Mrs. Budlong's pet Maltese kitten was done to nine deaths at once by the Disneys' fox terrier. She mourned the kitten, but there was consolation in the thought that she could now cut the Disneys off her list; but before she could get the kitten decently interred in the back yard Mrs. Disney was at the front door. She flung her arms round Mrs. Budlong and wept, declaring that she had resolved to give the murderous terrier to a farmer, and had already sent away for a pedigreed Angora to replace the Maltese. It would arrive the day before Christmas.

As if that were not enough for one day, in the afternoon Myra Eppley called. She saw Mrs. Budlong at an upper window and waved to her as she came along the walk. When the cook arrived upstairs, like a grand piano moving in, Mrs. Budlong said in an icy tone:

"Not at home."

"But I told her you was. And she seen you there at the windy."

"Not—AT—home!"

"But I'm afther telling her——"

Mrs. Budlong could be as stern as steel with her husband or her servants. She cowed Brigida into lumbering downstairs with the message. Mrs. Budlong went to the window to watch her victim's retreat.

Instead, she heard a light patter of footsteps and Myra Eppley hurried into the room.

"Oh, my dear, are you ill? Pardon my coming right up, but I was so worried for fear you were—but you aren't, are you?"

Mrs. Budlong was at bay. She glared at the intruder and threw up her chin. Myra Eppley stared at her aghast.

"Why, you aren't mad at me, are you?"

Mrs. Budlong smiled bitterly and said nothing. Myra Eppley shrilled:

"Why, what have I done?"

As a matter of fact, what had she done? All that Mrs. Budlong could think of was her husband's suggestion for a war with Sally Swezey. She spoke through her locked teeth:

"It's not what you've done but what you've said!"

"Why, what have I said?"

"You know well enough what you've been saying behind my back, and you needn't think that people don't come and tell me! I name no names; but I know—oh, I know!"

Now, of course, everybody says things behind everybody else's back that nobody would care to have repeated to anybody. Through Myra Eppley's memory dashed a hundred caustic comments she had made on Mrs. Budlong. She blushed and sighed, turned away and closed the door after her, like the last line of an elegy.

A surge of triumph swept over Mrs. Budlong. Success at last!

Then the door opened and Myra Eppley reappeared with a look of angelic contrition.

"I hardly know what to say," she said. "Of course I must admit I did rather forget myself. It was at the last meeting of the progressive euchre club. Before you came everybody was criticizing you for having solid gold prizes when they were at your house. They said it was vulgar ostentation. I didn't say

anything for the longest time; but finally, when they all said your money had gone to your head and asked me, 'Hasn't it?' I admit I did mumble: 'It seems so.' But it is only what everybody else says all the time, and I assure you I didn't really mean it. Of course nobody can behave just the same after they are a millionaire as they did before. But I am awfully fond of you; and—and——"

"It was most disloyal!" said Mrs. Budlong. "And to think that, after tearing me to pieces behind my back, you could come and call on me!"

It was a fine speech; but after she heard herself say it Mrs. Budlong had a sinking feeling that if she herself had never called on anybody she had criticized she would have stayed at home all her life. Myra Eppley took another line, however. She threw herself on Mrs. Budlong's mercy—and if

Cut flowers were not easily obtained in late December—but Mrs. Budlong deserved only the best.

Mrs. Budlong boasted of one thing more than another it was her mercy.

"I have just been at the church," said Myra, "helping to decorate it for Christmas week; and I was hanging up a big motto, Peace on Earth, Good Will to Men!—and I think it ought to apply to women too. I grovel in apology and I pray you to forgive me. You can't refuse to forgive me when I ask you to, can you?"

Mrs. Budlong wanted to but could not, and the two women fell about each other's neck and exchanged tear for tear. As they were comfortably dabbing each other's tears from their cheeks and sniffing their own, and laughing cozily after the rain, Myra Eppley giggled and sobbed all at once:

"The idea of your thinking I didn't just love you—and me working my fingers off making a Christmas present for you!"

IX

The day before the Day Before Christmas found them in a panic. The Day Before found them grimly resolved to stand siege.

On the blessed Eve they sat by their cheerless fire-front and stared at the packages that had been pouring in all day long. The old postman had staggered under the final load and hinted so broadly for a Christmas present that he got one—the first breach in their solemn resolve. They had excepted

Guardians of gratitude—Christmas gifts were the only way Carthaginians could express their true feelings.

Ulie, of course, from the embargo; but they had been in such a flurry that they had postponed him until they forgot him entirely.

The doorbell was rung so incessantly throughout the evening that the cook sat on the hall stairs to be handy. She piled the packages up on the piano until they spilled off. The piano lamp was gradually sinking beneath the encroaching tide. Presents were brought in wagons, carriages, buggies, carts, by coachmen, gardeners, cooks, maids, messenger boys, and children of all ages and dimensions.

On any other occasion Mrs. Budlong would have been running here and there, peeking into parcels and restraining her curiosity until the next day, out of sheer joy in curiosity. Now she opened never a bundle. She could only think of the morrow, when all of these donors found that reciprocity had gone down to defeat! The Budlongs avoided each other's eyes. They were thinking the same thing.

The strain endured until it tested their metal to the breaking point. When two enormous packages were brought to the door by the Detwillers' hired man Mrs. Budlong broke out hysterically:

"I just can't stand it!"

"Hell!" roared Mr. Budlong. "Get on your hat and coat, we'll go buy everything left in town!"

X

Holiday bargains in Carthage were not brilliant. After being pawed over for several weeks they were depressing indeed. When the Budlongs strode into Strouther & Streckfuss' it was nearly ten o'clock at night. The sales-wretches, mostly pathetic spinsters of both sexes, were gaunt and jaded, and held on to the counters. Even Messrs. Strouther and Streckfuss had the nap worn off their plushy sleekness.

When the Budlongs made their irruption they were not received cordially. Word had gone abroad that the Budlongs were buying all their Christmas presents out of town. They must be, for they bought none in. This treachery to home industry was bitterly resented. Then Budlong galvanized everybody with a cry like a flash of lightning:

"I want to buy nearly all you got. Get busy!"

It was too late to select. Mr. and Mrs. Budlong, with their lengthy list in hand, sprinted up one aisle and down another, pointing, prodding, rarely pausing to ask, "How much?" but monotonously chanting: "Gimme this! Gimme that! Gimme two of these! Gimme six of them! Gimme that! Gimme this! Gimme them!"

They bought glaring garden jars and ghastly vases, and scarfpins that would disturb the peace, silly bisque figurines for mantels and what-nots, combs and brushes that would raise the hair on end instead of allaying it, oxidized-silverized leadpencils, buttonhooks, toothbrushes, nail files, cuticle knives, pincushions, inkstands, paperweights, picture frames, bits of lace and intimate white things with ribbons in them—Mr. Budlong turned away as his wife priced these.

The town clock was striking midnight as the Budlongs dragged themselves home. There was much yet to be done. Parcels must be opened, price tags removed, gifts done up in pink tissue paper and gold twine, cards must be inscribed and inserted, and the parcels rewrapped and addressed. The Strouther & Streckfuss driver had been hired at an exorbitant cost to sit up and deliver the many gifts. The horses had not been consulted.

The Budlong parlor was soon a hideous scene. The husband would open a bundle and sing out:

"Who's this big, immense, pink-and-purple cuspidor for?"

"That's a jardineer! It's a return for that horrible cat those odious Disneys are going to inflict on me. Here's the card, it's all ready."

She handed him a holly-wreathed pasteboard on which she had written: "For Mr. and Mrs. Disney, with most affectionate Yuletide greetings."

She indited cards as fast as she could think up phrases. She sought for variety, but the effort was maddening. She wrote: "Very merry Christmas." "The merriest of Xmases." "A merry, merry Yuletide." "A Happy Christmas and a Merry New Year." "Christmas Greetings." "Xmas Greetings." "Yuletide Greetings." "Wishing you a——" "With loving wishes for——" "Affectionate——" And so on, and so on, and on and on. She scribbled and scrawled until slumber drugged her and her pen went crazy. When she fell asleep she was writing: "A Yuly New-mas and a Hapry X-Year to Swally Sezey!"

The delivery man pounded on the door and, wild-eyed, Budlong let him in from the night. The man whispered that he'd have to start at once if he was to make the rounds before his horses laid down on him.

Mr. Budlong called his wife but she did not answer. He shook her and she proceeded to roll off the chair on to a divan. Mr. Budlong straightened her out and stared at her in hopeless pity. He stared at the chaos of bundles. He seized the pack of cards from his wife's fingers and ran here and there jabbing pasteboards into bundles haphazard.

This is how Sally Swezey acquired an ashtray lined with cigar bands and why old Mr. Clute was amazed to receive a card offering him Mrs. Budlong's "loving and affectionate greetings!" He was

more amazed when he opened the bundle. There were ribbons in it!

As fast as Mr. Budlong stuffed cards into bundles he loaded bundles into the driver's arms as if they were sticks of wood. The driver stacked them up in his wagon. He made seven trips in all, and some of the cards fell out and were stuck in still longer bundles than before; but both the driver and Mr. Budlong were too sleepy to care. The driver finally mounted his seat and called out from the dark:

"Say, Mr. Budlong, where do I leave these packages—on the porch or do I ring the bell?"

"Chuck 'em through the windows! The more glass you break the better I'd like it!"

"All right, sir. Get ap! Good night, sir—and wishing you a Merry Christmas!"

"Merry——" said Mr. Budlong, reaching for a rock; but even the stones were frozen to the ground and the driver escaped. As Mr. Budlong closed his front door a thread of crimson broke out in the east.

An hour or so later Ulie awoke and sat up with a start. To his intense confusion he bumped his little skull on the bottom of his bed. He realized that he had fallen asleep in his ambush. He peered forth to see if he had snared Santa Claus.

The stockings were empty.

With a shriek of disappointed rage Ulie dashed into his parents' room to protest.

Their bed was empty.

He ran through the house, stumbled downstairs and into the back parlor. His father was snoring on a mattress of Yuletide parcels. His mother was curled up on a divan under the smoking piano lamp. Her hands were clutching strands of gold cord, and her hair was pillowed in pink tissue paper. She was burbling in her sleep.

Little Ulie bent down to hear what she was saying. He made out faintly:

"Mishing you a Werry Muschris and a Nappy Hoosier!" (1911)

Gene Coughlin

The Wonderful Merry-Go-Round

There would never again be a November dusk like this one. Soft and satin-smooth, it had settled on the four of us as we turned away from the scrubby bank of Cicero Creek and our exploration of hillocks that, we knew, were Indian burial mounds, no matter what the older inhabitants of Tipton, Indiana, had to say. Our elders contended that Indians definitely had never lived nor even camped in our part of the state; they insisted that the nearest authentic mounds were at Tippecanoe, which was several hours distant on the swift electric cars of the Union Traction Company.

We didn't intend to argue with our elders, but we had the evidence to prove they were wrong. Jody O'Beirne had a piece of flint that must have been an arrowhead; Bob Glass had uncovered something like a clamshell that had served some brave as a spoon; Tommy O'Toole kept fingering a dozen beads that undoubtedly had graced the swanlike throat of a beautiful princess. I carried a clump of feathers, a little moldy and decomposed, stained with something that had to be war paint. To make the outing complete, we had located a tree loaded with papaws, supersweet in their green and yellow jackets. We used plenty of red haws, tiny and tart, to take away the cloying effect of the papaws, and we were a quartet of surfeited nine-year-olds when we turned into what could be called the outskirts of Tipton.

On Mill Street several bonfires of sycamore and maple leaves had been touched off. We loitered in the low-hanging smoke, coughing but happy in the knowledge that the odor would cling to coats and sweaters and make us smell like frontiersmen who hunkered nightly over campfires.

We had plenty of time to beat it to the unguarded grade crossing, but we waited for the Lake Erie & Western freight, its oil-burning headlight jiggling in the gloom, its fireman painted in bronze as he hurled coal into the bright maw of the firebox. The downdraft of smoke brought tears to our eyes, but still we were able to call off the initials and the numbers of the boxcars and gondolas as they clattered past, and also identify Mr. Higgins, the conductor, standing on the rear platform of the caboose.

"Goin' to the railhead," Jody announced solemnly. "Pushin' steel west, night and day!"

We nodded, knowing the train was going south and then only to Indianapolis, forty miles away. Jody had certain privileges in such matters, since his father was a passenger conductor on the road, a circumstance that kept us from mentioning in his presence that many people said the initials L. E. & W. really meant "Leave Early and Walk."

There was a Panhandle freight just pulling out of the siding down toward The Junction, but we didn't wait for that; we were loyal to the Lake Erie, and the Panhandle was part of the Pennsylvania system.

"Well," Tommy O'Toole sighed, "best head for home." The others turned on East Street, but I didn't. I had special permission to stop off at the coal yard and walk home with my father when he locked up at six o'clock. I hadn't mentioned it, but Bob Glass sensed my destination.

"You going to see The Invention?" he asked quickly, and I said, "I might. For a minute."

"We could go along," Jody suggested. "Just for a minute."

"Not tonight," I said. "It's nearly done, and you know how people are. If somebody got ahold of the patent——"

Whether for work or pleasure, horses were a common sight early in this century, indispensable to daily living.

"That's right." They all nodded, and we parted. My route took me past the power-and-light plant and up the wagon track between the coal bins and the big barn that, occasionally, contained ice that was retailed by the Coughlin Coal & Ice Company.

Old George, the huge Percheron, heard my feet crunching the cinders, and turned around to look, moving the wagon just as Delt McGill, the deliveryman, flung up a scoop of coal, some of which hit the wagon side.

"Hold still, you big galoot," Delt yelled, "or I'll whack you!"

I had two handfuls of red haws and crab apples. George made a vacuum of his massive muzzle, swooshed them down and thanked me by nudging me with his nose, knocking off my cap and leaving a glob of froth on the shoulder of my Mackinaw. I headed for the coal office.

The office was a frame box about nine feet square, with small windows on three sides and a row of sliding panes on the side next to the scales. My father would slide back a window to hand out a receipt to Delt or to receive money from him after he had made a delivery. He did the same thing usually to converse with cronies or customers who called in person; not that he was inhospitable, but there was almost no room at all for adult visitors in that little office, what with The Invention and its original wooden model, plus a desk, one chair, a little potbellied stove and a padlocked cabinet containing drawings and blueprints and other papers having to do with the patent.

I stood up on tiptoe on the beam between the scale floor and the sliding panes, and the first thing I saw was The Invention, which was to make us rich. As usual, it looked mean and ominous to me, its black and ugly hulk taking up more than the corner originally assigned it. It had gear teeth that gleamed and flickered in the uneven light of the kerosene lamp hung from the low ceiling.

I had a vague idea of what it did, or was supposed to do, but I considered it vastly overrated for its size, weight and the attention it got and the effort it had cost my father, who had made all of its parts by hand. And yet it held a tremendous fascination for me. It would accept a little nut a half-inch square that was fed to it, let it rattle down a slot all the way to its innards and then, after my father grunted and turned a crank, it would eject the nut with threads cut on the inside.

"Of course," my father would explain after a demonstration, "that was just a rough example of what this Nut Tapping Machine can do. Driven by steam, this machine will tap, or thread, more nuts in an hour than any other machine on the market today can do in a day."

When he talked like that I admired The Invention, and it was a pleasure to help wipe it with an oily rag. But there were times when I resented it as a selfish monster, content to sit there on its cast-iron bottom and settling that section of the office deeper and deeper into the Indiana soil. This resentment came after I had overheard aunts and uncles, among others, remark that The Invention, through the patent attorney, was devouring money that we could have used for food and clothing, with no end in sight.

My father was sitting at the desk, his derby on the back of his head, using his left hand to stroke the full mustache that was in need of another application of walnut oil to disguise the graying roots and tips. He wore the Celluloid collar, Size 17, and the sleeve garters that were part of his business costume, along with the glasses that came from the five-and-ten and which he did not need but affected because most Tipton merchants wore spectacles as symbols of solidity.

I eased quietly through the door just as he started writing the receipt for Mrs. Board's half ton of coal that Delt McGill was loading. He wrote a beautiful flowing hand, much better than I could ever hope to achieve with the Palmer Method. What made his penmanship even more distinctive was that he held the pencil between the stubs of the first two fingers of his right hand. He had lost parts of these fingers while switching bars on the Chicago & Alton. I was at his elbow as he signed, "Owen J. Coughlin."

"What does the J stand for?" I asked.

He started a little, took off the glasses, and his dark-brown eyes twinkled as he answered my question with one of his own. "What does the D stand for in John D. Rockefeller?"

I admitted I didn't know, and he nodded. "An initial," he said, "is something any man can own. Rich or poor."

"But rich men have more initials than poor men," I pointed out. "Look at J. P. Morgan——"

"And F. W. Woolworth," he put in. "I think that what happens is a man starts out with just a plain first name, like John or Jim, and then, when he becomes a success, he adds an initial or two to make his signature more dignified, I suppose. The J doesn't stand for anything. But it might come in handy."

He winked and looked at The Invention. I followed suit, and we were both dreaming when Old George walked onto the scales, making the office shake. My father weighed the coal, handed Delt the receipt and told him to put horse and wagon away and go home after the delivery. We were wiping the machine with oiled rags when the big bell boomed in St. John's steeple, two blocks away, and we stood erect, reciting the *Angelus* to ourselves. He clapped his hat back on his head, and I shook him a bit with another question. "We didn't get the church contract this year, did we?" I asked.

He stopped the breath that would have extinguished the lamp and gave me a quick look. "Who told you that, Eugene?"

I told him, "Lots of people."

But my main informant had been Delt McGill, who had been bitter in giving the reason. He blamed some of the wealthy farmers who made up the bulk of the congregation of St. John's Catholic Church, where the three of us Coughlin boys served Mass and where we rented a pew. Delt said these farmers had got into the habit of driving their grain wagons to town and loading their own coal at our yard. But they had the sly

Around 1911, coal delivery was a slow business, yet a lucrative one—if the big contracts came through.

habit of using only the fork, thus getting the big lumps of the soft coal and leaving the small pieces and slack for the town customers served by Delt. My father had chided them gently at first, pointing out that *he* had to pay for *all* the coal and slack in a car and that they should take some of the fat along with the lean. But they had persisted until the matter finally became an issue, and the self-serving farmers were told that the Coughlin Coal & Ice Company didn't want their business any longer.

Some of these ex-customers were trustees of the church and, when it came time to award the contract for coal to be used in church, parsonage and school, gave the plum to an outsider whose bid was very little lower than ours. Since several carloads were involved, the contract meant the difference between a success and a failure for a year for my father's business.

The key rattled in the lock, and he tried the office door twice before he said softly, "No, Eugene, we didn't get the contract. What all did you do today, and where did you go?" I told him, and the tension lifted as we walked home.

Round steak, a quarter's worth, was sizzling in two skillets, and the potatoes were boiling on the cookstove. Joe, eleven, and John, thirteen, were at the kitchen table, Joe writing a composition and John figuring collections on his paper route. My mother reigned in her rocking chair near the oven. She was slight and pretty, a gentlewoman whose folks—the Mullarkeyes—had owned hundreds of acres of lush farm land near Tipton.

A talented pianist, Ellen Bridget Mullarkey had been sent to a conservatory of music in Indianapolis, and there had been talk of a concert career until, on a visit to a cousin in Joliet, Illinois, she had met Owen at a Switchmen's Ball and married him with the stipulations that he give up railroading before he lost any more fingers or any limbs and become a merchant in

Tipton. Now she was content with her husband, her three sons, an upright piano she played occasionally and a firm belief in the basic goodness of her fellow men. Her gray eyes widened as I told about our exploration of the Indian burial mounds, and she was properly horrified when I displayed my tuft of feathers. The others of our group gathered around and were sure the stain was war paint, and I went to bed happy, full of steak and potatoes and the conviction that The Invention would take care of all of us.

This mood continued through Thanksgiving and well into December. And then, a couple of weeks before Christmas, everything went wrong. People stopped buying coal—or stopped paying for it—and hints were dropped to the effect that "Santa might be late this year—if he gets here at all." I still had high hopes that I would get a Flexible Flyer sled and maybe a pair of ice skates—until one night, when I was supposed to be asleep upstairs, I heard my father and mother murmuring in the kitchen. He told her the patent attorney had to make further search in Washington and that would take more money, and he didn't know where it was to come from. Her assurance that the Lord would provide seemed sort of faint.

On top of that I was suddenly notified to stay away from the office for a few days—some ultra-secret work had to be done on The Invention.

The outlook was very bleak when, two days before Christmas, the three of us were doing the dishes, and John asked if I had written my letter

The letter to Santa Claus gets harder to compose as the writer grows older and the legend loses credibility.

to Santa Claus yet this season.

"No," I said, "and I don't think I'll write one this year. Won't do any good."

I was too cautious to say I no longer believed in him. I had my doubts, but I was willing to give him a chance—if business had been a little better.

"Well, now," John said. "Old Santa has been pretty good to you and to all of us, Eugene. He'd feel hurt if you forgot him all at once."

I gave in and wrote the letter which followed a pattern that, apparently, had been handed down in the family. I don't recall being prompted; it just seemed to take form, and it went:

Dear Santa: I know you are very busy, and I will not take much of your time. I want you to take care of the poor boys and girls first and see that they get warm clothes and food. If there is anything left, I would like a Flexible Flyer sled and a pair of ice skates. There is a piece of mince pie and coffee for you on the kitchen stove. Thank you, Santa.

Christmas Eve I went to bed early and had a restless night, as befits a martyr. It seemed that I had just dozed off when the sound of tinkly music filled the house, and the three of us rushed downstairs. All the lights were on, the base burner was a cherry red, and in the warm glow glittered the most fascinating toy I had ever seen.

It was a merry-go-round, complete with concealed music box and a ringmaster with curled mustache, tipping his high silk hat every time he passed the tiny ticket box. Boys and girls rode the prancing horses; ladies and gentlemen sat sedately in the circling tubs, all dressed in clothing of every hue. At first glance it seemed huge on its packing-box platform although it turned out to be about thirty inches in diameter. I don't know how long I crouched in wonderment before I figured it out that this was the reason for my being barred from the premises. I looked at my father, beaming and wiggling his good fingers, a sure sign of excitement, and my mother, in her dressing gown, holding his hand in both of hers.

When it was my turn to wind it up I announced, "Santa Claus didn't make this! He couldn't!"

"Well, then, Eugene," my mother said, "who did make it?"

I found out I couldn't talk. I pointed at my father, and he swung me up higher than his great shoulders, and when he rubbed the bristles of his mustache

The first glimpse of the tree and toys—Christmas in all its glory—is overwhelming.

against my cheek they were moist from a sudden tear—I guess it was. Then he ordered us gruffly to get ready for Mass, which we did.

Usually on Christmas our various gangs took turns visiting homes and inspecting gifts, but we hardly got out of the house that day. Jody and Bob and Tommy, plus pals of Joe and John, descended on us to watch the merry-go-round. Each demanded the privilege of winding it up.

Grownups came too, and Mr. Glass, who made regular trips to Chicago, paid the supreme compliment. "You can't get anything like that at Marshall Field, even," he said. "And if you could, I bet they'd want $100 for it!"

Getting ready for bed that night, the three of us wondered at the skill and the patience represented in the masterpiece, and John asked me, "Are you still mad at The Invention?"

I said I didn't see what that had to do with the merry-go-round, and he explained. "Well, pop never had any manual training, never knew how to do anything with his hands but pull switches and give signals. He didn't know the first thing about carving or carpenter work until he got the idea for The Invention four, five years ago. Then he taught himself how to do things with wood and iron. He carved that wooden model down at the office, and he cut the metal parts for the working model. So, when he had to do something extra special for this Christmas, he knew how to do it. He made a merry-go-round that the best carpenter in Indiana couldn't make."

I understood his point, and I relented somewhat in my attitude toward The Invention. But it was still on probation until, on New Year's Day—my birthday—I got the Flexible Flyer after all! (The skates could wait.)

After that I never entertained a mean thought regarding The Invention. It never did make us rich; it didn't even get into production. When, seven years later in 1918, the power-and-light company took over the coal yard, it still squatted there, sinking into the soil and smiling benignly as it showed its teeth.

In those seven years, as far as I was concerned, it was just as much a member of the family as Old George, who hauled the coal faithfully even when hay and oats were hard to come by, or Prince, the collie, who sometimes figured we were having too many meatless days and would deposit not one, but two freshly killed chickens on the back porch. (1961)

CHRISTMAS SCENES OF THE PAST

Author Unknown

Christmas at the White House 100 Years Ago

Christmas at the White House one hundred years ago was a remarkably gay and festive occasion. Thomas Jefferson was then President, and hospitality was dispensed at the mansion with a freedom which found no subsequent parallel until the arrival of Mr. Roosevelt, whose ideas on that subject seem to be remarkably like those of the author of the Declaration. Then, as now, every agreeable stranger who "dropped in" at the White House was invited to make himself at home, and it is a matter of historical record that as many as fifty persons at a time were sheltered under the Executive roof-tree—though how it was managed nobody can say for sure!

Contemporary, and still-extant, descriptions of the White House in those days, its family and its domestic doings, make it easy to give a fairly accurate account of the way in which Mr. Jefferson and his household spent Christmas Day one hundred years ago. For one thing, it is known that his two daughters, Mrs. Randolph and Mrs. Eppes, came up to the capital to spend the holiday, bringing with them their husbands, both of whom were Virginia Congressmen; and Mrs. Randolph also brought her six children, who were their grandfather's very particular pets.

Jefferson introduced the first children into the

Jefferson had his own brand of "open door policy."

White House. He was a widower, having lost his wife twenty years earlier; but his daughter, Martha Jefferson Randolph, spent the bulk of six years with him in Washington, and her sister, Mrs. Eppes, came now and then, bringing her children, so that there was no lack of family atmosphere. Mrs. Randolph, indeed, was the mother of the first child ever to be born in the White House, the happy event occurring in the winter of 1805-6.

Mrs. Randolph cared little for social pleasures, in the fashionable sense of the term, and could not be persuaded to assume the responsibilities of mistress of the White House. She was a very motherly sort of woman, and devoted to the children, for whom a schoolroom was fitted up at the west end of the second floor, she herself acting as teacher. Upon Mrs. Dolly Madison devolved the serious duties of entertaining, and it was she who presided at the Christmas dinner, as well as on all other formal occasions.

To make the picture of the Christmas vivid, one must recall, in imagination, the striking figure of Jefferson—tall and distinguished-looking, with red hair and spindle-shanks, his face much freckled, his hands and feet large, and his teeth noticeably fine and perfect. Extremely simple in his habits, and unaffected in manners, he often

Family ties were important to Jefferson, a widower.

market on the morning of that Christmas Day, a century ago, and picked out the geese for the dinner. He was fond of good cheer, and liked to exercise his judgment in the choice of a bird or a joint. Nowadays the White House steward, rather than the President, attends to all that sort of business. But those were days of greater simplicity in ways of living, and it was not considered (as now would be the case) that the President was derogating from his dignity in purchasing his own provisions.

It is chronicled that on the afternoon of that day Mrs. Madison took four of Mrs. Randolph's little girls to ride, and on the way back, over the old Georgetown Road, she bought boughs of mistletoe from an old Negro, decking the carriage with them. Doubtless gifts were exchanged—for the Jeffersons, being Virginians, believed, as the New England Adamses did not, in celebrating Yuletide in this and other ways—but, of course, the principal event was the dinner, which was held in the state dining-room, the private dining-room being too small to accommodate all the guests.

There was, indeed, quite a large party. Besides the President and his two daughters and their husbands, there were Mr. and Mrs. Madison, half a dozen other persons of distinction, and a number of relatives and neighbors from Virginia—not to mention at least six children, for each of whom a special cranberry tart was provided. Mr. Jefferson never forgot the little ones, and the tart, placed at each small plate, was considered indispensable to the happiness of the occasion.

The requisite illumination was furnished by eight large silver candelabra which stood on the table, holding dozens of wax candles, and the viands were dispensed with the aid of a dozen Negro servitors.

offended people by the frankness with which he expressed his opinions, which were certainly not modeled after anybody else's.

The White House, one hundred years ago, stood in the midst of a rough-looking and uncultivated area, which as yet had not been brought under subjection by the skilled gardener. Its principal entrance was at the south front (now closed to the public), and its interior had a rather bare and unfurnished appearance. The East Room was used only as a laundry, and the furniture of the other apartments was scanty.

Mr. Jefferson himself went to the old Marsh

John Adams established state dinners at the White House, their stiff formality delighting his highly conventional soul, but Thomas Jefferson abolished them. He preferred to entertain in a different style, and, being a very hospitable man, he made everybody welcome to his board. As above stated, he took great pleasure and pride in selecting viands for his own table, and those who dined with him were always sure of enjoying good cookery, along with first-rate wines.

There were no clergymen present at that Christmas dinner one hundred years ago. Jefferson, as is well known, had no affinity for the cloth. But, on the other hand, painters, Bohemians, adventurers, and deadbeats generally, foreign and domestic, were at home in the White House during his rule. He was easily imposed upon, and people whom he scarcely knew would quarter themselves upon him for indefinite periods. One family of casual visitors, from Europe, stayed ten months.

Presided over by Mr. Jefferson the Christmas feast could not be otherwise than a jolly affair. Of everything eatable there were huge quantities—and all of the viands were placed on the table at one time, the appropriate fashion of those days. The guests were encouraged to stuff themselves, and choice wines, in both decanters and bottles, were freely offered. Thomas Jefferson, a temperate man, abstemious for those bibulous days, when it was considered almost a duty for a gentleman to get intoxicated after dinner, enjoyed a social glass, and was by no means lacking in the convivial impulse.

The heavy drinking, however, was not begun until after the ladies, at a signal from Mrs. Madison, had left the table. Then a huge punch-bowl was brought on, and toasts were proposed, each one requiring to be duly honored with a brimming glass. Truly, what wonderful constitutions and capacities the gentlemen of those times must have had!

It may be taken for granted, then, that on this occasion, at all events, the men preserved a reasonable measure of sobriety; for presently they were obliged to join the ladies in the Oval Room, which is known to-day as the Blue Room, where much gaiety followed. There were round games, forfeits and various other frivolous pastimes for the grown-ups, the children having been sent to bed. By ten o'clock in the evening it was all over, and the guests were taking their departure—those of them, that is to say, who were not staying in the house.

Life was much simpler in those days than now, and late hours for entertaining were unknown. Such hospitality as the President dispensed was generous, but without attempt at any sort of display. Mr. Jefferson's salary was only $25,000 a year, and out of it he paid his own Secretary, as every President did up to Jackson.

It is worth mentioning that Dolly Madison presided at no fewer than fourteen Christmas dinners at the White House during the Jefferson and Madison administrations. One such celebration was missed because Mr. Jefferson spent Yuletide that particular year at Monticello, and another was missed (in 1814) because the British had driven Mr. and Mrs. Madison out of their official residence. (1903)

Tray upon tray of delectable fare—the Christmas feast.

René Bache

Christmas with Ben Franklin

hristmas, 1785, was probably the most enjoyable holiday Benjamin Franklin had ever spent. By that time, after his return from France, he had settled down to a peaceful existence in Philadelphia, and, realizing that now his struggles and anxieties were at an end, was enabled to devote his time to pursuing, in a leisurely way, the occupations most congenial to him, in the bosom of an affectionate family, cared for by a loving daughter, and finding special pleasure in the society of six grandchildren, four of whom had been born during his last absence abroad.

The gentle sentiments belonging to Yuletide were always held dear in that household, and Franklin's children and grandchildren had been brought up to celebrate the festival with the giving of gifts, the hanging-up of stockings for Kriss Kringle to fill, and all the other modes of merry-making appropriate to the old-fashioned holiday. This, too, notwithstanding the fact that his earliest years were spent in Boston, where (as was the case in all of New England in those times) Christmas was almost wholly neglected, the great feast day in that part of the country being Thanksgiving.

Richard, the baby, was only a year old in the winter of 1785. His sisters, Deborah and Eliza, were four and eight respectively. Louis was six, William twelve, and Benjamin Franklin Bache, the eldest (who had been abroad with his grandfather for eight years), was sixteen years of age. It had been unreasonably expected of Louis, by the way, that he would be a girl, and his mother had written to Doctor Franklin for a list of the

Marie Antoinette

Louis XVI

various names of Marie Antoinette to choose from; but the child turned out to be a boy, and was named after the King instead of after the Queen of France.

So many young people in the house must have made it a pretty lively Christmas. Doctor Franklin's wife had been dead for some years, and his household was managed by his daughter Sally, who, with her husband, Mr. Richard Bache, lived with him. The dwelling, on Market Street, which was fairly spacious, had been planned by the philosopher himself before he went for the second time to England as agent for several of the Colonies, and was built by his wife during his absence. After his return he added a library to it, which was his own particular "den" and snuggery.

The house stood on a patch of land which ran through from Market nearly to Chestnut Street, and in front of it was a considerable area of lawn, with a great mulberry tree, under which Franklin delighted to sit in warm weather, receiving his friends and drinking with them a cup of tea. He had acquired this habit of sitting outdoors during his long residence in Paris. There were flowerbeds of the old-fashioned kind, and a vegetable patch; but the latter, it seems, was eventually wiped out, for Doctor Franklin writes (in May, 1786): "Considering our well-furnished and plentiful market as the best of gardens, I am turning mine into grassplots and gravel walks." The market to which he refers was a wooden, shedlike structure extending along the middle of Market Street for several "squares," and endured, in a shabby and much-decayed condition, up to

After the church service, which probably lasted a couple of hours, worshipers headed home to Christmas dinner.

within approximately twenty-five years ago.

Such were the surroundings in the midst of which Franklin spent the Christmas of 1785, and, with the data accessible, it is not difficult to fill in the outlines and to compose a reasonably accurate picture of the holiday as it was enjoyed by the famous philosopher and his family.

The sage himself was an early riser, and breakfast was served at 7:30 o'clock, by which time the young folks had emptied their stockings—veritable "horns of plenty," filled for the occasion by their mother—and exchanged felici-

tations on the gifts received. These cheerful formalities past, the church bells rang out their notification of a more serious duty to be done, and all the members of the family put on their best "bib and tucker" and made ready for church.

The Franklin residence was on the south side of the street, between Third and Fourth. Christ Church, where the family had a pew, was only a few "squares" away, on the west side of Second Street above Market. One can readily picture in imagination the little procession churchward on that Christmas morning—the Doctor walking ahead, holding a child by either hand, his daughter and son-in-law following, and the other young people bringing up the rear. With due solemnity, doubtless, did they file into the sacred edifice and walk up the aisle to the ninth pew from the front, on the left, which to this day is occupied by some of Franklin's descendants.

It is a fact worth mentioning incidentally, that, when George Washington came to live in Philadelphia, as President, and rented the house at No. 190 Market Street, a block below the Franklin residence, he attended Christ Church, and it was proposed to put him in the front pew on the left, moving everybody else one pew back. This plan would probably have been carried out but for an objection by Sarah Bache, who said that it "would be just as preposterous as if a person should take an occupied corner house, and thus force everybody to move up." Accordingly, Washington was obliged to accept the use of Bishop White's pew, which was the third on the left of the aisle, six pews ahead of the one belonging to the Franklin family.

Doctor Franklin used sometimes to go to sleep at church, and possibly he did so on this Christmas Day, during the sermon of the rector, Bishop White. The service, which was that of the Church of England, was simple and bare of rites, as was usual in those days, with no exhibition even of cross or candles. Probably it lasted a couple of hours, and the children were glad enough when it was over. As for the philosopher himself, he did not attend divine wor-

ship merely for the sake of an outward show of respectability. He believed that it was right and useful to go to church. Notwithstanding an impression to the contrary that is somewhat widespread in these days, he was a profoundly religious man—though nonsectarian—and an earnest believer in an overruling Providence.

By the time the family had reached home again the hour for dinner had nearly arrived, and soon the guests, of whom there were a number, began to appear. Including the family, about thirty people sat down to table; for Doctor Franklin kept open house, his hospitality being always lavish, and the most distinguished persons who happened to pass through Philadelphia—statesmen, men of letters, and strangers of note in other walks of life—usually called on him, and were invited to break bread with him.

On such an occasion Franklin did much of the talking, and his daughter most of the carving. She was a fine-looking woman, and wore on her head a dainty white cap, while about her neck and shoulders a white fichu was folded becomingly. It was a huge roast of beef, solid and juicy, that she carved, and she stood up to do it, tucking up her sleeves to get them out of the way of the gravy. There were other meats on the table, including fowls, nearly everything being put on at once, after the manner of those times. The waiting was done by Negroes. Many people in the North owned slaves at that period, but the Doctor had manumitted the few he once possessed.

Half a dozen of the guests, perhaps, were men of noteworthy distinction—one or two of them Frenchmen whom Franklin had met while he was abroad. They all found much enjoyment in listening to the quaintly humorous remarks of the sage, who, while caring little for the more substantial pleasures of the table, dearly loved to talk to people who knew how to appreciate his discourse. He was a man with a good many hobbies, and when fairly set going on one of them he could keep on indefinitely. But he was so witty and amusing that his many companions were always delighted with

DRAWN BY GUERNSEY MOORE

Franklin's varied interests, homespun philosophies and quick wit made him a popular part of any gathering.

his conversation, no matter what the topic on which he chose to speak.

The furniture of the table included only a few articles of silver, such luxuries being rare in those days. There was a set of china (a few of the cups and saucers are still in existence) which had been given to the Doctor by his great friend and admirer, Madame Helvetius, widow of a famous Frenchman whose house in Paris he had frequented. The knives were of steel, and the forks of the same metal, with three tines—the height of elegance at that period, and so precious that they were kept, together with the knives, in a

pair of inlaid mahogany boxes made for them.

For supplementary refreshments there were mince pies and plum-pudding, both compounded by Sally herself; for at that epoch it was a matter of course that a good housewife should understand and practice all the domestic arts, including that of cookery. When the pudding was brought on brandy was poured over it and ignited, burning with a lambent and appetizing flame; but for the special benefit of the Doctor himself had been prepared a dish of "floating island"—a favorite dessert on state occasions. And, to embellish the feast at its conclusion, there were almonds, Madeira nuts, raisins, oranges and lady-apples—these last not very good to eat, but rosy-cheeked and pretty.

For drinkables there were on the table Madeira wine, port and curacoa; also ale, home-brewed by the hostess. In later years, when the brewing business had become a great commercial industry, it was cheaper and easier to buy ale in casks than to make it at home, and thus, like many another ancient occupation of the good wife, the manufacture of fermented beverages departed from the household. But at that period "home-brewed" was still a luxury, and Sally Franklin's hand was not least expert in its production.

For no great length of time did the gentlemen, on this festive occasion, linger over the walnuts and wine after the ladies and children had left the table. The host, with his son-in-law and the other men, soon retreated to the library, where he took advantage of the opportunity to exhibit to them his electrical apparatus—a veritable marvel in those days, you may well believe—and to administer a mild shock or two to those of them who were inclined to submit to the operation. Two of the machines which he used still exist, and are in a tolerable state of preservation.

About this time, probably, a couple of Negroes brought in the ingredients for a punch, together with a most curious punchbowl, which was one of the good Doctor's favorite possessions. It had the shape of a cask, though made of china, and held about two gallons. The ingredients were put in through the bunghole of the cask, and the punch was drawn off into glasses by means of a spigot. It is hardly necessary to say that the punch was a rum punch—rum being the favorite drink of the time—though fortified with a liberal modicum of brandy. Doubtless it was strong.

Franklin knew how to compound a first-rate punch. One can imagine him reciting for the entertainment of his guests, as he began to mix the punch, a bit of verse which he himself had composed on the subject:

Boy, bring a bowl of china here!
Fill it with water, cool and clear.
Decanter with Jamaica ripe,
And spoon of silver, clean and bright;
Sugar, twice fin'd, in pieces cut,
Knife, sieve and glass in order put;
Bring forth the fragrant fruit, and then
We're happy till the clock strikes ten.

The Doctor took but little of the punch himself, though it is not unlikely that some of his guests, tempted by the appetizing quality of his brew, may have become a trifle mellow. It was the fashion to drink hard, and none the worse was thought of a man who took a drop more than was good for him. Besides, this was Christmas.

Though in his youth he had been extremely abstemious, Franklin in later life held somewhat more liberal views. In his exquisitely humorous vein (while living in Paris) he wrote to his friend the Abbé Morellet: "*In vino veritas,* says the wise man. Truth is in wine. Before the days of Noah, then, men, having nothing but water to drink, could not discover the truth. Thus they went astray, became abominably wicked, and were justly exterminated by *water.*"

But to return to the little Christmas afternoon party in the library:

Doctor Franklin had composed a number of drinking songs, and he knew how to sing one when his audience was likely to be appreciative. It is not unreasonable to suppose that on this occasion he may have been inspired by a glass of the punch to render one of his own composition.

Well, what happened next? It is all a surmise, but it is not unlikely that the Doctor played, for the amusement of his guests, on the harmonica —an instrument of his own invention, which was a modification of the so-called musical glasses. The latter consisted of a series of glass receptacles containing different quantities of water, and by reason of that fact yielding different notes in the scale; but in Franklin's contrivance the glasses were of different sizes, containing no water, and the notes were produced by passing a moistened finger around their edges successively.

On that Christmas evening, after supper, several friends doubtless dropped in, and tables were set out for cards. Franklin toward the end of his life (he died in 1790) greatly enjoyed chess, and cards also. "I have, now and then, a little compunction in reflecting that I spend time so idly," he wrote to a friend; "but another reflection comes to relieve me, whispering, 'You know that the soul is immortal. Why, then, be a niggard of a little time, when you have eternity before you?' "

To another friend, at the same period, he wrote: "It is true that I enjoy here everything that a reasonable mind can desire—a sufficiency of income, a comfortable habitation of my own building, having all the conveniences I could imagine, a dutiful and affectionate daughter to nurse and take care of me, a number of promising grandchildren, some old friends still remaining to converse with, and more respect, distinction and public honors than I can possibly merit."

Doctor Franklin was very devoted to his family, no member of which was ever forgotten by him at Christmastime. His gifts on such occasions were always useful ones. To his younger sister, Jane Mecum, a widow who lived in Boston, he would send two or three barrels of best quality flour, which was accompanied by a draft for a round sum of money.

Much as he preached of economy and saving, he could be nobly generous, and the opportunity of which he most liked to take advantage for the bestowal of substantial tokens of his regard and affection arrived once a year, at Christmas—a festival which, for the sake of the kindly and cheerful sentiments associated with it, had a strong interest for the most sympathetic and good-humored of philosophers. (1904)

Rebecca Harding Davis

Some Old-Time Christmases

What usually happens when you uncover your real past to strangers? You show, for instance, to your neighbor a photograph of the old farmhouse where you were born. When you look at it you can smell the clover in the fields, you hear the cows lowing, you know that your mother is weeding in the garden yonder. You see yourself and Jack—two big, freckled boys, leaning from that attic window at night planning your lives out in the world, full of fighting and glory.

Just beyond that hill are the trees under which your mother has slept this many a year.

Jack lies dead in California. And your glorious life——?

All of these things are in that photograph for you. But your neighbor sees in it only a common frame house and barn that need repair badly.

The glories of the Christmases of my childhood, so splendid in my remembrance, would no doubt seem poor and cheap to this generation. For life was simple then as Charles Wagner would have it now, and bare of show and glitter. The nation was not as yet drunk with prosperity. The exchange of costly and beautiful things among friends and acquaintances—the gay, burdensome duty which now amuses and bores the whole country once a year—was then unknown. Then, only the few who loved you brought you gifts to remind you of the day when Christ was born. But what love went into the homely things! How you hoarded them!

Christmas trees then were unknown in this country outside of Pennsylvania. In Virginia we never had heard of Santa Claus. The stockings were hung in a row over the great fireplaces. But it was the fairies, we believed, who filled them so miraculously. We were told that they, too, rejoiced at the Infant's birth as did all living things. We believed that at sunrise the cows in the stable and the wild beasts in the mountains knelt, and even the dead arose and praised God that the Babe was born in Bethlehem. It was thought, too, that the sinner who left this world on Christmas morning was given a kindly greeting beyond the darkness, and that the gate of Heaven stood ajar for all comers during that hour in which the Son of God had passed through it on His way to save the world.

These superstitions belonged to the Scotch-Irish settlers of the Southern and Middle States. None of them, I think, ever penetrated into New England. Even Christmas itself was regarded by the descendants of the stern old Puritans there as a superstition, and, with Good Friday, Easter and all days set apart to commemorate religious events, was denounced as a remnant of "Popish idolatry." They rated the observance of them with gambling, dancing and other carnal delights. Even Sunday—under that name—they abjured and flouted. The Jewish Sabbath, a grim season of self-denial, they kept scrupulously. Thanksgiving was the one human festival of their year.

"I like Christmas," Henry Ward Beecher once said. "I can see the use and beauty of its observance. But it is new and foreign to me. I did not know it when I was a child, so my heart never warms to it as to Thanksgiving."

In fact, the day never has been acclimated in that chilly section of the States. I know at the present time large and important towns in New England in which Christmas is as foreign a festival as the *Jour des Morts*.

Hallmark Cards, Inc.

In New England, the time for merry-making and feasting was Thanksgiving. Christmas was virtually unknown.

In the South, to which the Cavaliers, with many ungodly habits, had brought a creed full of tender and holy superstitions, Christmas was always loyally kept. In the darkest districts of the slave-holding States that master was rated by his neighbor as hard and brutal who did not rejoice the souls of his people by gifts on that day.

In one of these South Carolinian or Georgian plantations the field hands would gather by daybreak in a ring around the lawn while the house servants, strutting among them, lofty and supercilious, drilled and ordered them about. The presents, given by the mistress or her children, usually were trifles—a red handkerchief, a pound of tea, or sugar or a lump of "baccy." "White meal," or wheat flour, was a highly coveted item, though no self-respecting Negro would eat the mawkish bread made of it. A loaf of this bread would fill the place of honor in a cabin for months. The proud possession of the luxury was held to raise its owner nearer to the social status of the whites.

More hearty kindness from one side and loyalty from the other went into these poor gifts than Northerners could understand. The day was given up on the plantation to idleness and fun, and that was a poor cabin that did not belch forth the fat smoke of 'possum and hominy as they cooked over the fire for Christmas dinner.

In Catholic Maryland and in German Pennsylvania the day was always set apart and scrupulously kept, though with different customs. With the mass of Protestant Irish in Pennsylvania and Virginia it was observed more as a family feast, a time when it behooved us to be forgiving and jolly together, rather than as a religious occasion.

Peace and good will always found vent in heavy feeding and drinking. The housekeeper whose turkeys and mince pies then fell short of her own high standard vaguely felt during the whole year following that she had utterly failed in a religious duty.

"I hope," an old fire-eater said anxiously once in my hearing, "that the Christian faith of my household is beyond a doubt. Never in my remembrance has a Christmas morning dawned when egg-nog was not brought to our bedsides before we were awake. The rule is absolute, sir, absolute! Let others do as they may, we never neglect to honor the holy day."

This man's house and heart were homes always open to the poor and wretched. He lived to help, to give his money, his thought, his care, to the needy. But it never had occurred to him that this habit of his life had anything to do with religion. It was through the turkey and egg-nog that he professed his faith.

This queer alliance of soul and stomach is quite as firm and general now as in old times. We all have a vague sense of Christian duty done while we go through the courses of a modern Christmas banquet.

But it was from the Pennsylvania Dutch that we borrowed most of our Yule customs in this country. The Christmas tree came to us directly from them.

The Mennonites have a queer legend about it. Martin Luther, they say, was once lost in the forest in a frightful storm on Christmas Eve. He fell, and would have died but that he saw a strange gleam of white shining through the thick darkness.

It was the light from the door of a woodcutter's hut, falling on the branches of a pine tree, which were covered with rime. He crept to the door and so was saved.

The pious Dutch folk now hang glittering tinsel on their Christmas trees in memory of that hoar frost, and insist that the custom of dressing a tree had its origin in the gratitude of Lutherans for this rescue of the great reformer. This could hardly be the truth, as the Christmas tree has been known to the Germans for centuries, long before Luther was born.

But it is true that Christmas, with all its good cheer for soul and body, appeals to the Pennsylvania German more directly than to other men. His faith is simple and strong; he likes to be happy and he also likes to eat.

He spends ten months in storing away food for the remnant of the year that is left. Whether his home be the big farmhouse of some rich Mennonite, or the abode of an Amish, he has sufficient store in it to stand a siege. His great red-roofed barns crown every hill from the Delaware to the Ohio; his cellars are packed with hogsheads of salted meat and huge bins of vegetables and fruit. He is always ready for possible war or famine or whatever the future may hold.

The Pennsylvania German is a generous fellow, too, always on the lookout for a chance to feed and comfort his needy neighbors. There are so few chances of merrymaking in his life that even a funeral is made into a feast for him. He stays his tears in order to feed the entire countryside for a period of two or three days.

Naturally, to this hospitable, devout soul Christmas has always been a more important day than to less kindly folk.

I remember its approach one year in a small community of so-called Pennsylvania Dutch. They were all well-to-do folk. Each family owned a spacious modern brick house set in the midst of a skillfully tilled farm.

In the house was the usual complement of rooms: a large parlor, a dining-room and fine, great bed-chambers, all handsomely furnished and kept in exquisite order. They never were used except at a funeral, a wedding and on Christmas Day. The family lived in the kitchen and the room above it.

Over the roof of each house swung a large bell which rang out loudly long before dawn for breakfast, at eleven o'clock for dinner and at four for supper. Before sundown, while the birds still were singing, the family all were snugly tucked away in bed. I never saw such bells in any other community. They had been rejected by the fire department of Philadelphia, and a shrewd agent had persuaded these farmers that the possession of one of them was as sure a proof of aristocracy as a coat-of-arms or crest. Consequently they listened to the incessant frightful clangor going on overhead with much innocent joy.

Preparations for Christmas began in October. Heavy fruitcakes and puddings had been compounded a year before. Firkins of choice apple-butter made rich by quinces, cans of pawn-haus and liverwurst, barrels of pork and hogsheads of loud-smelling sauerkraut, were set aside for *Kristkindtag*.

Two weeks before the holy day the master of the house went at night, candle in hand, through each barn and outbuilding, to whisper to every living thing, from the cattle and horses to the pigeons and pigs, the good tidings. He was coming. The hives were always visited first; the bees, as everybody knew, being a testy folk who held themselves to be the nearest friends of the family and would savagely resent any neglect.

The yearly love-feast was held in the square church on the hill a

week before the great day. The men, dressed in decorous brown, the full trousers plaited into a belt around their stout waists, the tails of their coats touching their heels, sat in the pews on one side; the women in short petticoats, capes of blue, and black coal-scuttle sunbonnets were ranged on the other.

Prayers were made devoutly and hymns sung. Then women, with decorous lawn caps and aprons, carried trays of pretzels and shining tin mugs of scalding coffee to serve to everyone.

In any other circumstance of celebration, this would be the time for socializing; the time when an austere people could give in to high spirits and a festive mood. But such was not the case.

This eating and drinking was done in solemn silence. When they had finished the servers took back the mugs and the company rose, sang a hymn, and parted, after a solemn shaking of hands, the richest man in the county greeting the laborer as "Bruder." It was not the Holy Supper, but a "love-feast," to enforce the truth that all Christ's children are brothers.

As Christmas approached the house teemed with fat dainties peculiar to the Dutch: cheeses compounded of pork and molasses, luscious pies filled with raisins, or with apples smothered in cinnamon syrup, crisp doughnuts in every shape, and a little sugar-cake called *Heitig kuchen*, which was made in enormous quantities and sent in boxes from house to house. On the day the chief actors were a young man who personated Kristkind tramping from farm to farm bearing gifts, and the wicked Belsnickel, clad in skins and armed with a whip to lash bad children.

It is certain that when I was a child the great religious festivals had fallen into neglect throughout this country. There was a feeble echo in a few sects to the sound of Christmas bells or the victorious Easter trumpets. But the ordinary American was too busy in his first century of work here to pay much attention to religion beyond the saving of his own soul.

It was Charles Dickens who first taught English-speaking peoples the meaning of Christmas Day. Call him a cad, or his art bathos, if you will. That one thing he did. The story of Tiny Tim perhaps now seems to you forced and unreal. But it went around the world, bringing hot tears to the eyes of men and women, making their hearts throb with pity for their poor brother and setting their hands to work for him. The good day, as never before, was recognized as the expression of Christianity.

This new zeal for Christmas was fresh in the hearts of our people when the Civil War broke out. Naturally, the two things jarred. "Yank" and "Johnny Reb" had trouble to bring for one day in December the spirit of love and peace into their long years of bloody battering of each other and fury of murder and rapine. But it is a fact that they honestly did try to do it.

I remember countless little happenings during the Christmas seasons of 1861-2, which showed how human, after all, were the awkward machines in blue and gray who were marching in huge masses through the country—how glad each man of them would have been to hear that the great riddle was solved, that he could settle down into Joe or Tom again with his wife and children, to find, perhaps, a crony and good fellow in that other Joe or Tom yonder whom he was sent out to kill.

In '61, too, the country had not yet begun to feel the stress of want. The crops of that year were large beyond record. The army was fed lavishly, and when Christmas drew near the stay-at-homes spent their zeal and affection in packing boxes for the boys in camp. And every woman, were she Dutch frau or New York belle, gave her time to baking cakes or knitting woolen socks enough for an army of centipedes.

Christmas boxes never had more meaning than then, to these thousands of half-frozen fellows in camp. After all, they were not soldiers, but college boys, thin-blooded clerks, fat, easy-going fathers of families who probably never before in their lives had slept out of their own snug beds. They broke open the

boxes, and inside were the fond, foolish trifles the women at home had sent—useless things, perhaps, at which the man playing soldier laughed as he took them out. But it was his old mother who had packed them—or his wife, or the children. As he looked up outside of the tent he saw the night, and beyond the fires of the enemy's camp. To-morrow—to-night might end it all, and he never would see mother or child again.

There was more meaning in these Christmas gifts than we shall find in ours.

I remember that an old Federal officer once told me of opening such a box on Christmas Day in '61. The camp was down in the mountains of West Virginia. There had been a fight between detachments under Generals Milroy and Johnson, of Georgia. The Union troops kept the pass. They buried the dead and took possession of an old barn for a hospital. One or two wounded Confederates were stretched in the straw alongside of their own men.

The box came at sundown, and the lucky owner opened it in the door of the barn so that the sick men could share in the fun.

"I really didn't think of the Rebs," he said. "They were nothing to me but two dogs who had tried to pull down the flag. They were mere filthy heaps on the floor; their old home-made clothes were stiff with mud and blood. I handed one of them a cigar along with the rest, but he shook his head and turned his back.

"But presently, as I was unpacking the bundles, I saw him up, leaning on his elbow, watching me, his eyes very bright.

" 'Cap'n,' he said—he had a low, womanish voice for such a huge fellow, 'thah's a picture thah—could I look at it? Just a minute. Thank ye.' It was a little photograph of one of the children. He handed it back with a long breath and then laughed. 'I thought it was my Jack. But it's a gell. My Jack's twice the size of her. He's bigger than other boys, let alone a gell.'

"I nodded and moved away from him. His filthy rags were ill-smelling, and he had

Traveling near and far to spend time with family and friends has become part of the Christmas Day agenda.

been justly shot down, busy at a bad work.

"Then it occurred to me that it was Christmas, and so——

"Well, I sat down in the straw beside him and asked about Jack, and we smoked together. He told me his name and the town in Georgia where he lived, and at last asked me, in case he did not get well, to send word to his wife and mother. I don't know why I felt as I did. He was dirty and ignorant, but there was something fine in the

man that brought him near to you. He died that night. I kept my promise, and when we crossed into Georgia I hunted up his people. His boy Jack is a friend of mine now. And it's odd, but I have come to think of his father as if he had been one of my kin.

"That all grew out of its being Christmas Day, I suppose," he added. "There's something in it different from other days that is impossible to explain." (1904)

Alister Burford

An Old-Time English Christmas

When the night ended and the day began no man could tell; for over London lay the fog. Dank and dun, it blotted out the houses; dense and impenetrable, it barred the streets. The lamps along the road glowed sickly yellow in the smother, and here and there a smudge of red showed where a candle flared.

Through the muffled air the shouts and cries of the venturesome came strangely hollow, and their footsteps echoed in the empty streets as if they trod the flags beneath arched cloisters. With outstretched hands the city groped through all the morning, every greeting an imprecation.

But on toward noon the fog began to lighten, and bit by bit the sun fought through. Then came the wind, and the last drifting scud blew into shreds. It brought a snap and sparkle to the dead air, a frosty nip, that rapid walking turned to tingling warmth.

The people rubbed their eyes and looked about them. Then, reassured that London town had not been spirited away by the genii of the fog, with one accord they reached for wicker baskets and started out. For in those good old days, when steam was but the waste of housewives' kettles, before the world turned topsy-turvy, the buying of the Christmas cheer was no light thing. Then were there twelve long days of merrymaking, and honest men had honest appetites.

As the night drew on the streets became more thronged. In every window candles twinkled; in every room a cheerful blaze danced in the grate, and sent out ruddy streams of light into the dusk. And everywhere was holly hung, and mistletoe.

Fat turkeys and lean turkeys, Falstaffian gobblers in all the bronze glory of their feathers, and plump hen-turkeys, picked clean to the white skin; rotund turkeys which had gorged the autumn away in Norfolk farmyards, and lean, blue birds which had scratched out a precarious livelihood on barren moors; turkeys piled high on every stall, and swinging head down from rows of hooks; turkeys before, behind, on both sides, wherever the eye rested; tons of turkeys, hills of turkeys, mountains of turkeys, that was Leadenhall Market on Christmas Eve. Nor was there lack of unctuous geese and Dorking fowl, of spicy brawn in rolls, and good roast beef in great, thick joints, the firm red flesh streaked and o'erlaid with yellow fat, all gay with greens and streaming ribbons, which fit the hearty tastes of those hearty times.

In and around the shops and stalls surged the whole quarter, jostling, crowding, pinching thin turkeys, prodding fat turkeys, and smelling suspicious-looking turkeys. There were round-paunched old papas, red-faced and jolly, dragging wondering children along on either side, with a porter, bowed under a roomy hamper, following on behind; there were fat old housewives, smiling all down their shining faces to their double chins, waddling from stall to stall, intent on the one great business of the moment.

On every side there rose the sound of bargaining, buying and selling, the shouts and laughter of the children and the more staid greetings of their elders. And here and there were ragged men and boys who cried out sheets of Christmas carols; and from a corner came the wheezing of a broken violin and the cracked voices of some

frowsy waifs bawling out the good old
God rest you, merry gentlemen,
Let nothing you dismay,
Remember Christ, our Saviour,
Was born on Christmas Day.

From end to end, the market smacked of Christmas. There was a breath of it in the pleasant smells that floated out from the shops where the fruiterers were entrenched behind barricades of oranges and apples and grapes and lemons; there was a jingle of it in the rattle of the canisters from which the grocers were weighing out the spices for the morrow's pudding; there was a suggestion of it in the piled-up sweetness of candied fruits and figs and plums; and everywhere there was the certainty of it in the greens.

At precisely one minute before ten the coachee of "the Fastflyer" came out of the tap-room of "The Bell and Hand," wiping his mouth on the back of a stubby paw, and gave a stolid stare around the inn yard. He was a short, stocky man, whom a swaddling greatcoat of rough blue stuff, with bright brass buttons, and a low-crowned hat, in which was stuck a sprig of holly, made shorter and stockier still. His face, what little of it showed below the hat, and above a gaudy "neckerchief," was veined and mottled red, like a map of an extensive system of lakes and rivers. And as he waddled toward the coach, he was surrounded by an admiring circle of stable-boys, and preceded and followed by a smell of gin.

The horses, with two hostlers at the heads of the leaders, were already in their places; the four insides, wrapped in traveling shawls, were snuggled down in theirs; the outsides, a fine, bluff, jolly old gentleman, to whom the coachee touched his hat deferentially, and three well-built, frank-faced schoolboys, were running back and forth alongside.

The top of the coach was covered and piled with boxes, baskets and hampers, and the guard and two porters were still stowing things away in impossible corners of the boot. There were barrels of oysters and hampers of game; there were hares and turkeys and geese swinging from convenient hooks. From a basket on top, the head of a great turbot stuck up and glared stonily at the snout of a stiff and stark sucking-pig that poked out from another.

"Up you go, now, young gentlemen," cried out coachee at last, and the three schoolboys bounced to the top like India-rubber balls. Up went the old gentleman, puffing and blowing, and then

the coachee, with surprising agility, jumped into his seat, just as the guard stowed the last bundle in the boot of the coach.

"Give 'em their 'eads, 'Arry," called the guard; and he grasped his horn.

There was a sudden shuffling of hoofs, and the hostlers fell back; there was a tightening of reins, and the leaders began to prance; there was a crack of the long-lashed whip, and the coach was off. Away they went, to the blast of the horn, hurtling along through the half-fog of the morning, and meaner vehicles turned from their way. Away they went, out of the smoke and soot of the city, along the winding country roads, where the air came clear and clean over the freshly fallen snow. Away they went, past lanes and hedges, down a long slope, over an old arched bridge, and then past a churchyard, where the rough gray

Twelve full days of merrymaking; holly and mistletoe abounding; markets overflowing with turkeys; street corners dotted with carolers—
that *was an old-time English Christmas.*

stones were stuck through the snow at queer, unsteady angles.

And now the shrill horn piped the entrance to a village. To every gate ran the housemaid and the cook, and giggled, and simpered, and cried "Oh, lor'!" as the coachee winked at one and leered at the other. From every ale-house the loungers came out and stared in stupid wonder at the charging coach.

Outside the village, the coachee eased his horses down and turned half out to let a mad procession by. Three old post-chaises, packed full of home-bound schoolboys, came racing up, the postboys standing in their stirrups and lashing the lean old brutes beneath them. With flags streaming, trumpets blowing, missiles flying, they came on, leaning far out the windows, and waving their caps. A sudden shower of missiles, a yell of "*Dulce domum!*" and they were past.

So sped the miles away, until at last the steaming horses drew up before the Abbey Inn.

From the Abbey Inn to the Manor House, where the fine old gentleman lived, the pair of shaggy ponies, which had been standing waiting for him, frisked and romped in no time at all.

"Hooray!" cried the lads in chorus, as the panting ponies stopped. And then the stout hall door flew open, and out burst a merry throng, blown on a gale of shouts and laughter. From mother to grandmother, from sister to brother, from uncle to aunt, from cousin to second cousin, the lads were bandied about and hugged, until they cried out "Enough!" and squirmed free.

From room to room, greeting the servants and admiring the greens, from stables to kennels, patting the horses and petting the dogs, they ran through all the afternoon. But with the twilight they came trooping to the spacious hall, where their elders sat in the deepening dusk.

Then the fine old gentleman, looking rosier and jollier than ever, advanced on the blackness of the yawning fireplace, holding tenderly in one hand a charred fragment of last year's Yule log. With this, that custom might be satisfied, he kindled a blaze that curled up and licked the rough bark of the good oak log. And soon the leaping flame lit all the hall, and danced back from the time-stained oak that wainscoted the walls.

Wax candles now were lit in every room, and from the farms around the tenantry came in, the men all stiff and jointless in their Sunday best, the women simpering.

Squeak, squeak! the fiddler was tuning up. Twang, twang! the harper was testing his strings, and impatient toes began to tap the floor. Then both together, in an ambitious flourish, and, at the head of the set, the silk-stockinged calves of the jolly old gentleman stepped in and out in gay anticipation.

Already the children were making merry. Unchecked by any frowning elder, a boisterous game of hoodman blind was in full swing, and youngsters were burning their fingers at snapdragon or sousing their heads playing bob-apple.

And so with games and dancing the evening wore away, until the butler staggered in under a great bowl of wassail, from which a spicy steam wreathed up. Then came more dancing and games and singing, and at last, when everyone was hungry and breathless, the jolly old gentleman led a fierce charge on a supper of cold fowl and beef, of venison pasties and pigeon and mince pies, with steaming punch or brown October ale to wash it down. Nor did a guest get up to go, nor a sleepy child submit to being led away, until the bells chimed out for Christmas morning. (1898)

Wallace Webster

Christmas with Royalty

No royal personage is more stately and conscious of his own importance than the German Emperor, who on Christmas Day, nevertheless, knows how to unbend, joining gayly in the jollification of the Court. This year he will celebrate the Yuletide festival at Potsdam with all of his children about him, including the recently-married Crown Prince and his bride. For each son and daughter there will be a tree, specially cut for the occasion from the near-by forest on the imperial estate, and a table at the foot of it laden with gifts. An eighth tree—the Emperor has seven children—will be largest of all, for Wilhelm II and the Empress, and its branches will bear presents for the various officers and ladies of the household, and royal court.

Hallmark Cards, Inc.

Emperor Wilhelm's children didn't have to "share" a Christmas tree—each of the seven was generously provided with his own.

The idea of the Christmas tree seems to have originated in Germany—a goblin that brings good luck into the house is supposed to dwell within its trunk—and hence the conspicuous part it plays in the imperial celebration. In obedience to custom, the eight trees will be set up in a large reception room in the palace, and nobody save the Empress and half-a-dozen servants will be admitted until the morning of the twenty-fifth of December. Then, when all the members of the household have assembled, including the officials of the Emperor's immediate entourage and the ladies in attendance, all will take part in singing the beautiful choral of Luther, at the conclusion of which the doors will be thrown open and the people will eagerly enter the great hall.

The scene, as may be well imagined, will be quite a brilliant one, the trees—forming a small forest, glittering with electric lights of different colors and hung with bright ornaments—being ranged along one end of the great room, with the presents laid out on tables beneath. As usual, they will be of different sizes, in a row from smallest to biggest, in direct proportion to the ages of the imperial princes and princesses, the tree of the Crown Prince being larger than any of the others, except that belonging to his father and his mother. Whether there is to be a tree for the new Crown Princess nobody knows; for all of the Christmas arrangements at Potsdam are kept very secret, in order that they may lose nothing of the charm of surprise.

When the gifts belonging to the princes and princesses and those of the Emperor and Empress have been examined and admired, her Imperial Majesty will proceed to distribute the presents intended for the various officials and ladies of the court, taking them one by one from the great tree. For the women there will be articles of jewelry, rare and beautiful laces, and other things dear to the feminine heart; and the men will get gold cigarette-cases and valuable trifles appropriate to masculine uses. But in each instance, where it is practicable, the object bestowed will have a personal significance in connection with its recipient—often jocular, too, as in the case of a chamberlain who (having been

The Emperor's gifts to his children were primarily practical— books, strings, tacks—plus a few frivolous toys.

engaged in collecting large sums of money for the churches of Berlin) last year received a cigar-case of silver in the likeness of a contribution-box.

It has never been the policy of William II and his wife to bestow costly gifts upon their young children. The Christmas presents of the princes and princesses have been, as a rule, of the inexpensive and substantially useful kind, including perhaps a box of candy, a toy or two, and a number of instructive books. It is said that on one occasion the Crown Prince received from his father, as a mark of affection at Yuletide, a hammer, a ball of string, and a paper of tacks. But each boy, on coming of age, gets one very magnificent gift, usually at Christmas: a completely equipped establishment of his own, for which an adequate revenue of maintenance is provided.

In the distribution of Christmas gifts at Potsdam nobody will be forgotten—not even the stable-boys and scullery-maids. There is something for everybody, and the list of people to be remembered is a long one, comprising over a thousand names. In order that presents may not in any case be duplicated, a book is kept—a sort of Yuletide register, which runs back for fifty years—showing just what each person has received. To the Kaiserin her husband usually gives a handsome article of bijouterie, almost invariably diamonds, while to each of half-a-dozen of his most intimate men friends he sends a coal-black charger. To the King of England, his uncle, he forwards a case of precious Johannisberger, with a few of his latest photographs for the ladies of the family.

If Christmas is an important occasion at Potsdam, it is a festival not less notable at Sandringham. In that great English country house, neither palace nor castle, Edward VII finds himself more at home than anywhere else in the world, and there he will spend the holiday this year in the bosom of his family. The Prince and Princess of Wales will be there, of course, with their children, and it is reasonable to expect that there will be great romps.

In Potsdam half the day will be spent in religious exercises, Wilhelm II being an earnest church-goer and believer, but in his uncle's establishment in England there is more jollity and less piety, and an effort is made at Yuletide to relinquish all cares both as to this world and the next.

Gifts fit for a queen—fine jewels, perfumes and laces— things other women only dreamed about.

There will be trees for the young folks—the Prince Consort, King Edward's father, who was a German, introduced them at the English Court— and the children will hang up their stockings on Christmas Eve. To his wife the monarch will give a dozen bottles of her favorite perfume, lavender water (his invariable contribution), and also a necklace of diamonds or some such trifle in the way of jewelry. Of course, Alexandra already possesses a vastly greater number of jewels than she can possibly wear; but a queen, after all, is a woman, and what woman ever had all the jewels she wanted? There will be presents, you may be sure, for all the family and for the lords and ladies in waiting, the gentlemen of the bed-chamber, the mistresses of the robes, the maids of honor, and so on down to the grooms and kitchen-maids. When Victoria was alive, every retainer who had belonged to the household during the lifetime of her husband received at Christmas a piece of plate, with a black-bordered card that read: "With the good wishes of her Majesty and the Prince Consort." She liked, you

see, still to associate the Prince with gifts conferred upon those who knew him.

But it is the Christmas dinner that will be the most important feature of the holiday at Sandringham. One hundred plum-puddings—just think of that, and smack your lips!—will be furnished by the kitchens, to make sure that everybody may have plenty and to spare. There is no fear of waste, for whatever is left over will be given to the poor. And such delicious plum-puddings, too! The recipe has been handed down as carefully as any substantial heirloom, from the time of King James I, who, indeed, is said to have been its originator.

On the sideboards in the great dining-hall, in obedience to ancient tradition and long-established custom, will be placed a huge boar's head crowned with holly, a vast woodcock-pie, and a cold "Baron" of beef weighing two hundred pounds. The beef must be from one of the King's own oxen. It will be cooked on the twenty-second day of December, so as to give it plenty of time to cool, the roasting being done over an enormous dripping-pan in front of an open fire; and finally, when sufficiently chilled, it will be served on an immense silver dish which once belonged to Henry VIII. There is a legend to the effect that Charles II, on a certain occasion, being overcome with delight by the flavor of a loin of beef, drew his sword and, with much solemnity, knighted it in due form —whence the term Sir Loin. Whether this be a true story or not, it is not recorded that a chuck of beef was ever made a Baron.

The Czar of all the Russias is not likely to have a very merry Christmas this year, but he may derive some timely consolation from a dozen quarts of the finest Scotch whisky which, in accordance with long-followed custom, King Edward will send him. A huge stone jar of marmalade, specially prepared by the Queen's cooks, went to him annually from Balmoral Castle when Victoria was alive, but it may be that this tribute has been discontinued. Anyway, the present of Nicholas to King Edward will undoubtedly be, as usual, a dozen boxes of Cuban cigars, of a brand manufactured and put up expressly for the Czar by a firm in Havana. Five hundred boxes of them are shipped every year from Havana, in time for Christmas, and are distributed among relatives and among members of the Russian Court circle.

Not infrequently the gifts picked out by the Czar on such occasions are decidedly odd. For example, he will sometimes present to a favored courtier a herd of deer. When Queen Victoria was alive he would send to her at Christmas a fresh-caught sturgeon, packed in ice, and it is said the royal lady greatly appreciated the luxury. For the imperial children bonbons and toys are ordered from Paris; but the baby heir to the throne, though already a full general, is as yet too young to eat candy or to appreciate the meaning of Christmas—a festival which, it should be realized, is celebrated twelve days later by the Russians, in obedience to the rules of their Church, which put the date at our Epiphany.

Emperor Francis Joseph of Austria, will gather all his grandchildren around him this Christmas, as usual, and will make the day as merry as possible for them. He is getting to be an old man now, and his life has held many troubles; but in the company of the young folks he is able to forget his sorrows, and nothing delights him more than to go shopping for toys and other things likely to give pleasure to small boys and girls. To his fellow-sovereigns, and likewise to a few intimate friends, he sends, as a token of good will appropriate to the festive season, the greatest imaginable luxury in the way of drinkables—a dozen bottles of Tokay from the royal cellars.

The Sultan of Turkey, of course, being a Moham-medan and himself the Pope of that faith, does not celebrate Christmas; but, as a matter of politeness, he signifies his remembrance of the day by sending to each of his fellow-monarchs—well, what do you think? Why, nothing more nor less than a huge and beautifully-decorated box of candy, of the kind known as "Lokoom," or "Turkish Delight." In eating this candy, which is specially prepared by the Sultan's own confectioner, the recipients have the pleasure of knowing that they are partaking of the favorite sweet of the royal seraglio. A gift, specially appropriate to the person upon whom it is to be bestowed, is put into each box.

If common report does not belie the Belgian monarch, the opera-singers of Paris are often the beneficiaries of King Leopold's Christmas generosity, and to them he is liberal enough, though a notorious niggard otherwise. With most of his family he has quarreled, and his palace at Brussels this year is not likely to be the scene of any cheerful Yuletide festivities. But his choice of gifts, when he does bestow one upon a royal or other distinguished personage, is usually a handsome Brussels carpet.

Christmas Day in Madrid is a gloomy time, so far as its celebration by royalty is concerned. There is a great deal of religious ceremonial and very little fun. It is said that Queen Christine, when she was Regent, tried to introduce at court the Christmas tree, the sentiment connected with which had been dear to her heart when she was only a little Austrian princess in the nursery at Vienna; but the high clerical dignitaries frowned upon it as an emblem of heathen worship, and the idea had to be abandoned. The royal mother is a woman of simple tastes, and it is recorded that, a year or two ago, when her son, King Alfonso, asked her what she would like for a Christmas gift, she decided in favor of a white bison.

Little Queen Wilhelmina, of the Kingdom of Pays-Bas, as it is known in the language of the

Traditionally, stockings have been hung by the young—or the young at heart, such as Queen Wilhelmina.

diplomats—or of the Netherlands, as we should say it—though she has been a married woman for several years now, still has a Christmas tree and hangs up her stocking for Kriss Kringle to fill. She is very clever with her needle, and to her friends she sends at Yuletide numerous specimens of her own handiwork.

At Rome, as in Madrid, Christmas is a rather solemn holiday, celebrated by religious processions and by masses in the churches. However, in the evening, the King will give a grand dinner, which will be followed by a reception attended by a multitude of political and other dignitaries. The Pope will pass the day quietly at the Vatican, and the potentates and other per-

sonages who receive presents from him in recognition of the sacred anniversary will value them rather for the sentiment they convey than for their intrinsic worth. His personal blessing, with an autographed letter, and accompanied by a few jars of wine made from grapes grown on the Pincian Hill, comprise the only gifts which he feels able to bestow. His predecessor, Leo, sent snuff to Queen Victoria every Christmas, recommending it to her as a sovereign cure for catarrh and other such ailments, and thus it was that her faithful companion and factotum, John Brown, obtained his supplies of the article. But the consignments of sneezing tobacco, it is said, have been discontinued under Pius X. (1905)

Acknowledgments

Text Credits:

"The Christmas Hunt" by Borden Deal. Copyright © 1960 by The Curtis Publishing Company. Reprinted by permission of the Borden Deal Family Trust (Borden Deal, Trustee).

"The Christmas Racket" by Jim and Allan Bosworth. Reprinted by permission of Allan Bosworth.

"Hard-Rock Candy" by Mack Thomas. Copyright © 1964 by Mack Thomas. Reprinted by permission of The Sterling Lord Agency, Inc.

"How to be Santa Claus" by Nat B. Read, Jr. Reprinted by permission of the author.

"Johanna's Christmas Star" by M.G. Chute. Reprinted by permission of the author.

"Silent Night" by Paul Gallico. Copyright © 1962 by The Curtis Publishing Company. Reprinted by permission of Harold Ober Associates.

"Women Want the Oddest Things for Christmas" by Peg Bracken. Reprinted by permission of The Lescher Agency.

Photo Credits:

Page: 19, 37-41, 126, 130, 139, Hallmark Cards, Inc.; 72, American Airlines; 83, Sylvania/GTE Products Corp.; 125, Culver Pictures; 128, Cardavon Press.

An effort has been made to trace the ownership of other text and photographs included. Any errors or omissions will be corrected in subsequent editions, provided the publisher is notified.